UNEQUAL CONTEST

The marquess laughed at the flashing of light in Tessa's eyes. He pulled her full length against him and bent his head to capture her lips with his.

Tessa was overwhelmed by a paralyzing giddiness. The marquess's full, firm mouth was strangely hot, somehow sweet, and his kiss was demanding. Her blood surged forward all at once and, ignited by his kiss, seemed to lick her veins with fire. She gasped, heard the sound, realized she'd made it—and she kicked him.

"Ow!" The yelp was Tessa's. Her bare feet were no match for his shining, black boots. Again he laughed at her, his mouth only a tantalizing few inches away from hers.

Tessa was beginning to learn that in love, nothing was fair. . . .

EMMA LANGE is a graduate of the University of California at Berkeley, where she studied European history. She and her husband live in the Midwest and pursue, as they are able, interests in traveling and sailing.

SIGNET REGENCY ROMANCE
COMING IN MAY 1990

Dawn Lindsey
The Talisman

Dorothy Mack
The General's Granddaughter

Mary Balogh
The Incurable Matchmaker

The Scottish Rebel

by

Emma Lange

A SIGNET BOOK

SIGNET
Published by the Penguin Group
Penguin Books USA Inc., 375 Hudson Street,
New York, New York, 10014 U.S.A.
Penguin Books Ltd, 27 Wrights Lane, London W8 5TZ, England
Penguin Books Australia Ltd, Ringwood, Victoria, Australia
Penguin Books Canada Ltd, 2801 John Street, Markham, Ontario,
Canada L3R 1B4
Penguin Books (N.Z.) Ltd, 182-190 Wairau Road,
Auckland 10, New Zealand

Penguin Books Ltd, Registered Offices:
Harmondsworth, Middlesex, England

First published by Signet, an imprint of Penguin Books USA Inc.

First Printing, April, 1990

10 9 8 7 6 5 4 3 2 1

1

To all appearances, Lady Madelaine Landon attended as carefully as ever to her toilette on the morning of the fifth of June, 1810. Leaning forward so that the filmy silk dressing gown she wore parted, she smoothed a dab of rosy cochineal across her cheeks before she took up a heavy silver brush embossed on the back with her initials.

Looking into her pier glass, she turned her head as if to judge the effect her efforts had achieved, but her eyes refused to attend to their task. It was past Lady Madelaine's image they looked, an appreciative, sensual gleam in their dark depths.

The one other occupant of her boudoir was clad in only a pair of skin-tight buckskins he was at that moment buttoning. Lady Madelaine watched him. He'd little difficulty; his hips were taut and lean. Her glance dipped. And his long legs well formed. Active by nature, the man needed no false padding. He drew the ladies' eyes to his unmentionables without effort, infuriating their husbands.

Madelaine half smiled. Those ladies' eyes would pop now, she vowed, could they but stray as hers did above his breeches to the gentleman's bare chest. His surprisingly fair skin, where it was not covered by a thick mat of black, curling hair, was entirely sleek and looked as if it would be as smooth to the touch as Lady Madelaine knew it, in fact, was.

The man turned his shoulders to her. They were fine and broad, his back strong, as the play of his muscles revealed when he leaned over to pluck a shirt from the carelessly disposed pile of clothing at his feet. Lady Madelaine's gaze

slipped again. There was no betraying pucker of skin over
his flat belly. The man's fit frame carried not an ounce of fat.

"Must you go so soon, Nick?"

Lady Madelaine's brush stilled in midair. She had not
meant to voice her thought aloud. The nature of her relationship with him did not allow for pleading.

"I must," Nicholas Gregory Charles Edward Steele, the
fifth Marquess of Kerne and eighth Earl of Stanbridge,
replied, his voice muffled as he bent to retrieve the neckcloth he'd discarded some hours before. "Having enjoyed
myself thoroughly . . ." he turned, neckcloth in hand, to
give her a lazy grin, and the effect of that white, rakish smile
was to set Madelaine Landon's experienced heart racing.
". . . I must now put my mind to duty."

"We have enjoyed a fortnight only." Madelaine, in a most
uncharacteristic gesture, bit her lips as if she might still them
against further outbursts. Searching her companion's eyes—
eyes that startled, for they were the light blue of the sky at
midday—she was relieved to see they did not harden against
her. Still, rushing her words, she amended, "I know that
is all you promised, but I thought . . ."

"You thought correctly that I am tempted, Madelaine,"
Nick finished for her, and though he smiled, she suspected
unhappily that his gallantry was only a sop to her vanity.
"I cannot break my promise to Honoria, however. I owe
her too much." Before she could speak again, he crossed
to her, turned her face up to him with his hand, and dropped
a kiss on her willing mouth. "She did make her request of
me some months ago, you know."

When Madelaine nodded, quiescent for the moment, Nick
looked over her head at his reflection in her pier glass and
in a few careless movements achieved a graceful, if unstudied, effect with his neckcloth. Madelaine watched his
capable fingers at work a moment, then turned her attention
to his face.

Her eyes lingered longest upon his mouth. Full but firm,
it held the promise of a sensual nature. His other features

were, admittedly, merely regular—a straight nose, strong chin and jaw, and wide brow—but, in all, combined with his fine mouth and brilliant eyes and his hair as black as midnight, they produced an arresting countenance.

"What can your godmother mean sending you, of all people, Nick, to fetch her young niece?"

Nicholas Steele grinned, upsetting Lady Madelaine's pulse again. "The lion going after the lamb?"

Madelaine managed a laugh. "Precisely."

He shrugged lightly before he took himself off to seek out his boots. When he was seated on the edge of her massive, quite rumpled bed, Nick looked again to Madelaine. "I suppose Honoria trusts that I would never serve her such a bad turn as to compromise her niece. It would be poor compensation indeed for the care she gave my mother during her illness."

Knowing, as did all their circle, how devotedly Honoria Gaston, Lady Alderly, had attended to Nick's mother after she was invalided by a carriage accident, Madelaine only nodded absently. "Yes, but the girl . . ." She allowed her voice to trail off, when she realized she intended to say, in so many words, that Nick was irresistible to women.

If he guessed the reason for her sudden distraction, he gave no hint of it. Grimacing, he pulled on a tasseled Hessian and then took up where Madelaine had left off. "The girl, it would seem from Honoria's account, is actually no lamb. With her grandfather's death, my godmother is her closest living relative and her guardian, but when Honoria sent Alderly's nephew, George Pierpoint, to fetch her down to London, the girl would not accompany him."

"She refused?" Madelaine's carefully plucked eyebrows lifted. "I do not know Pierpoint well, but I should have thought him up to a mere girl."

Nick chuckled as he attended to his second boot. "And she was only eighteen at the time. Honoria says it is the grandfather who raised her, Honoria's own father, who is responsible. A fierce old relic of Culloden Moor, he seems to have passed his prejudice against the vanquishing English on to his granddaughter.''

"But if the girl promises to be so difficult, why does Honoria not simply leave her in Scotland where she wishes to be?''

"The girl's the only family Honoria has left to her,'' Nick replied as he shrugged into a coat of blue superfine cut to fit without a wrinkle across his enviable shoulders. "My guess is she hopes to mother her. Lacking children of her own, Honoria has had to make do with Kit and me, and I suspect she yearns for someone she can shepherd about.''

Madelaine chuckled softly. "No, that would not be you, Nick.''

"No,'' he agreed, his rakish grin flashing only briefly but long enough to affect Madelaine. "At least Kit married, much to her satisfaction. He and my sweet gossip of a sister-in-law along with the children will be at Tarlton Hall to welcome this Miss Strahan to England.''

"You are taking her to Cheshire first?''

Nick adjusted the sleeves of his coat to his liking, appraised his appearance in the pier glass a final time, then, satisfied, turned away to give, Madelaine predicted correctly, his looks not another thought that day. "Honoria and I agreed she might need a respite after her journey and before entering the fray here in London. Honoria and Alderly, if he is well enough, will come up as well.''

"I see,'' Madelaine said slowly. "I had thought that by taking the *Sea Witch* for her, your journey would last no more than a se'enight at the most.''

Though Nick's expression lightened momentarily at the mention of his yacht, he did not pretend to misunderstand Madelaine. "I have agreed to allow the War Office use of the *Sea Witch* in July and August as they are hard pressed for ships of her draft to patrol our home waters. She'll only bring us as far as Edinburgh. From there we shall travel by land to Cheshire.'' His steady gaze held no apology. "I shall not return to London until well after Richard returns to you from the Peninsula."

At the mention of her husband, Madelaine made an abrupt, dismissive gesture with her hand. "You know Richard and I have an understanding whether he has absented himself to play at soldiering or not."

Again she had transgressed against the unwritten rules of an affair such as theirs. She had never done so before. At the end of her other affairs, if anyone had begged for it to be continued, it had always been the other party. Shifting restlessly, Madelaine recalled how annoying she had found those scenes.

But if Nick felt annoyed now, he did not show it. "You'll have forgotten me before the *Sea Witch* raises sail," he said, giving her a smile she or any other saw but rarely. Of great sweetness, it caused Madelaine only pain, as if a great fist were squeezing her heart. "Nor do I believe Richard's return will leave you as indifferent as you pretend, my dear. I suspect you've been piqued these two years that he did not elect to take you with him to Portugal."

"I've made do well enough," Madelaine responded with at least some of the languid sophistication for which she was renowned. But the attitude that was habitual with her did not come easily that day, and she could feel tears, embarrassing and unforgivable, pricking at the back of her eyes. "Kiss me and be gone, Nick," she demanded abruptly. "Else I shall embarrass us both."

Nick's kiss held passion, but too soon for Madelaine's liking he obeyed her wish. "Good-bye, sweetheart." He kissed her forehead lightly and was gone.

2

*S*ome eight days later Nick sighted Kilmorgan Castle, home to Thérèse Strahan, the girl he'd agreed to escort to his godmother. Standing sentinel on the cliffs above a deep, midnight-blue loch, the fortress was scarcely distinguishable from the high rocky crags surrounding it. Only its rounded towers attested to the work of men; otherwise it was as forbidding and indomitable as the stones used to construct it.

The castle's generally sound repair surprised Nick, for he knew it had been put to the torch by Cumberland's men after the battle of Culloden Moor. Somehow, someone had rendered it whole and defiant once more. But not entirely untouched, Nick realized, as his gaze traveled back a pace or two. To the side of the castle loomed the ruined remains of a charred tower.

Nick abruptly kneed the Highland pony he rode. There was little use wondering now about a girl who had grown up in the shadow of such a thing. He would see her soon enough.

The door of the castle, rather like the building itself, could not but daunt. Carved out of single huge fir, it was studded with great, sharp spikes, and groaned in loud protest as it swung open. Affected by the landscape, the castle, even the ruined hulk behind, Nick half fancied he would be greeted by an old crone muttering spells.

He nearly laughed aloud to see, instead, a young, winsome, red-haired lass, with eyes that had widened to the size of saucers at the sight of him. His stray hope the blushing child might be Miss Strahan was dashed when the girl, ducking her head shyly, replied in a whisper that she was not Miss Tessa and proceeded without identifying herself to show him

10

to a round solar room whose windows looked over the loch.

When she departed in a flurry of skirts, Nick was left alone to take stock of his surroundings, and found that if the castle resembled a thing of nature on the outside, inside it revealed human touches.

The thick walls were draped with fine tapestries from Gobelins, and about the stone floors were strewn rich carpets from Persia. Altogether, with the harsh natural building materials as backdrop for the luxurious appointments, the effect was startling, almost barbaric in some way.

Above the huge fireplace that dominated one side of the room hung a portrait Nick stepped up to examine, for the lady in the center of it might have been his godmother but that she was slightly taller. Otherwise, her thick auburn hair, bright blue eyes, even her sweet smile made her the mirror image of Honoria Ganston.

She could only be Joanna Strahan, Honoria's younger sister. And Thérèse Strahan's mother, Nick was reminded, when he noted that a young girl of perhaps thirteen years stood beside the woman.

The girl's hair was as bright and abundant as her mother's, but there was little else the two had in common. Joanna Strahan had a wide face and even, generous features Nick found pleasing to the eye. Her hands clasped sedately before her, she looked down at him and any other with something of the serene look of a madonna.

Her daughter's face, by decided contrast, was piquant and sharply drawn so that at thirteen she'd the look of a wood sprite. Quite unlike her mother, she stood half turned from the viewer, poised on one toe with her skirts lifted, as if she might at any moment skip out of the confining picture altogether. Glancing back over her shoulder, she regarded the world with bright, laughing gray eyes.

Sparkling brilliantly, they seemed to dance with challenge, and Nick could almost hear her calling. "Catch me! Catch me if you can!"

"Milaird! We dinna expect ye to coome up here to Kilmorgan!"

Startled from his reverie, Nick swung around to encounter a pair of bewildered brown, not gray eyes. They belonged to a small, neat, gray-haired woman, whose obvious agitation caused Nick to smooth the frown from his brow as he bowed with lazy grace. "Good day to you, ma'am. I am the Marquess of Kerne come to fetch Miss Strahan as I informed you I would do by letter."

"But Miss Tessa is nae here!"

"Not here?"

"Nae." The woman wagged her head firmly. "She sent ye a letter doon to Lunnon town." Seeing irritation flash in her guest's eyes, the little woman lifted a hand to her mouth. "Miss Tessa hae gone to Skelgara to meet ye, milaird! She thought to save ye the trouble o' ridin' up to the castle."

Thinking of the bumpy ride he'd had on the small but sure-footed Highland pony, Nick could only wish he'd received Thérèse Strahan's letter. The *Sea Witch* was docked at Skelgara, the largest town nearby, and had he met the girl there today, they might have left the north of Scotland on the next morning's tide. As it was, he must spend the night at the castle, make his way back down . . .

"Och, an' ye'll be thinkin' I've no manners at'll!" The woman threw up her hands before she made a belated curtsey. "My mind's t'let, but I do beg yer pardon, milaird! I am Mrs. Dunadee, housekeeper at Kilmorgan. I was to companion Miss Tessa, but when I come doon wi' a cold, she'd nae hear of my goin'."

Nick's eyebrows arched sharply at the thought of a young girl saying she did not need company. "Miss Strahan awaits me alone?"

"Aye, nae!" Mrs. Dunadee looked amazed by the suggestion. "Ye've no call to worry, milaird. Her girl, Nan, be wi' her. They'll abide safe enough in Skelgara until ye join 'em. 'Tis a pity ye did nae get Miss Tessa's note, but fer all tha' we've a good bed for ye. Ah, here's tea."

The young girl who had opened the castle door to him hurried in with a heavy silver tray. Mrs. Dunadee nodded to a table before the fire, and when the girl had left, seated herself to pour for her unexpected guest.

Nick looked back at the portrait over the fireplace, more curious than ever about the girl who was not where she was supposed to be. His brow lifted again. He'd missed the huge black mastiff that gazed up at her adoringly. "Is the animal her pet?"

Mrs. Dunadee looked up from pouring the tea to smile wispily. "Oh, aye, though he has gone now! A lamb he was with Tessa. 'Tis the same wi' all the animals." As composedly as if she had said, perhaps, that the girl carried herself well, Mrs. Dunadee added, "They mon feel she's a wee bit like 'em, half wild an' all. Will ye take cream, milaird?"

Nick said he would and dropped into a chair beside his hostess to accept his cup. His eyes straying again to the portrait and the girl, he wondered whether she had realized the promise of her beauty, or whether she had, like most young girls, faded before she had even fully bloomed.

It was not a question to ask the girl's housekeeper, however, and Nick asked instead, "Miss Strahan is unusual then?"

Mrs. Dunadee cocked her head and, looking at the girl above them, nodded unreservedly. "Oh, aye. Miss Tessa be tha'," she agreed. To Nick's surprise the older lady's eyes gleamed with sudden humor. "With Angus Ross for her grandfather she could nae help but be out o' the usual. Och, but he did love her somethin' fierce! Passed on his oon wild nature to her he did and encouraged her mayhap too much."

Nick was not well pleased with that, for though Thèrese Strahan at thirteen had possessed a certain coltish grace and decided animation of expression, those qualities, if she even retained them, were not sufficient to cause his godmother's social set, the most exalted in London, to excuse ungoverned behavior.

"Nae, ye needn't look so, milaird," Mrs. Dunadee chided with just the hint of a chuckle. "Miss Tessa ha' learned the social courtesies from her mither first, an' later from a governess Angus did bring to Kilmorgan. A fine woman, Miss MacIverson, who performed wonders wi' Miss Tessa 'til Angus learned her mither was English an' dismissed her."

"I see," Nick said slowly, reminded of the charred ruins left standing outside his rebuilt castle.

Mrs. Dunadee gave a nod, as if she'd read Nick's thoughts. "Aye, the hate he bore ye Sassenach, beggin' yer pardon, miliard, was black as night. But ye mon understand he had suffered mooch harm at Cumberland's hands."

Curious, Nick asked, "But why did Miss Strahan live here at Kilmorgan, Mrs. Dunadee? Did not her mother and father live in Edinburgh?"

"Aye, they did, and she lived wi' them when she was a wee bairn. But Mr. Strahan died when Miss Tessa was nae older than three, and afterward Lady Joanna, the lass's mither, married a man who did nae care to have another's offspring by him. They sent Miss Tessa to Angus here at Kilmorgan. She visited her mither, o' course, an Lady Joanna came away up here on occasion, but Miss Tessa grew to be more Angus's child than hers. He was a strong mon, if ye ken."

Mrs. Dunadee turned to look at the far wall, and following her lead, Nick realized a second portrait hung there. Angus Ross, Earl of Traquir, was depicted in his prime as a large, vigorous man who held himself as if he anticipated an imminent battle. He was the one, Nick saw, to give his granddaughter her gray eyes. Unlike her, however, he did not smile, but looked out at the room with an unflinching, steely gaze that challenged the viewer's purpose at Kilmorgan.

"Aye," Mrs. Dunadee said when Nick shifted in his seat.

"He was nae an easy mon." She sat staring at Angus a moment longer, and then, as if she'd made up her mind about something, she turned and leaned toward Nick. Her voice, when she spoke, was low, as if she did not wish old Angus to hear what she would say.

"Ye did see the old tower ootside?" When Nick nodded, she frowned sharply. "Not wishin' us to forget the wrongs done us by the Sassenach, Angus ordered the thing left as 'twas. Miss Tessa spent a deal o' her life lookin' at the ugly thing, as you must guess, and to please her grandfather, for she loved him as he did her, she vowed to hate the Sassenach as he did. But the lass has nae room for true hatred in her heart, not like Angus. If ye ken what I mean, milaird, ye'll go easy on the lass in the beginnin'. She'll coom 'round in time." With no apologies for the scrutiny to which she subjected a peer of the realm, Mrs. Dunadee leaned closer to search Nick's eyes so deeply he was reminded how he'd expected to be met by a crone casting spells. "Aye," the older woman nodded, seemingly satisfied by what she'd discerned. "Ye'll be the makin' o' her, if ye've the patience for the task."

3

"*O*ch, Miss Tessa! The skirt's nae long enow. 'Twill ne'er do for ye to be seen like tha'!"

Tessa Strahan's gray eyes sparkled vividly as she laughed. "And here I thought ye'd approve my dainty ankle, Nan MacDonald!"

Her maid, a plump girl with blue eyes and carrot red hair that proclaimed her Scottish heritage but belied her disposition, shook her head morosely. Two years her mistress' senior and a stout Scot, she did not hesitate to lend Tessa her advice. " 'Tis a wild start, I tell ye," she warned, though with little hope Miss Tessa would grow suddenly cautious. "The laird yer aunt's sent to fetch ye'll know the difference betwixt us. I am nae lady!"

"A pox upon ye, Nan, for your lack o' spirit!" Dismissing Nan with a toss of her bright auburn hair, Tessa frowned into the murky pier glass with which their small room was supplied. A great deal of her ankle did show beneath Nan's skirt, and she was not pleased that she must tack on a ruffle at the bottom, for she was no seamstress. There being no help for it, however, she whisked off the skirt before seating herself cross-legged upon the room's one bed to attend to her task.

She never considered forcing Nan to the chore, though the girl's needlework was quite fine. Nan would only grumble and dally so long, the thing would never get done at all. As her governess, Mrs. MacIverson had used to lament, a Highland servant was no servant at all, only a free man who lent his services as he pleased.

Tessa had dearly enjoyed MacIvey, as she had dubbed the

16

spare elderly woman Mrs. Dunadee had prevailed upon
Angus to import. The lady's keen wit and forthright attitude
had appealed to Tessa, and listening out of respect to
MacIvey's strictures, she had absorbed a great deal. But when
it came time to practice the refinements MacIvey preached,
Tessa did so only when it suited her.

Just as Mrs. Dunadee had failed to prevail in her time,
so MacIvey could not curb her young charge's tendency to
swear in imitation of her grandfather, or break her of the
habit of running as wild as she pleased over the heather and
crags about her home.

Only old Angus had had the power to rein in his granddaughter, but he had been too proud of her spirit to do so
with any regularity.

Nan, who had been born at Kilmorgan, knew all that very
well. Still, the matter at hand seemed worth another effort
to sway her mistress. "I canna think this pretendin' to be
me an' all is the way to gae on, Miss Tessa! If ye must gae
to Lunnon, then ye'd best face it."

It being an old argument, Tessa did not bother to raise her
head as she stitched. "I'll nae gae to London, Nan." The
assurance was made in a flat, certain voice. "I canna believe
Angus meant to leave matters like this. He would nae hear
Honoria's name spoken—and she his own daughter—after
she married her Sassenach lord. I am certain, absolutely
certain, Angus intended to leave my affairs in the hands of
his cousin in Edinburgh. He did nae do it only because he
was too stubborn to admit how ill he'd become. Now I must
contrive the best I can to outwit the Sassenach law. It may
designate Honoria my closest relative, but for all she was
born sister to my mother, she bears no true kinship to me.
And I do nae care to live with her!"

"But I dinna see how dressin' up as me will keep ye here!"
Nan burst out. "Aye, I ken ye've some daft notion that ye'll
play a trick on the Sassenach laird, and because he's not
watchin' ye overclose on account of he thinks yer me an'
I'm ye, ye'll do someat, but what? If ye run to Edinburgh,

they'll only fetch ye down from there. Lord Angus ever said his Ross cousin was nae able to stand against the Sassenach."

"But I shall not go to Edinburgh!" Tessa revealed with a triumphant grin. " 'Tis what they'd all expect, but I shall go the other way to Ayton, where MacIvey lives. She'll take me in, I'm sure of it, and Honoria knows naught of her. I shall stay there until I reach my majority and may return to live at Kilmorgan unhindered." Tessa continued with a confident smile. "I only need some means to come close to her town, ye see. Even I admit I could nae travel over the wild Grampians alone, and so I shall allow this Sassenach dandy to take me 'round to the Lowlands by ship. Once there, with the mountains safely behind me, I shall escape and go my own way."

Tessa paused in her sewing to examine her stitches. They were crooked and uneven, but served the purpose of holding the ruffle in place and she was not displeased. "Nae, Nan," she exclaimed, sighing when she glanced up to see her maid still wagged her head dolefully. "Ye're only fashed because ye must play my part. But, truly, ye needn't worry. Ye've only to play ill as I said. He'll pay ye no heed, thinkin' ye're weak and infirm, and of me he'll take nae notice at all. MacIvey said it was the Sassenach way to ignore those in their service. They look through them as if they were not there, she said."

Tessa chuckled richly at the thought of her plan, but Nan was not yet convinced. " 'Tis all well and good for ye, Miss Tessa, but 'tis I who shall face him when ye're gone!"

"Ye'll have no difficulty with him, lass!" Tessa tossed aside her sewing to go and give the other girl a reassuring hug. "The painted dandy will not notice a servant's run off. Ye'll see. He'll scarce miss me. And when ye reach Honoria, ye've only to throw yerself on her mercy and tell her I ordered ye to the deed. I canna believe she'll have forgotten entirely what loyalty means. Now, help me to put on yer skirt."

Standing before the pier glass a few moments later, Tessa

drew Nan's belt as tight as she could around her slim waist, and tucked her thick auburn hair beneath the maid's mob cap. "There! Now I'm off. Oh, nay, Nan, ye canna come." Tessa shook her head when Nan fell into step beside her. "Ye must stay and play at yer illness. I've expected this booby of a lord these two days or more. Now, ye're nae to worry, my dear." Tessa gave Nan an irrepressible grin. "I'll be away only a short while, and with Jamie Robertson gone fishing, there's none in Skelgara to look twice at me dressed in your clothes."

With a delighted laugh for the blush she'd brought to Nan's round cheeks, Tessa skipped out the door and quickly made her way from the tiny inn where she had decided to meet her aunt's godson.

She could not have assumed Nan's identity with Mrs. Dunadee looking on, and though everyone in Skelgara knew her, no one had reason to take the time from their busy labors to scrutinize a passing maid.

Tessa's mouth curved into a gamin's mischievous smile as she recalled how she'd persuaded Mrs. Dunadee to let her come to Skelgara. As if she would ever think to save a Sassenach lord a ride! Angus would roll over in his grave at the thought.

At the thought of Angus, the sparkle faded from Tessa's eyes. Though she had lost her grandfather to a fever a year and a half before, she yet mourned the proud, vital man who had been a father and sometimes a mother to her.

In her mind Kilmorgan and the country around it was inextricably bound with Angus, for he had ruled it all, though the Sassenach had sought to strip the clan chieftains of their power. Glancing up, Tessa could discern the outline of Kilmorgan Castle in the far distance, and a shaft of longing so intense it hurt lanced through her. She could not be gone long. She loved her proud home at the head of Skelgara's magnificent loch.

This unknown aunt, Honoria, thought to tear her from Kilmorgan and turn her into a simpering Sassenach miss married to a mincing Sassenach lord. Tessa knew this because in her first letter Honoria had made the mistake of confiding that she wished to take Tessa about London to balls and assemblies, "where there are a vast number of agreeable young men." As if Tessa would have a Sassenach for a husband!

Nimbly making her way to a fast-flowing burn that splashed noisily over the rocks, Tessa tossed her head in disgust. The Sassenach, particularly the men, were one and all, members of a hateful, vindictive race! Look how they stooped to killing women and children to bring Scotland low. Now, fat on their winnings, the Englishman had grown effete. Angus had told her how, though their country was at war, most sought to avoid service in her armies. In particular the wealthy, the very ones who ought to be leading their men, shirked thier duty.

This Lord Kerne, to be content running silly, useless errands for his godmother, must be the weakest among them.

Bah! It would be as simple to escape him as it had been to defy the first gentleman her aunt had sent. She had only to hold fast to her will. And she'd plenty of that, she knew.

Seated upon a rock by the stream's edge, Tessa removed her shoes and stockings and dangled her toes in water so cold it burned, but when she spied a huge, fat trout across the way, she laughed and threw herself full length upon the bank. Unmindful that her skirts slipped up to her calves, she went as still as a statue.

Nan's older brother, Robbie, had taught her how to catch a fish with her bare hands, and though she had only succeeded once, she had always enjoyed the game.

To Nicholas Steele, who came upon her by purest chance, she was an enchanting sight with half her charms on display. Her auburn hair, long since freed from Nan's confining mob cap, shone with a rich gloss in the sunlight. Lush and thick, her gleaming tresses would slide heavily through the fingers, Nick guessed.

His gaze moved lower, and his mouth curved. The chit's legs were as bare as an urchin's. And quite the most delectable sight he had enjoyed in days, for she had slim, delicate feet, and her legs were, in a word, beautiful. Long and slender, they were exquisitely curved just where they should be.

For the Highlands it was a warm day, and having bumped along on his pony a good portion of the morning, Nick had thought to refresh himself in the stream that ran parallel to but some distance below the road. Though he had made no effort to be silent, the girl concentrated with such intensity on something in the water, she did not hear him.

Suddenly, taking him by surprise, she exploded into movement. Rising in a swift blur, she plunged her arm into the cold stream, wetting her sleeve to the elbow.

"Damn and double damn!"

Her voice was clear and pleasing, its accents as refined as her words were not. Nicholas laughed aloud.

In one motion Tessa jumped to her feet and spun around. A tall man with shoulders broad enough to block the sun though he stood some distance away, was smiling down at her.

In the next instant he leapt with lazy ease from the boulder on which he stood to land directly before her, obliging Tessa to arch her neck to look him in the eye.

Tessa ought, perhaps, to have been afraid. He was a stranger, and though he wore clothes so well cut she knew they came from Edinburgh, she could tell he did not lack for strength.

But she had never seen a man so fine. He had something of a gypsy about him with his hair as black as a raven's wing and his loose-limbed grace. But he was no gypsy, despite the evidence of his bold smile. His eyes gave the lie to the premise. They were startling, brilliant blue, and just then were dancing irresistibly with humor.

Faced with such a smile, Tessa grinned impishly back. It was then Nick recognized her. Before, he'd been taken in by the costume she wore—her maid's, he thought—and by her body. She was no longer an uncurved adolescent. Her breasts had rounded to a pleasing fullness, and her hips flared gently. But—and Nick could only appreciate nature's exception—she had retained her lithe, supple waist. Indeed, it was so small, Nick knew without any question he could span the width of it with his hands.

Yet her wide, sparkling gray eyes were the eyes of the girl in the picture at Castle Kilmorgan, and her smile was still quicksilver bright.

"I can ne'er remain still long enow to catch one o' the darlin's," she announced, gesturing behind her to the stream and the trout in it. Despite the overwhelming presence of the stranger, Tessa did not forget to speak in a serving girl's lilting brogue. "Can ye?"

Nick's eyes gleamed with amusement. She was her picture come to life. Against the odds, while she had more than realized the promise of her beauty, she had retained the bright gamin's spirit he had found engaging, though he had been introduced to it only by an artist's rendering.

"I can think of better things to do along a riverbank with a pretty girl than lay in wait for a fish."

If he had pulled a pistol from his pocket, Nick did not think he could have wrought a greater effect than he did by merely speaking.

He was a Sassenach. Tessa stared in dumbfounded amazement before, closing her mouth with a snap, she whirled away to grab up her shoes and stockings. How such a fine-looking man could be Sassenach she did not know. Her aunt's first emissary had been as weak and feckless as Angus had said all Sassenach were. Beneath her breath she cursed the stranger with particular violence, as if he'd set out to fool her on purpose.

Her reaction, though he'd been given warning by everyone from Honoria to Mrs. Dunadee, took Nick by surprise. He was not particularly conceited, but neither was he accustomed to having women stomp disdainfully from his presence.

A half smile tugged at his mouth. Lord, how entirely the

accommodating lass had disappeared. Her eyes fairly shot sparks at him as she grabbed up her belongings, and her mouth, formerly curved in an inviting smile, was tightened in a quivering line.

As she turned back toward him, Nick realized the portrait painter, though he had captured Miss Strahan's spirit entirely, had omitted a particular physical feature. A tiny, natural beauty spot lay nestled just above the right corner of her mouth. Perhaps the artist had deemed it too provocative for a thirteen year old. Certainly it made the eye linger on her lips.

His eyes upon that tantalizing little mole, Nick caught Tessa by the arm when, wrapped tightly in a cloak of speaking silence, she made to pass by him. Outraged, she drew herself up into a bristling line, only to find to her fury that her head reached no farther than his chin.

"Loose me this instant, you fool!" Tessa spat indignantly.

Nick's blue eyes danced in answer. "Not before I've had a kiss, my pretty." If she wished to play at being a servant, she could, but she would learn there was a cost to such tricks. "I've been in Scotland long enough to know that if you find a nymph, it is good luck to taste her lips."

Nick laughed at the wild flashing of light in her eyes and held her arm tighter. Jerking back, Tessa attempted to pelt him with her shoes, but he caught that arm as well and brought her up full length against him. He left her in no doubt as to what he would do. His eyes caressed the little spot Tessa had always considered a blemish before he bent his head to capture her lips with his.

Kissed only once before by a boy her age and with little effect, Tessa was for a moment overwhelmed by a paralyzing giddiness. The stranger's full, firm mouth was strangely hot and somehow sweet and his kiss demanding. Her blood surged forward all at once and, ignited by his kiss, seemed to lick her veins with fire. She gasped, heard the sound, realized she'd made it, and recalled who it was that forced a kiss from her.

She kicked him. "Ow!" The yelp was her own. Her bare

feet were no match for the man's shining black boots. Again he laughed at her, his mouth now only a tantalizing few inches away from hers.

"Let that be a lesson, little wench," he chided softly, his blue eyes holding hers. "You should never lie about in the hills unless you've all your clothes on. Now, before I am tempted beyond chivalry, go on to safety."

With a light smack to her soft bottom Nick sent Tessa on her way down the hill. She ran like a deer until she judged herself distant enough to chance a curse over her shoulder. "A pox on ye, ye Sassenach devil!" she yelled, lifting a laughably delicate fist toward him. That her lips still trembled from his kiss and her soft backside glowed with the feel of his hand only added to her fury. "Ye've nae heard the last o' me!"

A smile tugged at his mouth as Nick thought how much more truth there was in that last statement than Miss Strahan could know. While she clambered nimbly over the rocks and disappeared from sight, he contemplated her probable reaction when she realized he was the man who would escort her to London.

He'd little confidence he could persuade her to believe he'd stolen the kiss in an effort to teach her, in the most direct way possible, of the dangers that lurked in the world for unescorted young girls.

Unexpectedly Nick grinned. He had trouble convincing himself.

4

"*M*iss Tessa!" Nan sprang up, spilling the dress she had been mending. Not heeding it or the flush staining her mistress' cheeks, she rushed to take Tessa's hand. "The Sassenach laird's coome! He sent a note sayin' he would see ye when he was settled!"

Tessa took a breath to steady herself and to put the hateful man she'd met in the hills from her mind. The real test before her was not some passing stranger whom she would never see again, but the enemy her aunt had sent to carry her off to hated England.

"And how did ye reply?"

"Just as ye told me," Nan reported faithfully. "That Mistress Strahan ha' taken ill and could nae go down."

"Aye, yer a bonnie lass to be sure, Nan MacDonald!" Tessa's infectious laugh coaxed a responding grin from Nan.

The second note delivered an hour later by a young serving girl conveyed the Marquess of Kerne's regret for Miss Strahan's poor health and inquired if she were well enough to take tea in the inn's private parlor so that "travel arrangements might be made." The note was signed Nicholas Steele, in what Tessa considered to be a pretentiously bold hand.

Tessa dispatched the girl with the reply that Miss Strahan's maid would be down shortly and went to adjust her maid's costume. Curls hidden and belt retightened, she grinned at her maid. "Behold, Nan! Am I not the meek, inconspicuous maid who comes as called to be advised of my mistress' travel schedule?"

Laughing, Tessa whirled out the door before Nan could

answer, which was just as well for the girl could only have said, were she to be truthful, that her mistress could never, however humble her costume, be inconspicuous.

Tessa knocked on the door of the inn's only private parlor, and when she was bade to enter by a distant voice, she entered quickly, curious to judge this latest enemy her aunt had sent against her. The man stood at the far side of the room, looking out the window toward the mountains behind Skelgara, but Tessa did not need to see his face. His gypsy-black hair and tall, lean build were enough.

"You!" she breathed, forgetting to use brogue in her extremity.

Amusement, unmistakable and unforgivable, gleamed in Nick's blue eyes as he turned with what she considered mocking indolence and bowed. "Nicholas Steele, at your service, Miss Strahan."

Tessa was recalled to her role. "Do nae be daft, milaird!" she snapped, wishing she had the means to wipe the smirking smile from the man's arresting face. "I am nae Miss Strahan but her maid, Nan. Mistress Strahan is abed with a soreness of throat."

Double damn, Tessa swore to herself as the dratted man's eyebrow lifted. What a fool she was to have trusted her aunt's second emissary would be as feckless as the first. She ought to have struck off for MacIvey's alone. Crossing the wild Grampian mountains could not have been as problematical as traveling with this arrogant Sassenach rogue with his knowing eyes would be.

Already he had very much taken notice of the servant he was to have all but ignored. "Miss Strahan canna travel for several days more," Tessa heard herself saying. She had no rational plan in mind as she gave Nicholas Steele a defiant look, only the thought that she must have time to think what to do.

"Tomorrow, my dear, ah, Nan. She will travel tomorrow."

"But she cannae!" Tessa objected instantly.

Nicholas smiled. "The ship on which we travel will be as comfortable a place as any for Miss Strahan to recover from her illness. It is past time that we began our journey."

" 'Tis yer fault we're late!" Tessa retorted. "And my mistress is too ill to travel!"

Nick did not reply to the accusation that he had delayed them. He'd wait awhile yet before he revealed that he had been to Castle Kilmorgan and knew very well that it was Mistress Strahan who stood before him, not her maid. "I shall come and fetch Miss Strahan myself if she is not ready by precisely nine o'clock."

His tone was pleasant, but Tessa received the clear impression the infuriating man would carry Nan to his ship if he thought he must. "But she can nae travel with ye! 'Tis a rogue ye be. Ye did nae treat me with respect!"

The smile she had thought bold before and now considered wicked flashed out at her. "Ah, but Nan, you are not your mistress. Mistress Strahan, I assume, does not make a habit of allowing any passerby a view of her bare legs or give any complete stranger a fetching and most inviting smile."

"Nae!" Tessa's outrage was not feigned. None of the young men who either lived near Kilmorgan or who had visited it in company with their families had ever forgotten Angus' legendary temper. However appealing they had found her, they had kept their distance. The result was Tessa truly had no notion how open to interpretation her teasing smile was. "Ye're a great boobie, ye are, if ye think I invited ye to take liberties!"

The novelty of being called "a great boobie" caused Nick, to Tessa's considerable surprise, to throw back his head and laugh outright. "If I'm a great boobie, whatever that may be, then you are a great babe, my dear. A smile to a stranger is always an invitation."

Tessa glared in mute response. The Sassenach's words had the hateful ring of truth to them, but she would roast in hell before she conceded as much.

She deeply regretted smiling at him, but not only, or even

mostly, because the result of that unstudied act was the mortifying interview she currently endured. Most of all, Tessa regretted failing Angus. His hatred of the conquering Sassenach had been a palpable thing. "Och! They're a murderin', thievin', dishonorable race intent on beggarin' Scotland to enrich themselves, Tessa," he had said more times than she could recount. And she had smiled in all friendliness at one of them!

"No retort, my dear Nan?" Nick challenged, and watched, amused, as Tessa's gray eyes stormed at him. "Then I shall surmise you have learned your lesson. As to your mistress, I shall treat her as I treat all gently behaved ladies: with courtesy." There was a threat in that assurance, and Tessa read it correctly. Should a lady not behave gently, he would not behave courteously. Satisfied from the tightening of her lips that she understood him, Nick continued, "As for tomorrow, you and your mistress may prepare yourselves to depart, or I shall do it for you. The choice is yours, but either way we shall depart for Edinburgh at the hour I stated. And now, dear Nan, would you care for some tea? Mrs. MacInnes has gone to great lengths to provide us an elaborate tray, I believe." Tessa blinked. She'd quite forgotten tea. "The scones look quite delicious."

Nick's efforts to tempt her into pleasantness failed. "I'll nae take tea with ye, ye cowardly Sassenach!" Tessa cried, indignant at the very thought, and without waiting for a dismissal she whirled from the room, snapping the door closed behind her with a sharp bang.

Nick grinned at the sound. Honoria had been more accurate than she knew when she'd guessed her niece was not in the common way. Lord, she was so uncommon Honoria might well regret taking her in. But that was his godmother's problem. His was to get the chit to her, and as it seemed the task would require all his strength, Nick did not neglect to thoroughly enjoy the tea tray he had rightly suspected would be delicious.

* * *

"Nay, ye must dry yer tears now, Nan! There'll be nae trouble, ye'll see! This Sassenach lord is still abed, I know it. Angus said they sleep as late as they are able."

The sun had only just risen when Tessa pushed Nan, cloaked and veiled, from their room. After a long night spent in restless consideration of her situation, she had conceded that she could not organize an escape from the Marquess of Kerne before the hour when he had said he would come to fetch her, and so she had put her mind to deciding how best to continue her reversal of roles with Nan, for, though the marquess had undoubtedly noticed her, she believed she possessed the advantage if he thought her only a serving girl.

Gulls screeched overhead as the two girls hurried through the little village of Skelgara, but as Tessa had hoped, there were few people about to look curiously at them. When she caught the scent of salt air, her spirits rose despite the circumstances. Several times she had journeyed to Edinburgh by ship, and always she had enjoyed the experience.

She would not be going to see her mother this time, however. Like Angus, her mother had died of the fever. So many had gone, Tessa thought, seeing now not the small lanes of Skelgara and the loch beyond, but the faces first of her parents and then her grandfather. Alone, she was left to the dubious mercies of the Sassenach.

Tessa's nose, slightly tipped at the very end, lifted defiantly. She might be the last of her line, but she was not the least. She would enjoy her trip upon the Sassenach ship, and then, in the Lowlands, when it suited her, she would make good her escape.

Turning a corner, both girls pulled up short. Before them was a sleek ship with raked masts. Well cared for, her black paint glistened in the early morning sun, and the gilt lettering on her prow proclaimed her to be the "*Sea Witch*." Jutting forward over the loch was her figurehead, a full-breasted woman with black, swirling hair and the most diaphanous of gowns, Tessa noted with a censorious eye.

"Miss! Ma'am!" A seaman hurried to them as they came

up the gangplank. "We never expected you so early like."

"Have you a cabin made up for my mistress?" Tessa demanded, though her tone was not as haughty as she had intended. The young seaman was blushing so profusely she could not help but feel sorry for him. "She is nae feeling well and needs her bed."

"Yes, yes, of course." The young man bobbed his head, and after a furtive glance at Nan, who stood silent and mysterious in her veils, he led the way down a narrow set of stairs to a large cabin.

"Why, 'tis grand!" Nan cried in wonder when the young man had departed.

"Nae bad," Tessa agreed grudgingly as she took in the cabin that accommodated a single enormous bed carved of mahogany, as well as a desk and a dining table and chairs, all of the same costly wood. Covering the floor was a fine carpet from, she thought, China.

Nan sank upon the bed with a blissful sigh. "I dinna think I shall find travelin' in a tiny sliver o' wood so terrible as I feared. The bed's soft as down."

As her maid's spirits rose, Tessa's kept pace by falling. "We are still in the harbor, dinna forget," she muttered, crossing to look out the porthole. The cabin was more luxurious than any she'd ever seen, and she wished to know who had paid for it.

Was it her money that had been used to sweeten her journey south? She did not care for the thought, though she had the wealth to afford it. Her father's family, the Strahans, had been clever enough early in the previous century to invest their monies on the Continent and so had not been affected by Prince Charles Stuart's defeat at Culloden Moor as severely as the Rosses. It was her father's money that had been used to rebuild those parts of Kilmorgan that had succumbed to Cumberland's torch, and on his death his fortune had come to Tessa.

Looking out at the loch waters, ruffled slightly by a building breeze, she wondered if Nick Steele knew she was an heiress. He must. Her aunt would confide that. Did he wish a wealthy wife? Was that why he had put himself out to do his godmother's bidding? Did he intend to woo her?

Tessa whirled from the window. Let him try! The Sassenach marquess would never succeed with her.

Her mind occupied with a fierce rejection of Nicholas Steele's suit, Tessa did not hear until too late the knock at the door. Even as she called, "Just a moment," and rushed to hand Nan her veils, the door swung open.

"Miss Strahan, at last we meet."

Nicholas Steele, sparing not a glance for Tessa, entered and advanced steadily upon Nan.

When the poor girl shrank from him, her eyes very wide, Tessa swore to herself. Nan was not prepared for the full effect of the Marquess of Kerne, and the responsibility for that could be laid at Tessa's door. Deliberately, fearing Nan would be frightened into refusing to play her part, Tessa had withheld a full description of the rogue. Intending to be more precise when they were safely out to sea and Nan could not threaten to return to Kilmorgan, Tessa had said only that the marquess was not quite the weakling she'd expected.

Smiling courteously, Nick took Nan's hand before she could snatch it back. Too late Tessa noticed how rough and red her maid's hand was, but she breathed a sigh of relief when the marquess did not seem to notice he lifted no lady's hand to his lips.

"Miss Strahan, I am pleased to find you eager for your journey. You must be feeling more the thing if you are able to rise so early."

Nan could only gape as Nick smiled down at her, and Tessa thought it time to intervene. "Miss Strahan is nae well at'll! We've come aboard sae early on account o' she slept poorly. 'Tis verra bad!" Tessa improvised as Nick slowly turned his head to give her the blandest of looks. "My mistress ha' lost her voice. She needs rest."

Dismissing Tessa without a word, Nick turned back to Nan. "You are lucky to have so solicitous a maid, Miss Strahan. I am certain she's in the right of it, too. You do need your rest, but first, I am persuaded, you need to break your fast. To sail upon an empty stomach is unwise, as I am certain you know, for you have sailed to Edinburgh before have you not?''

Nan's glance slid to Tessa before flicking back to the totally unnerving man before her. Quickly she managed a mute bob of her head.

"Good." His white smile dazzled her. "Ah, and here is Jakes now. Let him in, will you, Nan?''

Force of habit prompted Nan to move in response to the marquess' command, but she drew up, blushing, when Tessa shook her head frantically and hurried across the cabin.

"Shall we be seated?'' the marquess asked, the gleam in his eye so unsettling Nan that she could scarcely make herself move to the chair he held out for her.

To the girl's trembling relief, his lordship's disturbing attention was diverted from her when a trim, wiry man with twinkling brown eyes entered the room carrying a large tray. "Just put it here on the table, Jakes,'' the marquess directed. "Miss Strahan can pour.''

Nan's gasp was audible. She had no notion how to pour tea in the manner the marquess would expect.

"Miss Strahan is too ill to pour.'' Tessa came to her rescue. "I shall do it.''

"Nonsense.'' The marquess carelessly waved her off. "You would coddle your mistress. Miss Strahan looks well enough to pour.'' He smiled winningly at Nan who stared back as though he were an adder and she a mouse. "There, you see.'' A wicked gleam dancing in his eye, Nick turned to Tessa. "Your mistress does not argue. Indeed, I do not think we need your services at all just now, Nan. You may as well go along with Jakes and get yourself a bite to eat.''

Nan reacted by swaying dramatically. "I told ye!'' Tessa leapt to her maid's side. "She truly is nae well, milaird. She needs rest and quiet.''

But Nick was not moved by Tessa's words or her furious gaze. "And she will have both in only a few moments, when we have breakfasted. Just now she needs to eat.''

Tessa was sorely torn. She doubted Nan would get along well without her, but she did want the marquess to accept her as an inconspicuous servant. "As you will, milaird," she said, though she could see Nan give her a wild look.

"I have looked forward to meeting you, you know, Miss Strahan," Tessa heard Nick say as she went to help Jakes with the dishes. "Your aunt, my godmother, is almost like a mother to me. I admire her greatly, as I am certain you will do, for there has never been a kinder person."

Tessa wanted to snort in disgust at the suggestion that she might admire Honoria. Glancing over her shoulder to see Nan's response, she saw instead that the marquess had arranged the pot of coffee and cups before the girl.

Nan regarded the delicate china as if it might bite her. She had seen her mistress pour, but she had never paid close attention. Uncertain how to grasp the handle of the pot, she closed her shaking hand like a fist about it. The cups seemed impossibly small, and the marquess, she was sickeningly aware, studied her closely as the pot rattled in her hand.

"You know, I find it most odd, Miss Strahan, that you look nothing at all like your aunt."

"Ahhh!" Jerking violently, Nan splashed a stream of hot coffee on her hand and then promptly burst into tears.

"Now look what ye've done!" Tessa glared accusingly at Nick as she flounced over to comfort Nan.

"I do not think it is what I've done, Miss Strahan," he said mildly, lounging back in his chair and observing the sobbing girl with calm detachment. "I think it is what you've done."

A rejoinder upon her lips, Tessa looked up from attending to Nan only to realize it was she that he had addressed as Miss Strahan.

"How long have you known?" she demanded, her chin jutting up belligerently.

"From the first. I missed your letter and so journeyed to Kilmorgan where I saw your portrait in the solar. You have changed, Miss Strahan, but not that much."

5

"*A*bominable Sassenach cur!" Tessa trembled with the force of her anger. The rogue had known precisely who she was when he had forced his kiss upon her. "You'll not take me with you!"

Her skirts swirling around her ankles, Tessa got as far as the door before she heard a man cry, "All clear!"

Eyes blazing, she rounded on Nick. "You have kept us down here on purpose!" she said accusingly before dashing out of the cabin.

On deck she saw the foresails had been raised, and they were already some twenty feet of frigid water from the dock.

"Too far to jump, I think."

Tessa clenched her hands into fists. She did not know whether she was angrier that he had played her for a fool by the burn or that he mocked her now. "You are detestable!"

Nick's eyes gleamed. "And you are wiser, my dear. Now you know at first hand that it will not do to traipse about alone, shedding your shoes and stockings and hiking up your skirt as high as you please. You are asking for serious trouble with such behavior."

Tessa responded with a scathing look before she treated him to a view of her proud profile. She would not engage in banter with the Sassenach villain who meant only to put a good face on outrageous behavior. Whatever he might pretend aloud, he should never have kissed her. He had treated her as if she were a trollop!

A most unrepentant grin tugged at Nick's mouth as he eyed the angry flush coloring Tessa's cheeks. "If you are anticipating an apology, Miss Strahan, you wait in vain. For one thing, you brought the whole upon yourself, and for another,'' he paused, and though she was not looking she could almost feel his smile, ''I cannot honestly regret such an enjoyably returned kiss.''

''Oh!'' Tessa whirled upon him. ''You lie! You attacked me, you Sassenach rogue, and I—I despise you!''

''You despised me before you ever saw me, my dear, and if you have learned from our encounter to comport yourself properly, then I have taught you a great deal at no cost.'' Nick's bold eyes dropped to her lips, reminding her that said lesson had, by his account, been a pleasure to him, but before Tessa could call him all the vile names crowding her tongue, his mood changed. ''Now then, if you have decided you'll not jump overboard, I suggest you return below to your meal. We shall encounter the swells of the North Sea very soon, and your maid, in particular, if I don't miss my guess, will need sustenance to fight their effect.''

''I shall stay where I am until we leave the loch. I wish to say farewell to my home. Undisturbed,'' she added, her eyes narrowing when Nick made no move to go.

For a second it seemed that he might argue with her, but in the end, he only inclined his head. ''As you will,'' he said, leaving her and disappearing down the stairway of the cabin house.

Her emotions stirred to a high pitch, Tessa searched for the faint, blurry outline of Kilmorgan standing sentinel in the distance. Tears pricked her eyelids at the thought that she might never see her home again, and in the next instant she banged the rail with her fist. She would return! No mocking, insufferable Sassenach would deny her her home.

Behind her, Tessa heard the sailors heave in unison to raise the mainsail. Almost at once the ship lifted to meet the swells of the open sea, and the rising motion had a felicitous effect upon her spirits. However despicable the Sassenach lord was —and he had lied, she had not returned his kiss, she had only been caught off her guard and had pushed him away later rather than sooner—he could not diminish her pleasure in the sea voyage. She enjoyed the tang of the salt air and the rocking motion of the ship too well.

Nan was not so well pleased, as Tessa found when she returned to their cabin. "Have ye had coffee or scones, Nan?" Tessa asked upon seeing the greenish cast to the girl's complexion. "They will help ye get over that queasy feeling."

Nan's reply was faint but unequivocal. "Nae! Nae! I canna eat, Miss Tessa."

Eventually Tessa prevailed, and as she watched Nan take tiny bites of her scone, she recommended going on deck when they were done. "Just breathing in the fresh air will help ye."

"But I only wish to lie down."

A veteran of several sea voyages, Tessa insisted. "Truly, Nan, ye'll feel better there."

"Och! 'Tis nae only my illness!" Nan cried, the truth bursting from her. "I canna face his lairdship!"

Tessa was not well pleased to find that the marquess had so deeply affected Nan. "Do nae be daft!" she scolded impatiently.

" 'Tis not I who be daft!" Nan grumbled, her queasy stomach and lowered spirits prompting to her to be less accommodating than was her want. "Did nae I say our tradin' clothes was foolish? Aye, I did. But ye would nae listen, and I made a fool o' myself!"

When Nan burst into tears for the second time that morning, Tessa, feeling entirely contrite, went to embrace the distraught girl. "Hush, hinny," she crooned softly. "Ye were nae foolish! I swear it! 'Twas me that Sassenach devil wished to bring low, nae ye, lass."

Nan sniffed as she accepted Tessa's handkerchief to dry her eyes. "Why did ye nae say ye had met the laird when ye walked out, Miss Tessa?"

Recalling her meeting with Nick Steele, Tessa tossed her head in a gesture familiar to Nan. "I did nae know the man I encountered upon my walk was Lord Kerne, blast his soul."

Tessa's dark frown did not encourage further questioning. "I'm thinkin' the Laird Kerne be nae weak mon like ye expected, Miss Tessa," Nan observed a trifle wearily. "Nor the fool. He's bound to search for ye if ye run off."

Little to Nan's surprise, Tessa's mouth tightened in a stubborn line. "Ye may as well save your breath, Nan. There's no persuadin' me. I shall nae go to Lunnon. Now, if ye're through with that bit of scone, 'tis time to forget the Sassenach and go above. Ye'll ride easier there, I promise."

Her stomach increasingly affected by the roll and pitch of the ship, Nan hadn't the will to argue, and with Tessa's assistance she dragged herself onto the deck.

Though a bank of clouds loomed on the western horizon, the sky immediately above them was clear and blue, and Nan, breathing deeply of the briny air, conceded her mistress had been right. She felt well enough, indeed, to smile a little at the stocky, squarish man with keen eyes who introduced himself to them as Captain Reed, the master of the vessel.

A man of few words, he impressed both girls as capable of guiding them through the difficult waters off Cape Wrath, and even Tessa was able to overlook his nationality sufficiently to accept his offer of escort to an awning that had been erected at the stern of the boat. Beneath its protection Nan lay down to doze, but Tessa kept her fascinated eyes upon the sea, the sailors, and the stark shore of northern Scotland.

There was so much activity to observe, she was surprised when Jakes, announcing it was midday, brought them a cold collation. Though Nan could only manage a few nibbles, Tessa ate a full meal and pronounced herself well pleased with her journey until she saw that Nick Steele had returned to the deck.

Tessa watched warily as he went to speak to the captain and then came toward her. Prepared for battle, she was not certain how she felt when he did not so much as glance at her but went to relieve the man on watch at the wheel.

Looming directly before her as he was, Nick upset Tessa's

peace entirely. Even when she jerked her head to the left
to stare at the vague purplish shapes she knew to be the
Hebrides, she could still see him from the corner of her eye.

In the end, when her neck began to hurt, Tessa gave up
and allowed her gaze to turn where it seemed to want to go,
consoling herself as she stared a hole in Nick Steele's back
with the thought that it was wise to know one's enemy.

To her surprise, he seemed entirely at home on the deck
of a ship. Perhaps the journey north had accustomed him
to the sea's motion, for he stood easily at the wheel. And
he seemed to know what he was doing there as well. Captain
Reed, amidships, issued no orders as the marquess glanced
from the sails to the sea and adjusted the large wheel
accordingly.

He was strong. His coat fit so well, she'd no difficulty
seeing the play of his shoulder muscles as he kept the *Sea
Witch* on her course, and, grimacing, Tessa recalled the first
gentleman who had played her aunt's messenger. George
Pierpoint had been slightly pudgy and his skin a pasty white.
Tessa scornfully suspected Mr. Pierpoint disdained any
activity more strenuous than lifting his extravagantly starched
neckcloth to his throat, and she could not imagine him
standing on the deck of a ship. At the least, he'd have been
horrified to have his carefully tended hair disarranged by the
breeze. The marquess, by contrast, seemed not at all aware
that a lock of his black hair, ruffled by the wind, lay on his
brow.

When he turned, Tessa could see, the set of this second
messenger's lean jaw. It attested to an above-average strength
of will, and argued against the notion he was afflicted by
the degeneracy Angus had said all the Sassenach nobility
suffered from. Certainly the Marquess of Kerne's body could
be termed nothing but fit. He'd powerful shoulders any man
would have envied, a narrow waist, lean hips, and long,
sinewy legs.

Because she was staring at Nick's tight breeches, Tessa
realized only after the fact that his feet were no longer

pointing forward. Her eyes flew up at once to see he had
handed the wheel to another man and stood looking down
at her.

Color washed her cheeks when she detected the gleam
lighting his eye. Blast the man! she swore beneath her breath.
He thought she'd been lost in admiration of him. The
horrifying notion caused her to tilt her tipped nose and turn
pointedly away from him to stare at nothing at all. How dare
he think she did anything but disdain him!

To her vast irritation the Sassenach did not meekly accept
her snub. From the corner of her eye, she watched his glossy
boots advance until he stood directly before her.

"I am glad to see you are enjoying the day," he said
pleasantly, though Tessa refused to look at him. "Captain
Reed warns that a storm is brewing in the west, and tomorrow
will not be half so nice."

"A s-storm?" Nan had awakened in time to hear the
unhappy forecast. "Will it be bad, milaird?"

Nick's smile was meant to soothe and succeeded. "Nothing
we cannot survive, Nan. Captain Reed will see us safely
through. I shall be joining you for dinner to see that you eat
well, however, for we may not be able to light a fire in the
galley tomorrow."

The announcement brought Tessa's head whipping around,
but Nick was already striding away, calling, "Until then,"
in a mocking voice over his shoulder.

Her face set in a most mutinous expression, Tessa
determined that he might force himself upon her at dinner,
but he could not force her to receive him happily. In
consequence, when Nick entered their cabin that evening,
dressed in elegant clothes she realized now had been cut not
in Edinburgh but London, she did not bid him good evening.

Nan, however, did, though she kept her voice quiet and
her head turned from her mistress.

"And good evening to you, Nan," Nick returned with a
charming smile. Pointedly refraining from extending any
greeting to Tessa, he asked Nan if she would care for a glass

of ratafia. "Jakes has brought some along, I believe."

Flustered, for she had never been treated so courteously by such a man, Nan ducked her head affirmatively. Nick, unasked, poured two glasses, and Nan took one to her mistress.

Tessa accepted it with a terse thank you that did not extend to Nick, and silence reigned until Jakes entered with a tray of food for them. The fish was good, but though Nan nervously praised the meal, Tessa continued to maintain a grim silence. She would not pay tribute to prison food, she told herself.

The Sassenach lord at whom she would not look, but of whom she was intensely aware, allowed them to finish their meal without forcing conversation. Through her thick lashes Tessa saw that he ate everything on his plate, as if the tension in the air did not affect him in the least.

To prove she was equally unmoved, Tessa ate, if not all, then as much as she would normally eat. The lemon tart they were served at the end was so good that she did not notice Nick push his aside and lean toward her.

As a result, she jumped when his voice broke the silence. "You've not asked after your aunt, Tessa. Are you not curious about her at all?"

Not happy to have been startled, Tessa rounded upon him furiously. "I am Miss Strahan to you, Sassenach! And no, to answer your question, I am not the least curious about my aunt! I know all that I need to know about her."

All of a sudden the gleam in Nick's eye was not nearly as amused, though his voice, when he spoke, was even. "I do not think you know very much at all about Honoria. She is a fine lady, whatever your grandfather may have told you."

Tessa came out of her seat as she slapped her napkin down upon the table. "I shall not listen to the likes of you disparage Angus Ross!"

She whirled away, intent on departing the cabin altogether, but was not quick enough. Nick caught her arm and with an insistent pressure brought her back to her seat.

"I had no intention of disparaging your grandfather," he told her levelly. "The earl and his daughter had their differences, but I do not believe their quarrel should keep you from judging her for yourself. She is a woman of much generosity, as you will see if you but give her a chance. You are her only living relative, you know, for she could never have the children she wanted very badly."

With a violent jerk Tessa freed her arm from Nick's grasp. What he suggested was no less than a betrayal of Angus. "I do nae want to go to my aunt, do ye hear! She drags me to her against my will. If she is childless, then 'tis God's punishment for hurtin' Angus in the way she did."

Surging to his feet, Nicholas crashed his fist down upon the table. The dishes rattled wildly and Nan cried out, but Tessa was held motionless by the fury blazing suddenly in the eyes of the man towering over her.

"You will never say such a heartless thing to Honoria, do you hear me? As God is my witness, Therèse Strahan, you will bitterly regret it if you do. Honoria will not be obliged to endure such spite as that."

Disgusted, Nick threw down his napkin and strode to the door without awaiting a reply. When he had jerked it open, he turned to impale Tessa with a hard gaze. "Remember my words, for I mean them. If you should hurt her, I swear I shall take you over my knee and give you the lesson in comportment you are long overdue!"

Nan, when the door crashed closed, uttered a frightened cry, and even Tessa flinched. The truth was, she had spoken without thinking, for she could not wish barrenness even upon an aunt who had betrayed her family and her country. But she would never repent her words to Nicholas Steele. Let him think of her what he would, she did not care!

6

*T*essa was awakened from a confusing dream about rocking horses by a piteous moan. One look at Nan's face and she leapt from their bed, caught herself to keep from falling when the ship rolled sharply, and only just returned in time to hold a basin beneath the girl's head as Nan lost the dinner she'd enjoyed the night before.

Nan murmured an indistinct sob of distress when Tessa wiped her face with a cold cloth, but she was soon silenced by her mistress. " 'Tis often enough ye've cared for me, Nan MacDonald. Lie still now, that I may attend to ye."

No sooner had Tessa done so than a knock sounded at the door. Donning a thick nightrobe, she went to find Jakes there holding a tray, his legs planted wide against the heaving of the ship.

She smiled as she bid him good day, for though he was Sassenach and in Lord Kerne's employ, Tessa found his merry brown eyes a welcome sight that dreary morning. "Have you any medicine for seasickness, Jakes? Nan is very ill, I fear."

The amiable man looked with quick sympathy at the bed, where Nan lay in unheeding misery. "Aye, miss. I'll bring a medicament to make 'er sleep sound as a tick." When he'd set the tray upon the table that he had, by some seaman's magic, freed to swing with the rocking of the ship so it did not spill its contents, he apologized for the meager breakfast he had brought. " 'Tis not much. Cook dared not trust more than one fire in the galley with this wind ridin' us, but I did manage to bring you a pot of hot tea to warm the bread and cheese."

42

"I am so hungry the tea and bread will suit me admirably. Thank you, Jakes," Tessa assured him, earning herself a nod of respect.

When he returned, Jakes was not at all surprised to find she had polished off her simple meal. Had a temper did the missus, but she was a born sailor.

After Jakes had explained how she should administer the medicine he'd brought, he looked sympathetically toward Nan. "I well remember the first time I went upon a ship with 'is lordship, Miss. I was bad enough to pray for death."

To ask Jakes the particulars of that first trip or any other he had taken with his master would be to admit to curiosity about Nicholas Steele. Tessa subdued the unworthy impulse and asked instead if she would need a cloak when she went on deck later.

Jakes looked aghast. "The deck's no place for you today, miss! It'll be that dangerous. His lordship wishes you to stay below."

Tessa heeded his lordship's command most of the morning. She'd little choice, really, for Nan did not respond immediately to Jakes's remedy and required the basin and a cold cloth repeatedly. When at last, after a second dose of the dark liquid, she did fall into a sleep the tossing of the ship did not seem to disturb, Tessa uttered a groan of relief.

With nothing to occupy her, however, she had the leisure to notice how sour and heavy the air of the cabin had become. The portholes might have provided relief, but with the sea foam spraying relentlessly, there was no question of opening them.

To her further irritation, Tessa found she could not read to pass the time. The constant pitching of the ship made following the words on a page an impossibility.

Though in truth it was sizable, the cabin slowly seemed to shrink to the size of a tomb. The desire to be free of it became irresistible, and after a check on Nan, who slept as soundly as a babe, she sought out her cloak.

Seeing no one in the corridor, Tessa negotiated it as quickly as she could and, holding tightly to the railing, made her way up the steps of the cabin house to the deck. Here again luck was with her. No one appeared to forbid her her freedom.

When she peered around the corner of the cabin house toward the stern, the wind struck her full in the face, ripping the hood of the cloak from her head. Far from resenting its force, Tessa lifted her face to it and inhaled deeply. As she did, she glimpsed the man who stood at the helm. Nick did not hold the wheel that day. He stood behind it, shouting terse orders first to the men in the rigging and then to the helmsman. He was so obviously in command Tessa wondered if Captain Reed had become ill.

Surely they did not share the captaining of the vessel. She had never heard of such a thing, and, anyway, such an arrangement implied more exertion than she could imagine a Sassenach lord would care for, though she did admit that the particular English marquess standing just then with his head lifted and his legs easily braced against the stern deck did not look much like a gentleman who craved leisure.

Well, whatever the truth, Tessa shrugged to herself, that same marquess would not succeed in denying her a long taste of the wild elements. Casting about, she looked for a spot that would be sheltered from both the wind and Lord Kerne's eyes.

She was still deciding where to shelter when a heavy gust of wind sent the ship pitching steeply sideways. Unprepared, holding to nothing, Tessa was sent sliding across the deck. Her slick-soled slippers found no purchase on the wooden planks; rather, they seemed greased so quickly did she fly toward the ship's sea rail. She hit it hard, jackknifing over it so the breath was knocked from her. Below, the sea boiled madly and reached up for her.

Tessa flailed, searching for a foothold. Her fingers, trapped beneath her, were growing numb. The ship rolled violently again. She slipped . . .

When a pair of strong arms caught her by the waist just

as she thought she would be tossed overboard, she had no thought but to cry out and fling her arms tightly about her rescuer's neck. Even when she looked up to see it was Nick Steele who carried her to the relative safety of the area before the cabin house, she did not loosen her hold.

It had been a very close thing in all, and she did not need the Sassenach lord's thunderous expression to tell her how near to being lost overboard she had been.

"You little fool! You nearly got yourself drowned."

They were in the lee of the cabin house, and without the wind driving by her ears, Nick's furious shout was deafening. He'd have been surprised to know Tessa had the fleeting impression he sounded exactly like Angus in a temper.

Tessa did not muse over the impression for longer than a heartbeat, as Nick was, without faltering, swinging her through the cabin house entryway. Before he could take the first step into the gloom below, she cried, "No! Wait!"

He halted, frowning. "Now what?"

Lingering memories of Angus were sent flying when Tessa looked up to address Nick. His face was so close she could feel the warmth of his breath on her cheek.

"Put me down!" she demanded. The unsteady feeling she experienced she quickly ascribed to the ship's motion, but when Nick did not at once release her, she repeated more sharply, "Put me down, sir! I can stand unaided." Something in the way Nick's mouth lifted at the corner caused her to tense, but then he was setting her feet upon the floor. "Thank you," she said quickly.

"You ought to thank me." Nick's ill humor had, it seemed, returned. "You were nearly thrown into the sea! I told Jakes to keep you below. I can't allow you on deck with this westerly crashing down behind us."

Thought of the airless dungeon awaiting her prompted Tessa to say at once, "But I am unharmed, my lord. Don't send me below! Please." The pleading word was out before she could bite it back, but seeing the stern look on Nick's face, Tessa decided her pride could stand a little more swallowing. "I could sit near you on the stern deck. There is a stout railing there."

Tessa's struggle to conciliate went for naught. Nick caught her arm and, turning to usher her below, dismissed her request out of hand. "I've a storm to outrun."

"You've a challenge to enjoy!" Tessa amended, eschewing humility as she wrested her arm from his grasp. "I saw you on the stern deck. You like this wild wind very well, yet you would send me back to a dark, stuffy cabin where Nan has been sick all morning. I won't go! She is sleeping now, and I'll only wake her. Besides, Captain Reed has the authority here, and he has not forbidden me the deck."

"I own the ship, and he will forbid you the deck if I demand it."

"Oh!" Tessa stared a moment as she came to terms with the revelation that her Sassenach enemy needed no one's wealth to sail his own beautiful ship. It must be his cabin she enjoyed, and his bed she and Nan shared. The thought unsettled her so, she blurted out abruptly, "Then you may decide to let me stay. Please! I promise I'll sit still as a mouse. Truly," she added when Nick arched his eyebrow skeptically.

"I thought you'd have experienced a lifetime of storms living at the head of your loch."

He was wavering! At the knowledge that she might not be banished to the cabin, Tessa forget herself to such an extent that she smiled. "Och, never say ye dinna ken, milaird," she chided, a suspicion of a sparkle appearing in her gray eyes. "On land, as ye must know verra well, there's nae movin' with the wind."

A gleam, perhaps of amusement, perhaps of something else, lit Nick's eyes, and Tessa's heart raced oddly. "Aye, I ken," he laughed, and the knowledge that she had won free of the gloom below pushed any consideration of her suddenly erratic heart rate from Tessa's mind. "I shall relent, as you have pleaded your case so well," Nick said, then his eyes narrowed. "But you must stay where I put you. If you move an inch, I'll take you below."

"Oh, yes! I promise."

True to her word, when Nick settled her at the rail that ran along the stern deck, Tessa never budged. She'd no need to actually, for she commanded a fine view of the entire ship. Fascinated, she watched the prow surge down into the sea before it reared again and sent sea spray flying. Men scrambled lightly in the rigging, tightening this line or loosening that one, and she wished she could be so sure-footed. Overhead, adding urgency to the scene, a thick canopy of gray clouds raced by as if whipped to flight by the irascible wind.

Tossing her head, she gave up the battle to hold the hood of her cloak in place. What did it matter if some Sassenach dandy did not care for her complexion? She liked the feel of the wind in her tumbled curls.

Tessa had the sense that were she to dare move more than an inch in either direction, Nick would pluck her up instantly and trundle her below, but in truth, he never spared a glance for her. His concentration was all for his ship, and as he was not more than three feet from her, she could not keep from hearing his shouts of command. Crisp and authoritative, they brought instant action, but—and Tessa watched carefully— the seamen did not seem to resent the ship's owner who played at being their captain.

Indeed, Tessa thought the grizzled old man who stood at the helm seemed to admire the marquess commanding him. Once, when the ship pitched with particular violence, he shouted above the wind, his voice rich with the accent of Ireland, " 'Tis a bit o' breeze, milord!"

"A vixen to be sure, O'Shaughnessy," came the reply, then, with immense satisfaction, "but what a devil of a ride!"

The older man guffawed, obviously well pleased, and Tessa, slanting Nick a quick look through her lashes, caught her breath. If he had been handsome before, he was more than that now with his hands on his hips, his dark head lifted to challenge the elements, and his bold smile lighting his face.

As quickly as she'd looked, Tessa looked away. Something had leapt in her breast, something very like a sense of kinship with the Sassenach. The notion was so daft it only showed how very unusual the circumstances were that day on the high seas off the east coast of Scotland.

When, after a long time, Tessa's stomach informed her it was time to go below in search of sustenance, she looked around to find Nick's eyes upon her. "Hungry?" he mouthed the words, and she nodded after subduing a spurt of amazement over the easy access he seemed to have to her mind. It was likely past noon by then. Anyone might have guessed she'd be hungry.

The wind had gained in strength, and Tessa was grateful when Nick wrapped his arm around her shoulders and held her tightly to him. She only regretted how aware she became of the strength of his hard body.

The moment they gained the stairway, she pulled free of him. "It is so quiet!" she said and hoped he would attribute her breathlessness to wonder at how different the conditions were now that they'd reached shelter.

Nick agreed absently, but his eyes—and hand as well, she realized with a start—had gone to her tangled curls. "You'll be hours getting this mess straightened."

Tessa ducked away from Nick's touch and began to descend the stairs. "Nan has had years of experience untangling my curls," she informed him over her shoulder. "If she is well, I shall look civilized in no time."

"She'll recover soon enough. We'll be putting in at Aberdeen in a few hours."

"Aberdeen?" Tessa turned at the bottom of the steps to find Nick had followed her down. She was obliged to arch her neck sharply. "I thought we were bound for Edinburgh."

"We were until this wind came up. Reed believes this is only a prelude to a more dangerous storm."

Tessa gave him a mocking look. "Do nae tell me ye Sassenach fear a bit o' wind then!"

Nick annoyed her by grinning. "Having had decidedly more experience of the high seas than a wee Scottish lass, Reed and I agreed this stretch of the journey would best be accomplished upon land."

When he had the effrontery to brush the tilted tip of her nose with his finger, Tessa jerked away with a scowl. "You're naught but a soft Englishman!" she muttered, stalking away.

Nick laughed. "If you cannot agree with our decision for your own sake," he chided, his long strides effortlessly bringing him even with her, "you might at least show some concern for Nan, Tessa."

"I did nae give ye leave to call me that!" Tessa impaled him with a fierce gaze, all the charity she had felt above decks, when he had granted her request to stay, forgotten. "I am Miss Strahan to you, Sassenach."

"When you behave like a Miss Strahan or even a Thérèse, then I shall address you as such, my dear. Until then, you can only be Tessa."

"Oh! You are a cad and and no gentleman!"

Tessa flung herself inside her cabin and slammed the door shut behind her with a satisfying bang. Unhappily, her satisfaction lasted only seconds, for in the ensuing quiet she'd no trouble hearing Nick's deep chuckle echo richly down the corridor.

Much later that afternoon, when she and Nan were snugly ensconced in a warm inn in Aberdeen, Tessa admitted to herself at least she was relieved to have disembarked from the *Sea Witch*, for the wind shrieked unmercifully and hurled sheets of cold rain against the windows.

Nan was outright joyous. "Och, an' I did believe my time had come, I did!" She shook her head adamantly. "Ne'er, ne'er will I go upon the sea again. I could nae eat or even think o' food, though now I feel I could eat three meals at once."

"Well, ye did miss two meals by my count, Nan. Go on

to the kitchen if ye wish. Our host said dinner is some two hours away yet.''

Tessa did not add that they were, by Nick's decree, to take dinner in their room. He had given no reason for his direction to the innkeeper, and she was uncertain what she thought of being told in so many words that her company was undesirable, though, of course, she was entirely delighted not to be obliged to dine with the arrogant Sassenach.

Free of him for the evening, she would have all the more time to consider her escape. She had, unfortunately, a very imperfect knowledge of the geography of her country, Angus having lacked any interest in maps and she was not precisely certain of the location of Ayton.

She thought it to be far from Aberdeen, south of Edinburgh, but she was not certain, and decided her first step must be to obtain a map.

Accordingly, with Nan absent, she went in search of her host. He was a busy, ruddy complexioned man, but he stopped when she called out to him. ''I hope the accommodations be suitin' ye, miss. If ye ha' any wishes, do nae fash yersel', but call at once.''

Tessa gave the man a very fine smile. ''The room is lovely, I assure you, sir. But I do want for one thing.'' When the landlord asked her what that could be, she said, ''A map. I do nae know much of the land from here to London where the English lord is to take me, and I can nae like to seem ignorant before him. Could you bring me one without his knowing? I've a coin to repay you.''

The landlord beamed fondly down at her. ''Ye're a proud lass, as well as bonnie! Nay, I've nae need o' yer coin. Just rest yersel' and I'll see the map we keep fer travelers is sent up to ye.''

7

*O*blivious to anything but a feeling of immense satisfaction, Tessa left the innkeeper and returned down the inn's lower hallway. She would have her map and Nick would know nothing of it. Sounds of revelry, unusual for the early evening hour, emanated from the taproom, but Tessa scarcely took note. She was trying very hard to swallow a smug smile when the taproom door opened and a man burst through it into her path.

When he caught sight of Tessa walking unescorted toward him, the man's bleary eyes brightened. Befuddled by the excessive amount of ale he'd spent the storm-bound day imbibing, he took her for a barmaid.

"Here, here, sweeting!" he cried delightedly, and before Tessa understood what he intended, he grabbed her tightly against him. "The toll for entrance to the taproom is a kiss, my sweet! Give it over!"

"Ye Sassenach buffoon! Let go of me!" Tessa, outraged, pushed at him.

Her resistance only seemed to inflame the man's interest. "A kiss, I say! A kiss!" he insisted, pressing his face to hers.

When she realized she could not wrench free of the oaf, Tessa, not thinking on the consequences, arched her head back and aimed as much spit as she could summon at his leering face.

In an instant his countenance flamed a beet red. Entwining his hands in her hair, he jerked her head up to his. "Think you are too good for an Englishman, is that it, wench?" he demanded, his reeking breath making her nauseous.

Tessa kicked his shins and prepared herself to bite the ugly, wet lips descending to hers when the man was suddenly jerked backwards as if he were no more than a offending fly.

Stumbling off balance, Tessa only heard the satisfying crack of a fist connecting with a jawbone and was just in time to see her attacker slide woozily down the wall and collapse in a heap upon the floor.

Over him, she saw next, stood the Marquess of Kerne. "The young lady is under my protection, you jackanapes. Attempt to molest her again and you'll breathe your last."

Whether the man heard the threat was debatable. His head reeled loosely on his neck and his eyes rolled back in his head. With a disgusted oath Nick rounded upon Tessa. His blue eyes blazing, he grasped her arm and half dragged her up the stairs to her room, where he threw open the door with a bang and unceremoniously thrust her inside.

"Damnation!" Nicholas shook her as if she were a kitten. "Can you not stay out of trouble?"

"That ugly scene was no fault of mine!" Tessa retorted, her gray eyes sparkling angrily at the unfairness of Nick's attack. "The drunken fool grabbed me."

Nick brought his face to within an inch of hers. "A well-brought-up young lady does not traipse about a strange inn alone!"

Tessa flung up her chin as if to ward off Nick's evident disgust with her. "My pardon, sir. It is taking me some time to realize you Sassenach think nothing of forcing kisses from any and all passing females!"

Nick's disparaging snort indicated no hint of remorse for the kiss he himself had forcibly bestowed upon her. "Now that you have been enlightened," he snapped furiously, "I expect you to have Nan with you at all times."

"Else you will punish me further?" Tessa demanded, making a show of rubbing her arm when he let go his grip on it. Mentally she added the bruise she'd likely sport to her list of grievances against him.

The look Nick gave her sore arm was without the least hint of sympathy. "You would be soothing a sore backside had I truly set out to chastise you."

The reply elicited a scandalized intake of breath. "You would not dare!"

"Be assured of it, Tessa," he addressed her snapping gray eyes in a tone so implacable Tessa was assured. She wheeled from him, an exclamation of frustration escaping her, and Nick watched her flounce angrily to the window before he spoke again, more reasonably. "If you would think on what I have said with an open mind, Tessa, you would grant that I only have your best interests at heart. The rest of the world is not like Kilmorgan. You cannot run free without consequence. Had I not come along, that swine could well have dragged you off to his room and done a great deal more than steal a kiss."

Tessa's cheeks paled, but unwilling to concede him that or any other point, she kept her back to him. Nor could she bring herself to thank him for his rescue. His insufferable arrogance prompted rebellion, not gratitude, and so she said in a caustic tone, "Speaking of such things, my lord, I cannot think it seemly that you are in my bedroom with the door closed. Surely my being alone with a rake would be enough to ruin my reputation."

"And what gives you cause to imagine I am a rake?"

Tessa did not have to look to know Nick was amused. She could hear the laughter threading his voice, and she regretted having made mention of rakes, a subject upon which he was likely to know a great deal more than she. She could see little recourse but to go on the offensive. "You are not married, are you?"

"No. Are all unmarried men rakes?"

"Old unmarried ones," she pronounced, turning to fix him with a triumphant gaze. "Were you not a rake, you'd have married by now and gotten an heir, as is the duty of any title holder."

To Tessa's vast disappointment, Nick laughed aloud. She had thought he might be offended by her characterization of him as old, but he was, infuriatingly, merely amused. "I salute your reasoning, my dear. Indeed, you sound suspiciously like my very Sassenach sister-in-law." Nick grinned down at the affronted look his comparison earned him. "Allow me to set your mind at ease, however, now that you've uncovered my true character. Have no fear that I've designs on your person, Tessa. Even were babes to my taste, I have given Honoria my word I will present you to her intact, and I always keep my word—as in the case from which you would divert us. You will keep Nan close to you, or I give you my word that I shall punish you in the way I described only a moment ago."

Tessa, hands clenched, resisted the impulse to dispute that she was a babe. If she did, Nick would know that he'd succeeded in needling her. Nor did she argue with him over the spanking he threatened. She did not really believe he would act so outrageously. She did, however, fear he would order Jakes to tag after her and so she nodded reluctantly. "I shall keep Nan close by."

Satisfied that she would keep her word at least as long as he was close by to make an issue of it, Nick gave her an oddly affecting half smile. "At least we've come to agreement on one thing." At the door, he glanced back briefly at her. "Enjoy your dinner and your rest, Tessa, and I shall see you on the morrow at eight."

Before Tessa could open her mouth to tell him that half past eight suited her better, he was gone.

Though Nick had managed somehow to find a roomy carriage, Tessa resented its confines horribly the next day. The rain had slackened sufficiently to allow them to travel, but not to the extent that they could lower the carriage windows to enjoy fresh air from time to time. Nor, with drizzle and mist obscuring her view, could Tessa see much. Only occasionally did the weather lift enough to permit her to catch a glimpse of the remote and imposing Grampian Mountains.

Aside from sleeping or reading, both of which Tessa found impossible to do as they bumped along over the less than smooth road to Perth, there was little for her to do but study the other occupants of the carriage. Having known Nan from birth, she had every excuse for allowing her gaze to rove to Nick, especially as he had obligingly fallen into a doze almost as soon as he had seated himself in the carriage at precisely eight o'clock.

Her eyebrow arched considerably, she noted he had surprisingly light skin, considering how black his hair was. And his lashes. They looked like sooty fans closed over his eyes, but perhaps it was the contrast with his skin that made them seem so thick and long. Tessa wished she might deride Nick's fair complexion and extravagant lashes as feminine. Certainly any female would have given her eye teeth to possess either one. That she could not, for his features were strong enough that she thought he could have worn a ribbon in his hair and looked dangerously masculine, left her entirely irritated at the quirk of fate that had wasted such lashes and such fine skin upon a man who had so little need of them.

Scowling at the thought that she could not but admit she found Nicholas Steele, her jailer as she thought of him, an attractive man, she turned to stare out the window at the wet day.

Unfortunately, Nick's face was reflected in the window, superimposed upon the drifting mist outside. He seemed younger and more boyish in sleep than when he was awake doing battle of one sort or another with her, and for some reason Tessa was reminded how Nan had rhapsodized only that morning over the man. "Aye, 'tis true he be Sassenach, Miss Tessa," the maid had allowed when Tessa had grumbled irritably about his high-handed Sassenach ways. "But there's nae denyin' he's bonny as a man can be. Why, all the servin' girls at the inn ha' been fallin' over themselves to come to his attention. An' the ladies too, mind," Nan added, nodding wisely. "When I returned the dinner trays down to the kitchen last eve, I saw sooch a one pretend to turn her heel as she came down the stairs. She knew his lairdship was at the bottom, o' course. He caught her too, and wi' such a smile it fair took my breath away!"

Tessa frowned darkly as she thought of the flirtatious smile Nick had bestowed upon a complete stranger. He was a rake. He had not denied her charge. And he was Sassenach, and he was forcing her to go where she did not care to go.

She quite detested him, in fact, and now she regretted that she had, as she thought of it, let down her guard with him the day before.

Still, Tessa defended herself as Angus's image rose in her mind, the circumstances had been unique. She would never again have the opportunity to ride such exciting seas. She had owed Nick the smile she'd given him. It would have been within his rights to banish her below. Now that she had time to think upon it, it astonished her that he had not. She suspected strongly that proper young ladies did not expose themselves to the elements and that their escorts always endeavored to protect them from those same elements.

Perhaps Nick did not think her worth protecting.

"Do you intend to scare the rain away with that sour expression, Tessa?" She jumped and jerked around to see that Nick had awakened and was watching her. "At a guess I should say you were plotting murder, but I know you've too sweet a disposition to contemplate anything so dreadful."

Tessa tightened her lips against a traitorous smile. "How humorous you are, sir. If you must know I was merely feeling bored to tears with this detestable, entirely undesired journey."

"Ah, well, if that's all, I shall return to my rest undisturbed."

Nick closed his eyes as if he intended to do just what he said, but Tessa had had quite enough of her own thoughts for the time being. "No!" she cried, and fearing when he opened one eye to look at her in mild surprise that she had sounded rather desperate, she said stiffly, "I only mean I should like to know where we shall stay the night. And what town you hope to reach tomorrow."

"An interest in your forced journey south? My, my, I am surprised."

"I am only trying to be civil! And to pass the time."

Nick subjected Tessa to a long study, but when she gave him look for look, he shrugged. "I plan to stop in Perth this evening, and after passing Edinburgh tomorrow, to reach Lauder, a small town near the border on the following night."

"We'll not stay the night in Edinburgh?"

"No." Nick watched her with an unfathomable expression. "I fear I've little fancy to sit by your door the night through to keep you from enlisting any close, but not-close-enough, Ross relatives in your cause against the Sassenach."

Tessa colored and abruptly found the gray view out the window riveting. She had, in fact, seriously considered attempting to reach her father's cousin when they stopped in Edinburgh. True, Nick would know where she was, but she was half inclined to gamble on the hope that he would not care to drag her screaming from the old gentleman's home.

When Nick laughed softly, Tessa contented herself with a lofty sniff. He may have foiled her plan to escape him in Edinburgh, but he had revealed something vital to the success of her alternate plan: their route after Edinburgh.

On the innkeeper's map Tessa had found Ayton to be a tiny dot close to the east coast of Scotland. Now that she knew where they would stop for the night, she had only to study the sketch she'd drawn, to know what road she must take to reach MacIvey and freedom.

From beneath half-closed lids Nick studied Tessa's profile. That the minx wished to escape him was as plain as the provocative mole that lay so close to her sweetly curved mouth. Perhaps avoiding Edinburgh would foil her, but perhaps it would not.

"Knowing how little you care to arrive in England, Tessa, I cannot help but wonder why you descended to Skelgara to save me the day's ride to Kilmorgan. Unless, of course, you did not care to have Mrs. Dunadee know you intended to pretend to be Nan." Nicholas paused, but receiving no answer, continued, "Which brings me to my next question. What did you think to gain by playing at being your maid?"

"Why, 'tis simple, sir." Tessa turned quickly from the window, for it was not a question she cared to have Nick consider. "I changed places with Nan for the simple pleasure of playin' a trick upon a Sassenach!"

Nan drew in a scandalized breath at such open baiting, but Nick only gave Tessa a lazy look. "Somehow I doubt that," he replied, and was treated to another view of her profile.

It was not a bad view, of course, Tessa's fine bones made an elegant profile. Indeed, Nick thought it entirely possible that she would take London by storm, for she'd the fire to make her beauty interesting.

He could not but recall how, entirely undaunted by her near brush with drowning, she had sat ensconced upon the stern deck, the hood of her cloak thrown back and her face lifted to the wind. He had been obliged to stare down the several seamen who had glanced up from their labors to gawk at her, but he had not blamed them. With excitement tinting her cheeks a rosy pink and making her gray eyes sparkle as if lit by some inner light, she'd been simply breathtaking.

Today, Nick thought smiling to himself as he closed his eyes, she was again merely beautiful—as well as, it was not to be forgotten, obstinate, rebellious, and decidedly up to something.

8

" "Tis time to rise, Miss Tessa. His lairdship ha' left betimes, and we're to follow in the carriage."

Confused dreams of Angus and storms and ships commanded by dark-haired Englishmen had kept Tessa awake a great deal of the night, and she was loathe to part with what little sleep she had been able to find.

Closing her eyes tightly, she burrowed her head under her pillow until suddenly the import of Nan's words registered. "The marquess has left?" she demanded as she sat up and rubbed her sleepy eyes. "Without the carriage? Why? When will he join us again?"

"As to tha' I canna say," Nan answered Tessa's last question first and went to open the curtains to let in the subdued light of another cloudy day. "At least 'tis nae rainin'," she sighed half to herself before she turned back to her mistress. "But Mr. Jakes ha' told me that last eve his master fell in with some Sassenach gentlemen that followed behind us from Aberdeen. 'Twould seem they played cards, and the laird was lucky as the devil, for this mornin' one o' the others is less a mount that Mr. Jakes says is fine as can be."

Tessa recalled the Sassenach who had accosted her in the hallway of the inn at Aberdeen, but dismissed the notion that Nick had trounced the man at cards in order to further avenge her honor. Surely the drunkard had not been so far gone that he could not recognize the man who had knocked him flat on his backside.

" 'Tis like the Sassenach to be wagerin' good mounts and such for naught but the thrill of the moment," Tessa muttered, put out at the thought that Nick had won his freedom from the closed confines of the carriage. " 'Twould be better for their country if they found relief from their idleness and boredom in her service, but they fear anything truly dangerous such as battle with Bonaparte's men."

"There is tha'," Nan agreed as she laid out Tessa's blue serge carriage dress, which was not only warm but turned her eyes a deeper shade of gray. "Still, I would nae say his lordship feared much, would ye?"

"I canna say. I dinna know him well enough." Tessa ended the conversation by going to rinse her face with the warm water Nan had brought. A vision of Nick dominating the heaving deck of the *Sea Witch*, his eyes gleaming with the challenge, rose in her mind, but she dismissed it. He'd seemed fearless then, it was true, but a strong wind was very little when compared to the charge of an enemy.

The low, brooding clouds covering the sky were perfect companions for Tessa's spirits as she and Nan rattled out of Perth. Though she could not actually see the Grampians recede, she could feel the Highlands slipping away from her.

The hills now were small and round and plentifully covered with tall firs. Tessa viewed the different terrain with a cold eye, seeing only that she was not in her home where she belonged. Every turn of the wheels took her farther from Kilmorgan, and her expression grim as the day, she wondered when she would ever see it again.

To have been torn from it against her will! To be sent south to live among strangers—enemies! She bit her lip at the thought that if the Sassenach succeeded in taking the last of Angus's line, their triumph over the proud old man would be complete.

"Look there, Miss Tessa! 'Tis his lordship."

It was, indeed, Nicholas riding his prize, a sleek, mettlesome black, toward them. That he sat the proud animal with the ease of a man who had mounted his first pony before he took his first step, Tessa noted before she could stop herself. And then she tossed her head.

Neither his horsemanship nor his seamanship could alter his relation with her. He was her arrogant, high-handed Sassenach jailer.

Tessa's mood was not sweetened by the smile Nick gave her when he drew alongside the carriage. He was obviously in high spirits over the fleet mount he'd won.

"Good morning," he called out amicably. "Are you hungry yet, Tessa? There's an inn up ahead with a fine view of the Firth."

"No, I am not hungry as yet, Lord Kerne," she responded with a cool look, though she would not have minded eating.

Nick's eyes narrowed a fraction, but he held his temper. "A pity, Tessa, for I am hungry, and I imagine both Nan and Jakes lack your fortitude as well. Perhaps you will enjoy a cup of tea to wile away the time as we stop to refresh ourselves."

Spurring his horse, Nick galloped away to arrange matters to his liking—just as he had intended to do whatever she said, Tessa thought irritably. Why had he bothered with a mere charade of courtesy?

Though she only grew hungrier in the half hour it took them to reach the inn, Tessa was careful to take only tea at luncheon, and as soon as the serving girl had poured it, she took her cup with her to the window. As Nick had promised, there was a sweeping view of the Firth of Forth. Bounded that day by a low, drifting mist, the Firth looked strangely mysterious. Almost, Tessa thought she could see a band of old Celts materializing out of the gray clouds to rescue her.

Absorbed in her vision, she did not realize Nick had come to stand behind her until he spoke. "I am glad we stopped here. It is a beautiful spot."

Startled, she glanced up to see he looked out at the haunting scene with a smile that sent an odd feeling through her. Not pleased to find his mood in harmony with hers, she said sharply, "I am sorry I am being dragged away from it and all Scotland."

Stomping off to the table, Tessa set her cup down with

a clatter and curtly bade Nan accompany her to the ladies
retiring room. "We would not want to keep Lord Kerne
overlong, for it is crucial the heiress be hurried to England
as soon as possible." Though she had spoken in a voice loud
enough for Nick to hear, she had addressed her remarks to
Nan, but now she spoke directly to her enemy. "For my
part the view I enjoyed most this day, my lord, was that of
Stirling Castle. It was there we Scots routed Edward's men,
as you may not know."

"In fact, I do know some of the history of Stirling, Miss
Strahan." Nick's voice held an edge that lifted Tessa's chin
at the same time that it kept her rooted to the spot. "The
battle to which you refer took place nearly four centuries
ago, I believe. In the interim there have been other battles,
some won and some lost by both sides. At present our two
countries live in a unity you would deny. And why, I wonder?
Is it that you are afraid to look at the world for yourself?
Your grandfather's doomed battle at Culloden Moor took
place over fifty years ago, and if you had the courage to throw
off the bitterness he bred into you, you might see that we
English, while no better than your countrymen, are of a
certainty no worse."

The door's sharp bang was Tessa's answer. Butcher
Cumberland no worse than the lowest Scot! How dare he
say such a thing—he, who had not been hunted across the
length and breadth of the land like an animal!

To no one's surprise, Nick chose to continue on his stallion
rather than join Tessa and Nan in the carriage after luncheon.
Nor did he wave farewell as he spurred his mount past them
and disappeared within moments from Tessa's hostile sight.

Tessa pulled her eyes from the bend around which Nick
had vanished. It was time to have done with the Sassenach.
Tonight, if she were to keep to her plan, was the night she
must escape.

The carriage swayed with the speed the coachman
maintained, and they made quick work of the approaches
to Edinburgh. An increase in traffic slowed them a little as

they neared the city, but they kept to the outskirts and were soon clear of it. Some time after the spires of Edinburgh had receded, Tessa made out the shapes of Lammermuir Hills in the distance. She knew the name from her map and knew as well she must cross them to reach Ayton.

Even from a distance, the hills looked lonely, but she did not let the thought daunt her. The fewer people about, the better, she told herself.

When at last they reached the village of Lauder, Tessa could have shrieked for joy or pummeled Nick, had he been handy. To avoid a stay in Edinburgh, he'd made them ride so long in the cramped carriage, she was not certain she could walk, much less escape later in the night upon a purloined horse.

Nonetheless, she took care to glance toward the inn's stables. When she saw, wonder of wonders, that some ten horses stood hobbled on a line outside the building, she smiled to herself. They were poor nags, of course, whose owners could not afford a stall, but she'd not quibble. They all looked strong enough to carry her to Ayton, and she would not be obliged to walk her choice out of the stable under the nose of the ostlers who slept there.

Nick met them at the doorway, but Tessa swept by him without a word and only heard him inform Nan their dinner would be served on a tray in their room. She was pleased, for she wished to save at least half of her meal to take with her for sustenance.

Tessa never looked at the bed she was supposed to share with Nan. She went directly to the window and saw that Providence had been kind again. Outside, within easy reach, there was a large oak tree with branches that descended accommodatingly one after the other almost to the ground.

The first inkling Nan had that Tessa intended to effect her escape that very night came after their dinner, when her mistress opened a small valise she'd specifically asked to have brought up to the room. Before Nan could ask what she sought, Tessa pulled out the complete set of boy's clothing,

including breeches, shirt, jacket, and cap she'd persuaded
Nan's youngest brother, Davey, to lend her.

"Och, Miss Tessa!" The red-haired girl cried, aghast.
"Ne'er say ye mean to run off this night! Can ye nae forget
the notion? 'Tis a daft start! His lairdship's nae a bad mon.
He ha' treated us wi' courtesy, though ye've been a trial to
him. If yer aunt be half so kind, ye'll lead a good life in
Lunnon. An' if ye make a fine match there, 'twill mean
there's more in yer coffers to help Kilmorgan and the
crofters."

"Ye would ask me to live among the Sassenach?" A flame
kindled in Tessa's eyes as she confronted Nan. "Ye canna
mean what ye suggest! Ye've fallen under the Englishman's
spell, and all because he is a practiced charmer. I am ashamed
of ye, Nan! Say no more to me about marryin' a rich Sassenach, I can nae do it."

As she always had, Nan wilted before Tessa's fiery will.
"Nay, do nae look a' me like that, Miss Tessa! I'll nae try
to keep ye. Only—only 'tis so dark now, and you may come
to harm!"

"Oh, Nan! Nay, lass, do nae cry!" Contrite because she'd
come close to accusing Nan of betrayal when the girl was
only concerned for her, Tessa ran to embrace her. "I shall
be safe, I swear. No one will guess who I am in those
clothes." Tessa gestured to the bed, her spirits lifting
measurably as she gazed at the little bundle of clothes.
Grinning saucily, she teased, "I daresay ye'll call me
Davey!"

When Nan made an effort to smile as she wiped her tears
with the back of her hands, Tessa hugged her again and then
began to undress. With Nan's assistance she was soon clad
as a boy, and she thought she made a fine one but that she
lacked a masculine pair of boots. That could not to be helped,
however, for her feet were too small for even wee Davey's
boots.

Too soon for Nan, the lights at the inn dimmed and the
noise from the taproom faded nearly to silence. "Tell the

marquess 'twas all my scheme, Nan. He'll believe you," Tessa said as she embraced her maid a final time.

Nan sniffed and wiped her cheeks, but Tessa did not see. She had gone to the window. Sitting astride the sill, she turned to give Nan a jaunty wave before, without the least trouble, she reached out and caught the nearest branch of the old oak. The bark scraped her hands, but she scarcely noticed. The branches took her weight easily, and she was soon swinging lightly to the ground. Crouched in the shadows, she waited to be certain she had not been observed, then cautiously made her way to the stables.

Luck was with her. No ostler was about as she crept stealthily to the long line of horses.

Craning out the window to watch, Nan marveled at how silently the horses stood. Tessa's way with animals was famous at Kilmorgan, but Nan had thought that animals who did not know her mistress might protest the appearance of a stranger in their midst.

Even when Tessa slipped a bridle she'd found by the stable door over the head of a sturdy mare, there was no sound. The animal docilely allowed Tessa to lead her away from the light to a tree stump. Using it, Tessa mounted the horse, and after another wave at Nan, she made her way out of the yard without the benefit of a saddle.

Nan remained a long while with her head out the window, though Tessa soon blended into the shadows. A dog howled, making her shiver, and when the wind, rising suddenly, made a moaning sound, she put her hand to her mouth.

It took only a knock at the door to make her cry out.

"Tessa? Nan?"

Nan covered her mouth with both hands. It was the marquess!

When he received no response to his knock, Nick rattled the door handle impatiently. "Tessa! I would speak with you."

There was nothing for Nan to do but trot to the door and shoot the bolt. "Miss Tessa's nae feelin' well, beggin' yer

pardon, milaird,'' Nan informed him in a quavering voice
after she had opened the door a crack.

Though the opening was meager, it was sufficient to reveal
how wide and frightened Nan's eyes were. Swearing a fierce
oath, Nick pushed past her and strode into the room.

''Where is she, Nan?'' he demanded, scowling at the
empty bed.

Nan shrank from him and shook her head, but Nick whirled
threateningly upon her. ''She has run off. Where? Tell me,
Nan!'' He took the frightened girl by the shoulders and shook
her. ''For the love of God, you must see that only harm can
come to her if she is out riding in the dead of night.''

Nan gave a miserable little cry, for the marquess's words
echoed her fears too closely. ''Miss Tessa'll have my head!''

Nick retained a hold on his temper, but only just barely.
''You know very well she won't hurt a hair on your head!
She may, however, lose her own, and she will be fortunate,
indeed, if that is all she loses!''

Nan shuddered at the visions the English lord conjured.
''She took one o' the horses from the line, milaird. An' . . .''
She swallowed convulsively. The thought of how fiercely
Tessa would hate her made the words clog in her throat.

''Where, Nan?'' The marquess's growl was fierce and his
urgent hold painful.

Nan crumbled. ''She goes to Ayton, milaird! To her
governess, Miss MacIverson.''

''Do you know the road she took?''

Nan nodded, and though she felt ever more the traitor,
she told Nick in a shaky voice what she knew of Tessa's
route. Not quite half an hour after Tessa rode into the dark,
Nick, mounted on his black stallion, set off in pursuit.

9

*T*hick black clouds raced across the sky, plunging the road into sudden darkness. Swearing beneath her breath, Tessa slowed her mount's headlong pace. She did not fear pursuit. Nick would not learn until morning that she had made good her escape, and even then Nan would not betray her destination.

She feared the weather. Already the rising wind tugged at her boy's cap and whistled by her ears, obscuring the sounds other travelers might make. Consideration of the sort of persons who might have need to travel in the dead of night unnerved her, and Tessa forced her thoughts elsewhere.

Leaning forward, she patted her horse's neck. She'd chosen well. The mare was responsive but docile. Thank heavens, Tessa sent a fleeting glance upward, she'd learned to ride a true horse as well as a Highland pony. On her fifth birthday, Angus had presented her with a full-blooded colt despite the objections of her mother, who considered her too young. "The lass could ride the wind if she wished," Angus had said with finality.

And so she'd had a horse, though such an animal was an exotic indulgence in the Highlands. Tessa's smile faltered. Had she heard a voice? She pricked up her ears. Too late. Out of the dark three riders, all upon sturdy ponies, appeared. The wind had hidden the sound of their approach from her.

She pulled down her cap, hoping to pass by with only a nod, but the men had other thoughts. They surrounded her.

"Aye, an' wha's this?" one called out, his slurred words sending Tessa's heart plummeting. They were hopelessly drunk.

Another caught her reins even as she attempted to spur her mare into flight. "Hie! 'Tish a bit of a lad to be ridin' sooch a fine horse!"

"Who besh ye, lad?" the third bellowed, craning forward. "How come ye to own sooch an animal? Mayhap ye stole it?"

" 'Course he ha'!" The man blocking her path laughed uproariously. "Whysh else'ld he be out on sooch a night? But I'm thinkin' we could use the animal ourselves. 'Twould outrun the magistrate ever' time, dosh ye not agree, lads?"

"Och, aye!"

The men's laughter had an evil sound.

"Nae!" Tessa yelled when the man to her right reached to lift her from the mare.

She had attempted a gruff note, but the man in front of her swore. "Damn, but he's a right strange voice for a lad!"

Before Tessa could duck away, the man on her left seized her cap. "Look ye!" he cried as her hair spilled down to her shoulders. " 'Tish a lassh!"

The clouds that had covered the moon deserted Tessa just when she needed them most. A shaft of silvery light revealed Tessa to the men. And they to her.

She cried out in fright as they sent up a lusty cheer. They were clad in rough, ragged clothing that bristled with pistols and knives. She'd the fleeting impression of grimy beards, leering mouths that gaped without teeth, and hot, gleaming eyes.

" 'Tis bonnie she is! Let's ha' her now!"

Tessa kneed her mare with all her might, but the man holding her reins proved stronger than the mare. "There'll be sport wi' thish wildcat!" he shouted, sweeping her from the mare's back as the animal reared.

Before Tessa could catch the breath her fall had knocked from her, the men descended upon her. Sheer terror sweeping her, she fought like a wild thing, flailing her arms and legs. She raked one villain's cheek with her nails, kicked another in the stomach, but in the end, panting and grunting with exertion, they dragged her to the grass at the side of the road.

Heaving frantically, Tessa cried out for help, but the wind caught her plea and tossed it high in the air for no one to hear. The man holding her arms slapped her hard and screamed to his confederate, "Have at her, mon! She's nae easy to hold."

"Nay!" Tessa thrashed so fiercely the two men holding her could scarcely contain her, but the third man let out a lusty roar as he threw himself to his knees between her legs.

Tessa could feel his loathsome hand reaching for her waistband when a clap of thunder shattered the night, freezing them all. The villain's hand twitched oddly, and as Tessa gathered herself to heave against him, he slumped not onto her, but backward in a heap on the ground.

" 'Tis the devil!"

"The militia!"

The screams confused Tessa, as did the still body at her feet. Her arms and legs were flung down, and she scrambled to her knees. Another explosion of thunder sounded, but now, jerking her head toward the road, she recognized it as the report of a pistol.

There she saw that the devil had in truth descended from the Lammermuir Hills to save her. Dressed all in black, his cape billowing behind him, a horseman sat upon a perfectly motionless ebony stallion. His pistol raised, he sent a final shot after the two men scuttling away into the concealing night.

Abruptly the horseman wheeled his horse about, prompting Tessa to cry out for fear he would leave her alone. Picking herself up, she sent a shuddering glance toward the man she realized had been shot dead before she stumbled to the road. A sigh of relief escaped her when she saw her rescuer had only gone to catch the reins of her mare and frighten the men's ponies into thundering headlong toward Lauder.

Wide-eyed, shaking from a delayed reaction to the assault she'd suffered, Tessa waited for the man to bring her horse to her. Though he stopped only a few feet from her, the clouds again covered the moon and she could not see his face.

"Are you hurt?"

Tessa gaped, witless as any fool.

"Speak!" Nick commanded in a harsh, cold voice.

Tessa started. "N-no."

"Shall I leave you to your brave countrymen, Tessa, or do you choose to come with a Sassenach?"

The men no longer had their ponies, but they did have their pistols. And they might have confederates. "I shall . . ." When her voice cracked, Tessa cleared her throat. "I shall go with you," she managed, her voice very low.

"Then mount this nag you stole."

It did not seem the time to say she'd left coins with Nan to pay for the animal. Nick did not dismount to assist her, nor did Tessa question the discourtesy. She wanted him high above the ground, keeping an eye out for the ruffians, though she knew it was as likely he left her to her own devices because he was too angry to treat her with any consideration.

They had traveled about a mile on the road toward Lauder, Nick following just behind her, when a real clap of thunder caused Tessa's mare to rear.

"Damnation."

Tessa echoed Nick's sentiments, though she said nothing aloud. The thunder acted as a herald. Following hard upon it came a cold, heavy rain. Each drop pricked like slivers of ice at the exposed skin of Tessa's face and hands.

"There's a croft up there. We've no choice but to try it."

Nick did not wait to see if Tessa followed. Turning off onto a track she had not noticed, he led the way up a hillock to a rude hut that appeared to be deserted.

Tessa slid off her mare and ducking her head against the rain, followed Nick to a lean-to for the horses before trailing after him into the croft. Tessa had the impression of dampness, then heard Nick rummage in his pockets. The sound of a match scraping against flint was one of the most welcome she'd ever heard, and soon he held a small flame aloft.

Though the small room was uninhabited, it showed signs of recent use. The fireplace held peat, a stub of a candle sat on the hearth, and a rude pallet lay in the far corner.

Nick lit the candle, then turned his attention to building a fire. The peat was damp, but he persisted and in a few minutes he had produced a smoky fire.

He warmed his hands a moment, then stood, sending a spray of raindrops flying as he removed his cloak. When he had hung it upon one of several pegs pounded into the wall, he turned at last to Tessa.

She shivered. Nick's blue eyes were colder than the rain beating upon the roof.

No spark of sympathy warmed them as he strode toward her. Tessa instinctively shrank back, but made no real effort to evade him when he caught her arm and pulled her roughly toward the fire. He was, she thought, merely concerning himself with her welfare.

She was mistaken. In a tone of voice that was all the more menacing for being soft, he said, "Do you recall, Tessa, what I warned you I would do if you broke your word and went out without protection?"

Tessa had not expected the question and could not think for a moment what he meant. When she did recall, it was too late. Nick had her arm in a tight grasp and was hauling her in the direction of a rough stool she'd not noticed.

"You would not dare!" She attempted to pull away from him, but Nick lifted her with such ease she might have been a feather and jerked her face down across his knees.

"If you act like a child, Tessa, you will be treated like one."

She flailed and kicked, but he paid no heed. Holding her arms in a viselike grip with one hand, he administered the spanking he'd promised her with the palm of the other.

Angry, Nick did not blunt his blows. Tessa's soft derriere soon smarted painfully, but the indignity of her position hurt as badly. "I shall hate you forever for this!" she cried out and meant it.

"I shall stop only when you swear on the memory of your grandfather, Angus Ross, who cannot have wanted you to get yourself brutally assaulted, that you will not, under any circumstances, do anything so foolish again."

The particularly fierce swat that followed his demand wrung a gasp from Tessa, but no craven pleading for mercy. She bit her lip so she tasted blood to keep from crying out. Another fiercer blow followed and another.

"I swear!" Tessa's voice, bitter as gall, was clogged with tears. At once Nick stayed his hand, but he did not release her.

Swinging her off his knees, he pulled her between his legs so that she knelt like a supplicant before him. To Tessa, Nick's revenge upon her was utterly complete. At such close range he could not miss the tears swimming in her eyes.

If he saw them, he did not appear moved. "Once more, Tessa," he demanded harshly. "And use your grandfather's name."

"You would humiliate me!" She tried to strike him, but Nick held her arms to her sides.

Their gazes warred as his blue eyes implacably returned her wild, impassioned, resentful glare.

"Have done, then!" she spat at last, her shoulders sagging in defeat. "I do swear." He shook her so her teeth rattled. "Upon Angus's name!"

At once Nick released her. Unprepared, Tessa fell to the mud floor, only to leap up quickly when her abused posterior stung at the unexpected contact. Her eyes flashing with hatred, she glared furiously at Nick's back as he moved to stir the recalcitrant fire.

Had she had a knife, she'd have gone for him, but when the ruffians had attacked her, she'd lost the dirk she'd secreted in her boot.

A sudden, anguished cry rose in her throat. Biting down hard on her hand, she smothered it. Dear God! Those dreadful men. Her escape had been so narrow. How could she think Nick's punishment anything in comparison to the fate they'd intended for her?

When Nick heard Tessa gasp, he turned from the fire and stared at her. His grim expression did not soften, though she stood holding her bowed head in her hands.

"You do know what rape is?"

Gasping, Tessa flung up her head. "Yes!" To her mind, the cruel question was the verbal equivalent of rubbing salt in her wounds. "I am aware how grateful I must be to you."

Nick's sardonic smile did not reach his eyes. "Should be but are not?"

"It is difficult to summon a wealth of gratitude after the beating you gave me!"

"A beating you richly deserved. Not only have I lost a good night's sleep, I am wet and I am cold, all because, having childishly chosen to cast yourself as the tortured heiress in some fanciful play of your own creation, you must parade about in the dead of night clad in the flimsiest disguise it has ever been my misfortune to see!"

"No one ever guessed I was not a boy before!"

"Did they not?" Deliberately, insolently, Nick flicked his gaze to the swell her breasts made beneath wee Davey's tight jacket and then allowed his eyes to travel down to her hips, whose womanly flare was emphasized, not concealed, by the breeches she wore. "How old were you when you last played at being a boy, Tessa? Twelve perhaps? You've ripened a trifle since then."

His eyes piercing her, Nick did not fail to see hot color flood her cheeks and uncertainty darken her large gray eyes.

"Damnation!" he swore so savagely Tessa took a step back. "Did they keep all pier glasses from you in that remote fastness where you were raised? You've only to take one look at yourself to see you fill those idiotic clothes in the most suggestive possible manner."

Galled by a tone more scathing than any she'd ever endured, Tessa clenched her fist. She had had quite enough of this discussion. "You do not need to belabor this subject, sir! I have learned my lesson!"

"I should hope you have!" Nick fired back, still full of

venom. "Else I should say you desired that trio of unwashed vermin to take you with their grimy hands!"

"Stop!" The shrill cry carried an element of the panic Tessa had felt on the road, for the memory of callused hands grabbing her, holding her helpless, was not old.

At the sound of her cry, Nick expelled a long breath and swore again, but more softly. "Forgive me. I am, as I said, tired and cold and wet, though that is no excuse for such lack of sensitivity."

Tessa could not hold his gaze. She'd not expected an apology or the ragged note in his voice. Until then she'd not spared a thought for the dread she must have caused him. Perhaps the marquess had worried only for her aunt's sake, but even so, he could not have looked forward to finding her broken and discarded upon the road.

Though her head was bowed, she was aware of his gaze upon her. "I . . . I am indebted to you."

Even to Tessa her voice seemed impossibly small, and when Nick made no immediate response, she glanced through the veil of her thick lashes to see if he'd heard her.

She could not say with any certainty. He was staring at her with a grim expression that tightened the line of his jaw. Abruptly he shrugged and made a noise that seemed to dismiss her thanks.

Immediately afterward, he strode out of her line of vision, and she, trembling with a sense of release, was left to contemplate the ironic twist of fate that had left her so deeply in a Sassenach lord's debt.

10

*T*essa heard Nick return to the hearth and looked up to see he'd found a bucket of peat to add to the fire.

"How was it you discovered I had . . . departed?"

"Escaped, you mean?" Nick glanced around with an uncompromising look. "That is what abducted heiresses do, is it not?"

"I stand corrected," Tessa retorted, holding his gaze though she felt her cheeks heat.

"Nan did not run to betray you, if that is what you wish to know." Nick turned to feed peat into the fire. "Knowing the storm approached, I stopped off at your room to inform you that you might sleep late as you wished. I actually thought to spare you another day in a carriage closed up against the rain." Though she could not see the expression on his face, Nick's voice was laden with sufficient irony to make Tessa flinch, but she was not given long to contemplate the consideration she'd not been on hand to enjoy, for he turned then and arched an authoritative brow at her. "You are not to blame Nan for revealing your route, Tessa. She endeavored to keep the truth from me, but she is no actress. Her agitation was obvious, and when I found you missing, I'd have stopped at nothing to learn where you'd gone. I only thank God you had divulged your plans to her in such detail."

Tessa looked away from Nick's censorious gaze without reply. If Nick new of Ayton, then she had no secret refuge. Despair made her bite her lip against a cry of frustration. Now she could not escape the Sassenach.

"What, Tessa?" Nick's voice dripped ice. "You seem

despondent. Would you rather I had left you to your own devices?''

Her emotions raw, Tessa jerked around and stabbed him with a murderous glare. "I said I was indebted to you! Would you hear me pronounce my gratitude again? Thank you, my lord. Thank you. There! I've said it four times by my count. But before you swell with satisfaction, Sassenach, know this: I wish to God it had been anyone but you who came to my aid!''

Nick's eyes flashed with an emotion powerful enough to cause Tessa to draw back, but in the next instant his expression became so shuttered, she was not certain if she had imagined his fury. "How unlucky for you that the Almighty seems arranged upon the side of your enemy, Tessa.'' Nick's tone, though it carried an edge, was controlled. "Having learned that lesson, however, I trust you to remember it. And this one as well: I shall bring you to Honoria as I agreed to do, even if I have to drag you before her trussed up like a partridge.''

Tessa was the first to look away, but she did not allow Nick a total victory. Stubborn to the end, she lifted her tipped nose as if to say though he bound her with the strongest ropes, he still would not hold her prisoner.

Only when she heard Nick dragging something large across the dirt floor did Tessa condescend again to look in his general direction. He was moving the narrow pallet from its far corner to a position before the fire. Feeling her gaze, he looked up. "I intend to use what is left of this wretched night to get some rest.''

Tessa dropped her eyes to the thin, lumpy thing. Clearly intended for a single occupant, the pallet was scarcely as wide as Nick's shoulders.

"I am not tired. I need only sit on the stool while you sleep.''

Nick gave a mirthless laugh. "Where you will be poised to flee at the sound of my first snore? No, my dear, you shall, if not sleep, then lie quietly at my side. To prove I am magnanimous beyond your deserving, I shall even give you the side closest to the fire.''

"I cannot lie with you."

"No need to allow your imagination to run away with you, Tessa. You will not lie with me, my dear, merely beside me. I assure you, it is not the same thing at all.'' Nick's mocking rejoinder was met with a dark scowl, and he laughed outright. "Alas, I see you need more convincing than my lesson in semantics. Well, then, here is the lowering truth: even were I the sort of man who took pleasure in forcing young virgins against their will, I would not think to follow my dastardly inclinations just now. Being without sleep for close to twenty-four hours has, I am ashamed to admit, quite sapped me.''

Tessa's face flamed with such embarrassment she whirled to stare into the gloom beyond. She had not meant—indeed, it had not occurred to her—to suggest he might take advantage of her. "I cannot lie with you, whatever your intentions,'' she insisted, her voice sounding odd to her ears.

"Leave off, Tessa.'' The command to her rigid back was harsh. "You cannot say you care a fig for the conventions, for you found no fault at all with traveling alone in the dead of night dressed in boy's clothes. Come. I know perfectly well you are reluctant only because you will be in proximity to my Sassenach self, but that is your penance for costing me almost an entire night's sleep. Now, take off that sodden jacket and those boots and lie down.''

There was a note in Nick's low-voiced growl that indicated he had come to the end of his patience and would, however she tried to resist, impose his will upon her. Wishing to preserve some measure of her dignity from the disaster of the night, Tessa decided not to afford him another opportunity to best her with his superior strength.

Her head bowed, she removed her half-boots, placed them by the fire to dry and hung her jacket upon a nearby peg. Nick had removed his jacket and boots as well, she found when she shot him a wary glance. He wore only his breeches and a shirt of cambric that lay open at the throat to reveal a patch of dark, curling hair.

Dragging her gaze from the unexpectedly masculine sight, Tessa found for once she was relieved to look into Nick's eyes. His flat, level look somehow steadied her, and when he said simply, "Come," she went to the pallet.

Tessa carefully lowered herself to lie on her side. Half on the pallet and half off it, she gave Nick as much room as she could without rolling onto the dank floor.

But when Nick lay down beside her and threw his cloak over them, she became as rigid as a board. The few inches she had expected to separate them had disappeared. They lay closer together than a married pair in a normal bed. Her forehead touched his shoulder, her legs pressed his legs, and her breasts . . . quickly she inched away, only to misjudge the width of the pallet and tumble to the floor.

As she crept, cheeks rosy, back under the cloak, Nick's sigh sounded very loud in her ear. "Tessa, have you some male cousin you know well?"

The question surprised her. "I know my father's cousin in Edinburgh, but not well. He is over sixty."

When Nick shrugged, Tessa felt his shoulder brush her nose. "He will not be of much use to us, then. I only wished to propose that you think of me as you might of a male relative you knew very well." Tessa could almost see Nick's dry smile as he added, "With a bed this narrow, there's little else to be done, or we shall not sleep at all. Come, you'll turn to ice with half of you lying out from under this cloak."

Though Tessa started tensely when he touched her, Nick summarily lifted her so that her body lay entirely upon the pallet and therefore tightly against him. Her head he situated on his chest.

Rigid, her eyes wide, Tessa considered gathering her forces to leap away altogether. Their position was more indecent than ever. Nick's hips pressed against her belly, and his stomach was a hard wall against her breasts.

But Nick's arm lay heavily across her shoulder. He might

not let her up without a struggle that he would undoubtedly win. His lean body had never seemed stronger to her than it did just then with her soft woman's body draped over it.

The seconds ticked away, and Tessa marked each one, awaiting she did not know what.

Slowly she became aware how the fire hissed and the wind whistled around the corners of the croft. Vaguely she noticed that Nick's cambric shirt felt uncommonly smooth to her cheek. She had not known a man's shirt could feel like down.

She quelled a desire to rub her skin over it, but did breathe deeply. She had not realized a man had a scent. A unique scent. Nick smelled of a combination of leather and peat and rain and something she could not put a name to, never having experienced it before. Nick's Essence, she thought, her mouth quirking slightly as she imagined a bottled scent bearing such a name. Women would . . .

Her mind shied from finishing that thought and fastened upon the sound of Nick's heartbeat instead. It seemed so strong and steady beneath her ear she could not think how she had missed it before.

The rhythm of it lulled her until she became aware that Nick's breathing had become equally steady. Her eyes flew open—which surprised her, for she had not realized she had closed them. Had he fallen asleep?

She was not certain whether she was piqued or not—an absurd quandary, as she admitted. She ought, without reserve, to be thanking the fates that looked after her for sending her a companion who was completely unaffected by her nearness.

She was a babe to him. But he was not to her. Tessa nearly flung herself from Nick's side. The last thought particularly stung, but the two together mortified her: to have him indifferent when she was not! Tessa was kept from acting with undue haste only because her agile mind divined yet another explanation for their differing reactions to their situation.

Intimacy with the opposite sex was natural to Nick. While

she was most certainly not accustomed to sleeping with men, he was, by his own account, quite accustomed to sleeping with women.

Tessa's eyelids drifted down as she decided not to think about Nick's experience. A tired sigh escaped her. It had been a long night. The dinner she had shared with Nan seemed to belong to another lifetime.

Darkness surrounded her. Grasping hands overwhelmed her. She struggled, but they pinned her down and she screamed.

"Tessa!" Warm hands shook her shoulders. Her heart pounding thunderously, she jerked up to stare blindly at Nick. " 'Twas a dream, Tessa. No more. You're safe now."

The firelight was too dim for her to see his face clearly, but Nick's voice was low and comforting. When he smoothed her hair from her face, Tessa turned her cheek into his steady hand.

"They won't find us here, will they, Nick?" she whispered.

"No. They won't." He took his hand from her before she was ready. "Come." Tugging gently, he tucked her head into the hollow of his shoulder. A perceptible measure of Tessa's tension drained from her when Nick lifted her heavy hair from her neck, then lazily caressed her back. "They feared I was the militia, and they fled in the opposite direction from us as quickly as they could. They are miles from here by now."

There was a long silence as Tessa digested that, then she asked softly, "And the man you shot, the one who—"

"They've taken his body," Nick said unequivocably. "Ruffians or no, they'd not have left him to the buzzards."

Tessa shivered at the thought, but after a moment she nodded her head. Nick's reply carried the weight of logic. And was what she had wanted to hear as well. She did not like to think of anyone, even the devil who had intended to assault her so brutally, lying exposed to the elements and wild animals.

"Listen to the rain."

Nick's voice was quiet, his hand very warm on her back, and the rain steady as it beat against the roof of the hut.

"Thank you, Nick."

Nick did not respond aloud, but he heard her. His hand tightened almost painfully on her shoulder, and he pressed her to him. Tessa felt herself melting into his warmth. Her eyes closed as she burrowed her head into the hollow of his shoulder, and as from a great distance she heard herself emit a deep, shuddering sigh.

When next Tessa became aware of anything, she was curled in a solitary ball and a voice was saying, "Tessa. Come on, girl. Wake up. It's time we left."

Confused by the male voice at her bedside, Tessa reluctantly lifted eyelids that seemed heavy as lead. Nick's face swam into her view, and, her defenses momentarily routed by grogginess, she felt her pulse leap at the sight of him.

He had just washed, it seemed, for his black hair was wet and lay close to his scalp, while his light skin glowed with the high color imparted by very cold water.

The last thought puzzled her. Surely Nick would not order cold water for his ablutions.

"No use frowning, Tessa. The rain stopped sooner than I expected, and we must go."

It was the touch of Nick's cloak that truly brought Tessa awake. When it chafed her cheek, she recalled all at once where she was and how she had gotten there. She was reminded as well that she had spent the night in Nick Steele's arms.

"It is early yet," she grumbled. If she was disconcerted by the memory of her head secure upon his chest and his arm wound tightly around her, she did not care for him to know it. "The sun's not yet risen."

It was Nick's turn to frown. "I want to reach our destination before too many people are about to recognize my companion for a girl rigged out in boy's clothes. Now get up." Ruthless, he pulled his cloak from her. Tessa groaned at such unfeeling cruelty, but Nick was not deterred from removing the thing from her grasp. "Up!" he commanded sternly. "I am ravenous, and there is no food at all in this place."

How like the Sassenach to profess a concern for her reputation when he was, in truth, more concerned for his belly. "I've bread and cheese in my jacket pocket," she informed him grudgingly.

Sitting up, she took in again, with much less pleasure, the fresh, clean appearance Nick presented. With his coat of superfine covering the wrinkled shirt he'd slept in, he looked almost as if he had been turned out by Jakes.

By comparison, Tessa's boy's clothes were irretrievably rumpled, her skin felt grimy, and her hair was a tousled mess.

When Nick eyed the bread and cheese he'd found wrapped in a napkin in her jacket pocket with a dubious look, she gave vent to some of her irritation. "If you were truly starving, as you suggested, you would not mind that the bread is not entirely dry and crumbly besides. You would be grateful. After all, it will go down easier soggy."

Nick, his eyes seeming particularly light that morning, shot her a narrowed look. "I would be grateful, my dear, to be in a warm bed, anticipating in my dreams the fine breakfast I am persuaded the innkeeper in Lauder intended to prepare for me. And what of you, hardened campaigner that you are? Do you care for a portion of this princely repast, or shall I make short work of it?"

A piece of lint on the bread, though small, was sufficient to cause Tessa to shake her head. "I can wait," she said as if there were virtue in delaying a meal.

"Then perhaps you would care to make use of the rainwater that collected in a bucket just outside the door while I eat?"

Not bothering to answer, Tessa tugged on her half-boots and shrugged into her still damp jacket. Outside a faint pink glow from the eastern hills heralded the dawn.

She drew in her breath when the water hit her face. Had

she scrubbed with ice, she did not think she could have been more chilled. Nor was there comfort when she was done, for without a towel she was obliged, after wiping the excess from her cheeks with her hand, to allow her face to dry in the raw wind.

She had no comb to smooth her hair and, having lost her cap in her struggles with the ruffians, had no way to hide it. Tired, stiff, and cold, she assigned the problem to Nick.

Let him worry with it. When he had recaptured her, he had taken on her problems.

Her wording was dramatic, but Tessa did not amend it. Just then she was feeling at war with the world and, kicking a stone, watched it roll away with a frown.

The truth was, in the thin light of dawn she felt abysmally disappointed in herself. Had she possessed half Angus' mettle, she'd have made an escape after Nick dropped off to sleep. He had said he was tired. He'd never have felt her slip away or heard the door close behind her.

She would have been free . . . and going where? she demanded angrily as she gave another pebble a vicious swipe. She had no place to go now.

But she needn't have slept so docilely in her enemy's arms! There was the rub. She had, in fact, been soothed to passivity sleeping in Nick Steele's arms. Perhaps it was natural that she would crave security after her ordeal, but Tessa had lived long with Angus's hatred of Englishmen. She felt she'd failed her grandfather in a way she'd never dreamed she would. There was no escaping the truth: she had actually sought— and had found—comfort with the enemy.

When Nick came out the door, she scowled at him, as if he were responsible for her betrayal of Angus.

He had a length of greasy string in his hand. "The only thing I can think to do with your hair is to tie it back with this."

"It is filthy."

It was then that Tessa realized what Nick's eyes on occasion reminded her of. Her mother had had a set of opals

Tessa had used to admire, and even now she could recall
how the light blue color on their surface was underlaid by
a tantalizing, fiery sparkle.

Just now the sparkle in Nick's eyes was unfriendly. "I
dislike disabusing you, Tessa, but your hair at the moment
is not precisely pristine." He arched his brow, daring her
to protest further. "Come here. There is no other choice."

Her fine lips set in a mulish line, Tessa stood where she
was, though she turned her back. If he were going to tell
her she was a filthy mess, he could come to her.

He did and, working efficiently, soon had her hair tied
in a braid.

"You won't set a fashion," he decided when he had
finished and turned her for a critical inspection, "but at least
you're tidy."

It was not a remark calculated to sweeten her temper, and
Tessa gave him a hostile glare. To her intense indignation,
a gleam of amusement flared in the back of Nick's eyes.

He gave her no opportunity to douse it. Even as she opened
her mouth to say that they made a well-matched pair, he
turned and strode to the leanto.

When he returned leading both horses, he looked at the
eastern horizon. "If we ride hard, I should say, we will reach
the inn where Jakes and Nan are awaiting us by eight o'clock.
Hopefully the Scots along the way are slug-a-beds or
incurious."

Tessa looked in surprise at the unexpected information.
"We don't return to Lauder?"

Nick's unfathomable gaze met hers. "I arranged with Jakes
to meet at an out-of-the-way inn to the south if I did not return
to Lauder with you in the night. Though it is not likely, it
is possible someone who knows me may have arrived in
Lauder while we were away. It is a major posting inn on
a major road, and I thought it best not to call attention to
our unchaperoned sojourn together."

"Oh." Tessa swallowed but held his gaze and finally said
stiffly, "Thank you."

Nick's mouth quirked. "You know, you'd not be obliged to express your gratitude to a Sassenach with such annoying regularity, my dear Tessa, if you could curb yourself of your penchant for haring off at every turn on wild starts."

Tessa's hands clenched around the reins she held. If there was one thing in particular she detested about the man smiling sardonically down at her, it was his infuriating ability to read her thoughts with such clarity.

Nick laughed, demonstrating that particular ability once again, and Tessa whirled around and mounted her mare. At least she'd not be obliged to ask for his help. A nearby crib that had likely held hay at one time supported her.

She had hoped to glare down upon Nick from her superior position, but when she turned back, she found he had mounted and was already leading the way down the hillock to the road.

11

They found Jakes waiting for them at their rendezvous when they arrived at a quarter of eight. As they pulled up, he hurried from the inn and took Tessa's reins.

"I'm that glad to see you, miss," he announced gravely.

Discerning no censure in his solemn brown eyes, Tessa favored him with a wan smile before half sliding from her saddle to stand beside the mare and await Nick's direction.

Her unnatural docility was a result of fatigue. They'd ridden three hours that morning to reach Nick's truly remote inn, and after riding more hours than she'd slept the night before, Tessa was swaying on her feet.

"The innkeeper believes I am arriving with my errant sister?" Nick asked of Jakes.

"Aye, milord."

"And Nan awaits upstairs with a change of clothing?"

"She does, and there's hot water for a bath as well."

"You may bathe and eat," Nick addressed Tessa as he took her arm and advanced her toward the inn, "but you'll not have time to dawdle. We leave in an hour."

Tessa possessed the strength only for a rankling glare. She thought Nick's haste designed to punish her. Knowing how dearly she longed to sink into a bed, he would deny her the pleasure.

It had been much the same since they'd set out from the crofter's hut. Nick set a determined pace, speaking only to address infrequent, curt commands to her: "We shall stretch our legs now," or, after a too-brief respite from riding, "Time to mount up."

Engulfed in his concealing cloak, Tessa had stared sullenly

at his unresponsive back. She did not care that he had not forgiven her for her attempt to escape. She told herself that stoutly.

She felt as gloomy as the gray day because she owed him so great a debt for saving her from her attackers. She did not know if she could bear such indebtedness to a Sassenach, particularly to the one who had wrested her from Kilmorgan.

How could she ever even the debt? Nick had saved her virtue and most likely her life. Her code of honor demanded that she give something in return.

What had she to give that he would want except her obedience? Tessa scarcely saw their host and did not note how curiously he eyed the sister who had unsuccessfully defied her brother. Preoccupied with her unhappy thoughts, she only realized he had offered to lead her to her room when Nick gave her a push. "Go on now," he bade her, and she dutifully mounted the stairs.

She would go to England. Her thoughts shied from Angus. She'd no other choice. Even had she not owed Nick an obligation almost too heavy to bear, she had nowhere to hide from her legal guardians.

The English earl who was her uncle had charge of her monies, and among her friends and relatives there was not one with the stature to battle him for it.

"Miss Tessa!"

Tessa looked up, startled, as Nan emerged from a door before her. Poor Nan. Her hands worked fretfully and her eyes were enormous.

"Nay, lass, ye need nae look so fearful," Tessa bade her in a voice rendered unusually quiet by fatigue. "I'll nae draw and quarter ye."

"I was so afeard for ye!" Nan cried, her eyes filling with tears. "And when his lairdship came, I could nae stand against him! He was verra angry, do ye ken?"

"Aye, Nan." Tessa managed a faint smile that faded almost as soon as it came. "I ken." Nick's face when he'd demanded she swear by Angus's name rose in her mind.

"Lord Kerne is a man accustomed to having his way. Truly, lass,"—she gave Nan a pat on the shoulder—"I've nae quarrel with ye. What ye did was for the best. Nay, I can see ye're curious, but I've nae desire to speak of my night. I would dearly love a bath, though. Is the water hot?"

Nan's head bobbed. " 'Twill be when the girl fetches it. The tub lies behind the screen there."

In only a few minutes Nan had Tessa soaking in a warm, fragrant bath, a cup of tea in her hand. Afterward, when her mistress was dressed again in a proper twill traveling dress, she brought in a breakfast, but Tessa would eat no more than a piece of toast.

"But, Miss Tessa, ye did nae eat much o' yer dinner last evenin'!" Nan remonstrated, obviously more herself.

Tessa eyed the eggs, the rasher of bacon, and the bread and jam upon her plate with vague distaste then shrugged. "I shan't shrivel and blow away just yet."

After an hour, Tessa followed Jakes downstairs meekly enough, but her foot faltered above the last step when she overheard the innkeeper saying to Nick, "Aye, the border be only thirty miles or so, milord. Ye'll be there afore noon most likely."

Nick nodded, glad to have his own estimate confirmed. He was anxious to be gone from the Scottish border area, for he thought it within the realm of possibility that they might yet meet the men who had attacked Tessa the night before. Were the ruffians to recognize them, it was inevitable an ugly scene would ensue, particularly if they had gathered reinforcements. He had shot one of their number dead, and they must wish for vengeance.

It was for that reason he'd forced the pace all morning, though he knew Tessa was faint with fatigue. Alone and in broad daylight he'd have been hard put to protect her.

Now, with Jakes and the postilions for support, Nick did not doubt who would emerge triumphant and admitted to a grim desire to rid the world of men who had dared lay hands on his charge, but he put aside his desire for blood. He did not care to have Tessa distressed by encountering the brigands again.

Then he saw Tessa hesitating upon the last step, her face pale and her eyes, the color of the sea in a storm, fixed upon the landlord. There was no doubting she'd heard him say how soon she would reach England. Her dismay was too obvious.

"Come on, then," he said, his voice gruff as he took her arm. "The carriage awaits."

They were in England when they stopped for luncheon. From the window of the parlor where they were served, Tessa could see the Cheviot Hills. The ones in the foreground were, like her, trapped in England, but those fainter ridges were in Scotland.

"That is all you intend to eat?"

Tessa glanced disinterestedly down at the piece of bread she had not finished. "Aye. I'm not hungry."

Because Nan had excused herself, there was only Tessa to answer when Nick observed, "I suppose they did serve you an unusually large breakfast this morning."

"Hmm," she said absently, and with no intention of giving him a false picture of what she'd eaten that day. She simply had no interest in the subject.

Her spirits lower than they'd ever been in her life, Tessa could not summon enthusiasm for anything, even food. What most affected her was her helplessness. She, who had, to all intents, ruled Kilmorgan Castle; she, who had dictated all her own actions; she had lost all control over her future.

Her aunt and uncle controlled her life now. They could dictate everything, even the man she married.

At the thought that he would likely be a Sassenach, Tessa closed her eyes. She felt entirely lost and tried to numb herself against the surge of despair that threatened to overwhelm her.

What was she to do now? She did not know. She had not thought beyond escape to MacIvey's.

In her mind's eye she saw Angus. His eyes were bleak

with disappointment at how completely she'd failed him.

Close to the southern border of Northumberland, they stopped for the night. Fatigued beyond bearing, Tessa only waited for Nan to help her don her nightclothes before she fell into her bed and was asleep before her head touched the inn's hard pillow.

By chance Nick was on his way to his own room when Nan, carrying Tessa's untouched dinner tray in her hands, slipped out the door of the room she shared with her mistress.

Nick looked from the tray to the girl. "Miss Strahan did not eat dinner?"

"Nae, milaird." Nan shook her head regretfully. "She could nae think o' food before she fell into sleep."

Sympathetic with Tessa's fatigue, Nick shrugged. "Well, I suppose the breakfast she ate will sustain her well enough."

It was Nan's turn to look surprised. "Nae, milaird, Miss Tessa ate only a bite o' toast then and drank a cup of tea to wash it down."

Nick frowned. The thought that Tessa meant to starve herself crossed his mind, but he dismissed it. Even she was not so stubborn as to refuse food as long as she was kept in England.

"Let your mistress sleep as late as she wishes tomorrow, Nan, but when she awakens, tell her I have asked that she breakfast with me. Do not tell her I am concerned over how little she has eaten today, only that I've something to discuss with her."

With a clear conscience Nan dipped an assenting curtsy. Having known her mistress since she was only half a day old, she knew that Tessa had never lacked an appetite before, and she thought it a critical situation that called for drastic remedies.

12

*T*essa slept soundly for twelve hours, and when she first awakened, before she recalled where she was, she experienced a surge of energy. When Nan cheerfully opened the curtains and revealed that the day was filled with sunshine not a cool Scottish mist, however, she sagged back on her pillows.

When Nan inquired what she wished to wear, Tessa responded, with a vague shrug, and when she was at last outfitted in a gray serge of her maid's choosing, she drifted listlessly down to the parlor, where Nan reported Nick awaited her.

As one in a dream she noted how different the voices emanting from the stableyard sounded. There were no lilting Scottish accents to be heard, only flat, terse English ones.

Her eyes downcast as Nick rose from his place to seat her, Tessa did not notice that he nodded over her head to Nan, nor that her maid departed.

The sight of four covered dishes on the table before her had the odd effect of causing her stomach to heave. Closing her eyes briefly, Tessa quelled the sensation then helped herself to a single hard biscuit for the sake of appearances.

"Good day, Tessa. I trust you are feeling more rested today."

Nick, she saw when she glanced his way, lounged comfortably in his chair and his blue eyes searched her in a way Tessa found disturbing. She busied herself with pouring a cup of tea. "Thank you. I slept soundly."

Nick watched Tessa stir her tea and sip idly from her cup while she ignored the covered dishes before her as well as the lone biscuit she'd selected from the bread basket.

"I thought that while we broke our fast you might care to hear about the people you'll meet at my home in Cheshire. I hope to reach Tarlton Hall sometime late tomorrow evening."

"Tomorrow?" Tessa repeated blankly. She had not thought they would reach their destination so soon. As long as they traveled, nothing was settled, but when they arrived at her aunt's—no Nick had said his—home, her fate, whatever it was, would be upon her. The thought made her faintly ill.

"I shall see them soon enough," she muttered into her teacup. "I needn't hear about them yet."

"Just as you needn't eat?" Nick inquired coolly. "You are not eating even that biscuit," he pointed out when Tessa glanced at him in surprise. "Nor have you eaten anything since what I imagine was a hurried repast the night you ran off."

Tessa pushed her plate away as if she found its proximity troublesome. "I am not hungry," she said simply.

"You intend to starve yourself for amusement perhaps? Or is this a ploy to force me to return you to Scotland, where you had no difficulty with your appetite?"

"Whatever ails you, my lord?" Sighing, Tessa gave Nick a weary look. "You've won entirely. I am in your England." Disinterestedly she looked past him toward the window and added under her breath, "Godforsaken place that it is."

Disturbed as much by her spiritless manner as by her lack of appetite, Nick did not allow himself to be drawn out. "Because we've not got mountains as high as yours or crags as craggy or skies as misty does not mean Northumberland is godforsaken. You might even enjoy gentle hills, a few trees, and sunshine, if you would allow yourself."

Tessa ignored the ironic remark as she poured herself another cup of tea. She appeared to regard their discussion of her lack of appetite as finished and did not glance his way as, thinking of nothing at all, she sipped the hot beverage.

"If I have to tie you to your chair and pour food down

your throat until you choke, Tessa, you will eat something substantial this morning.''

Tessa did not immediately comprehend the threat Nick had made, for he had spoken in such an even, pleasant tone, she had not attended to him at first. ''Beg pardon?''

''I know this journey has been difficult for you, but I cannot allow you to make yourself ill,'' was the steady reply, and Tessa realized she had heard him aright.

Her eyes flashed as a shaft of anger penetrated the numbing gloom that had enveloped her. ''What truly concerns you, my lord? Surely it is not my health. You know perfectly well I would do no harm to myself. Perhaps you worry that I may fetch a lesser settlement upon the marriage mart if I'm off my feed a bit?''

Nick cocked his head toward her untouched biscuit. ''A bit? I should say entirely. And you will fetch no settlement at all as a corpse, my dear. They are *de trop* this Season, I've been told.'' Tessa bit her lip in an effort to resist his black humor, but her eyes gave her away. ''I see you agree.''

Quickly she dropped her glance and made a show of stirring her cup. She denied that Nicholas Steele's eyes, lit with ironic amusement, could affect her. Her pulse had leapt in that unsettling way only because her emotions were unsteady.

To her relief the landlord knocked upon the door, drawing Nick's attention from her. ''Be there aught else ye need, milord?'' he asked.

''A glass of ale, if you please.''

Tessa shot Nick a look of surprise, for he had never taken drink so early in the day before, but he said nothing until the landlord had returned with the glass and departed again.

''This is for you.'' When Nick passed the glass of foaming liquid to her, Tessa stared at it dumbfounded. ''I think half the glass should do.''

''You are not serious?''

''But I am.''

''But . . . !''

''Drink.''

Nick never moved from his chair. He remained seated with

his legs stretched indolently before him, but something in the way his gaze hardened convinced Tessa he was utterly serious.

"This is preposterous! I have never had ale! Is it that you wish to render me pliable?"

Instantly Tessa regretted her query. Nick's eyes now glinted with a wicked light. "Careful, Tessa. Belabor me on the question of my intentions often enough, and I might think you actually interested. But you may be at ease just now. When it comes to it, the truth is that I've little taste for inebriated virgins."

"That is not what I meant!" Tessa thought her cheeks had never burned so hotly. "As you very well know," she added for good measure, though her voice insisted upon sounding very like a squeak.

"You must learn to be more precise, Tessa," Nick chided, his eyes still laughing at her. She sniffed indignantly and turned her head away, but Nick was not repulsed. Extending his arm he nudged the glass toward her with a finger.

"Think of the ale as a medicinal potion, my dear, and drink up. You will drink it, you know," he added, his tone firming when Tessa continued to ignore him. "Either you will lift it to your lips or I shall. The choice is yours."

She could not believe he was serious, but the flat look he gave her advised her he would get the ale down her if he had to call in Jakes to assist.

Slowly she lifted the dark brew to her lips and wrinkled her nose when the suds tickled it. Still Nick wore that unyielding expression. A tentative taste revealed that the ale was bitter and not at all to her liking.

Tessa condescended to cast Nick a pleading glance. "It is awful."

But he was proof against her. "More."

Her flashing eyes advised him she hoped he drowned in a vat of ale, but after a deep breath, she lifted the glass and drank deeply. "There!" Tessa slammed the thing upon the table and wiped her mouth with her napkin.

Nick grinned his approval. "You'll soon be ready for the taproom."

Tessa was shaken to find her mouth curving as if it had a will of its own. The ale's effect, she decided, had been accelerated by her empty stomach. "Is it a Sassenach custom to teach young girls to like ale?" she demanded, but her words came out less indignantly than she'd have liked.

Nick's lopsided—and appealing, she admitted—smile was testimony to the lack of temper coloring her inquiry. "Only if it will improve their appetites. Do these eggs tempt you now?"

He drew the cover off a dish of eggs. To her surprise, she found she was not repulsed by the sight of them. Nor did the platter of ham look so dreadful, though the kidneys that lay beneath the third cover held no appeal. Nick covered them without protest, but he did cut a serving of ham for her, though she had thought to refuse it.

When it came to actually tasting the food, Tessa did so carefully, as if each bite might attack her. When nothing untoward occurred, she ate a little more, only to discover that the more she ate, the more she wanted.

When she was done with everything upon her plate as well as two pieces of toast, the last laden with gooseberry jam, she pushed her plate away firmly, just as she had done earlier, only this time she sighed with satisfaction.

"Feeling better?"

Tessa forced herself to look at Nick. "Yes." There was a pause, then, "Thank you."

"If you don't eat for a bit, you can lose the taste for food."

Tessa wanted to ask how he knew that, but she also wanted to have done with the subject. "I see," she said before once more taking refuge in stirring her tea.

From the corner of her eye she saw Nick rake his hand through his hair. The gesture was so surprisingly uncertain she glanced up.

"Tessa, do you trust me at all?"

There could be no doubting the earnestness of his interest

in her answer. Nick's expression was as grave as Tessa had ever seen it. She considered the question, and found, reluctantly, that honesty compelled her to answer in the affirmative.

He had always been straightforward with her, except when she had first met him in the hills above Skelgara, and even then, though he had not divulged his identity, he had not given her a false one.

To Nick, Tessa said stiffly, "If you gave me your word, I would trust you to keep it, I believe."

Nick grunted, as if not entirely satisfied with the way she'd couched her response but not utterly displeased either. "Well, then, it occurs to me you are concerned that Honoria and Alderly have it in mind to press a particular suitor upon you whether you approve of him or not. Truthfully, I cannot say I share your concern, but if my assurance will help to reconcile you to this journey, I will give you my word I shall intercede on your behalf should you find some candidate of theirs unacceptable."

"Nae!" Tessa's chair crashed to the floor behind her as she leapt to her feet.

Nick looked slowly from the chair to Tessa, whose eyes were a decidedly stormy shade of gray. "I beg pardon?" he inquired in an imperturbable manner that set her teeth on edge.

"Och, mon! Can ye nae see?" she exclaimed, reverting to Scottish brogue. "If ye do this for me, I should be indebted to ye even more than I am now. As 'tis, God spare me, I owe ye my life!"

"You would owe me nothing for this." Though Nick's tone was final, Tessa looked a wary question at him. "I do it for myself. It would not please me to see you caged in a distasteful union."

Her slender body going absolutely still, Tessa stared. Why should Nicholas Steele care what sort of union her marriage was?

"All I ask in return is that you conquer the dismals you've been in since we left the crofter's hut. You needn't worry over your future. It will be as you wish it to be. Or almost," he amended with a very smile. "You are still obliged to linger in England a time."

Tessa released the breath she had not even realized she held. Of course, he wished to ease his own life. He could not have found it a pleasure to watch her mope about so listlessly that she could neither speak nor eat. And he must have worried that his godmother would reproach him for bringing a bag of bones to her.

Nonetheless, whatever his motive, Tessa believed Nick would do what he said. He always had in the past, as she knew more to her chagrin than her pleasure. But now, with this pledge, she needn't worry that Honoria would marry her off to a pompous Sassenach lordling she detested. She need only bide her time for two years until she reached her majority, and then she could return free as a bird to Kilmorgan.

Tessa inclined her head slowly. "I shall do my best."

Nick's sudden grin caused a strange feeling to attack her midsection. Choosing to ignore the odd trembling, Tessa smiled back in celebration of their pact, but she was not sorry when Jakes knocked at the door to announce the carriage awaited her.

As she left the inn a little time later, Tessa entertained the notion that in future she would be advised to measure her doses of Nick's company. Somehow, in some way she did not care to consider with any precision, she sensed their relationship had changed. Their sojourn in the Lammermuir Hills came to mind in a most tentative way as a reason, but she did not even care to delve into causes. Her only firm thought, really, as she allowed Nick to hand her into the carriage that had been home for a little under a week, was to make a mental note to advise Nan that in England it was expected that a maid would stay with her mistress when said mistress would otherwise be alone in the company of a gentleman.

And if Nan should look surprised at Tessa's sudden interest in convention, well—Tessa arched a brow—then her mistress would inform her that when one was in Rome, one did, as much as one was able, just as the Romans did.

13

*T*hey traveled at a crisp pace all day, but Tessa found she enjoyed her blurred view of the moors of Yorkshire. Her mood lightened considerably by her pact with Nick, she forgave the stark scenery its lack of mountains and sea and found it interesting even if it was English soil.

The next day, however, when they came into country that was softer, greener, even warmer, Tessa was less sanguine. This land, with its gently rolling hills and neat, well-tilled fields prettily marked off by fences all covered with flowering vines, seemed distinctly alien to a girl from Scotland.

There were more people too. They passed a greater number of vehicles upon the road, and Tessa could see little villages dotting the landscape like raisins in a sugar bun. Each one would be filled with Englishmen, as would Tarlton Hall.

She regretted having cut Nick off when he had thought to tell her whom she'd find at his home. Grimacing to herself, Tessa allowed that pride had its drawbacks. She had no notion now if she should brace herself to encounter only her aunt or an entire Sassenach greeting party.

Luncheon was a much briefer respite than usual that day. When Tessa entered the private parlor reserved for them, she found Nick marking its confines with long, impatient strides. Before he took the time to greet her, he signaled that the roasted fowl he had ordered be served. In the blink of an eye, or so it seemed, Nick was handing her into the carriage again before climbing in behind her.

"I cannot say much for your idea of a rest stop, my lord." Tessa turned on him at once. "I scarcely had the opportunity to stretch my legs."

Nerves lent an edge to her voice, but Nick did not seem to take offense. "Frankly, I cannot endure another night in an inn," he told her. "If we keep up this pace we should reach Tarlton Hall before nightfall. You may rest there as much as you like while you accustom yourself to English ways."

"Accustom myself to English ways!" Tessa's temper flared. "Why is it you Sassenach imagine that we Scots have no ambition whatsoever but to become as English as a . . . oh, you? We desire nothing more than to be left alone to be as Scottish as we please."

"I do fear this MacIvey of yours was not as precise with her language as she ought to have been." Tessa could see her temper had not affected Nick in the least, for he was half smiling. "I said 'accustom,' not adopt, which is very different. I don't care a fig whether you choose to adopt more English ways than all Scots already have—look outraged all you like, my dear, but I think you would find you've more in common with me, say, than a Marmeluke of Egypt or even a Frenchman from Marseilles. But I digress. I only intended to say originally that I believe you will appreciate the opportunity to observe in an unhurried atmosphere the customs those of us who have the ill fortune to live south of the Grampians have adopted."

"How thoughtful you are."

Nick ignored her ironic tone. "I have tried to be. And in that spirit I shall tell you whom you may expect to meet at Tarlton Hall, though you maintained in a temper you've no interest in the subject."

Tessa folded her hands primly in her lap and looked directly into her companion's blue eyes. "I am all ears."

When he laughed aloud at her exaggerated display of restraint, Tessa found the sound so infectious, she had to fight to restrain an impish grin.

"Honoria, it goes without saying, will be on hand, though Alderly's appearance is more doubtful, for he has been much afflicted by gout in recent years. However, I am certain my younger brother, Kit, will have come from his estate in Wiltshire to make the house hospitable as I asked him to do. He'll have with him his wife, Susannah, a"—Nick paused, his eyes twinkling as he considered his sister-in-law—"ah, a, let's say, scatter-brained charmer. My advice to you there is to listen to Susannah with only half an ear, but bask in the confidence that she will support you whatever comes."

Her curiosity piqued, just as she suspected as Nick had intended, Tessa gave him a wry look, but—all innocence— he contented himself with a grin. "They've two children, James and Cecily, one six and the other three without whom they cannot seem to travel. The Steeles of Wiltshire are, in short, a delightful family, all kind to a fault, and all entirely unprepared to do battle with a latter-day Scot rebel."

Tessa widened her eyes as she asked with false sweetness, "Afraid I shall murder them in their beds, my lord?"

Nick did not take the question lightly. "You shall treat my family with utmost courtesy and respect while you are a guest in my home."

"I am not a savage to be instructed on the duties of a guest!"

Nick was entirely unaffected by Tessa's affronted outburst and continued as if she had not interrupted the flow of his remarks: "You will not refer to them or anyone else as Sassenach." Tessa's eyes flashed at that. What were they but Sassenach? As if he read her thoughts, Nick said, "On your pretty lips the word is a curse, and I shall not have Kit or his family sullied by the sound." Thrown off stride by Nick's remark on her lips, Tessa lost the chance to argue the point. By the time she managed to dismiss the compliment as a diversionary tactic and not a true reflection of his thoughts, he was already saying, "There will be no murderous looks, Tessa, no remarks such as 'devil take ye,' and no speaking silences.

"In short," Nick continued smoothly, "you shall be the model of courtesy, sweetness, and light. By the by, you will henceforth address me as Lord Kerne and I will refer to you as Miss Strahan.'' His bold gypsy's smile flashed, catching Tessa off guard so that her unprepared pulse leapt. "You see, I must make concessions as well." Before she could take herself in hand and make the sort of response he deserved, Nick was entirely serious again. He'd even that hard look she'd come to associate with serious intent in his eyes. "I hope you do understand, Tessa, for I promise that if you should willfully disobey me, I shall administer the same punishment as I did when you thought to escape into the Lammermuir Hills in the dead of night."

Color charged into Tessa's cheeks, but, keenly aware that Nan, sitting not three feet away on the opposite seat, was not in the least deaf, she did not launch into a potentially mortifying argument. She'd no wish to admit, even to her trusted servant, that she'd been spanked like a child. Nor, she admitted gloomily, could she see much point in challenging Nick. He'd do as he threatened no matter how strenuously she objected.

Situated at the end of a winding, impressively long drive, Tarlton Hall proved to be a gracious three-story mansion built in the shape of a U. Ivy clung to its mellowed brick, and the afternoon sunlight reflected off a quite astonishing—to a Scottish girl—number of windows. On one side of the house, rolling lawns descended gradually to an ornamental lake, and on the other a deer park stretched as far as Tessa could see. The entire, most charming view spoke of comfort and ease, and could not have seemed more different from Kilmorgan.

The welcome they were accorded was in keeping with the unpretentiousness of the house. There were no lines of servants to welcome them, only three liveried footmen hurrying to hold the horses and open the carriage door. Behind them two children burst out the door, followed at a more leisurely pace by a tall gentleman more comfortably than fashionably dressed.

"Uncle Nick!" the boy cried as he scampered down to

embrace his uncle. His younger sister, finding she could not negotiate the broad steps as easily as her brother, begged her father to swing her up in his arms.

While Nick laughingly fielded his nephew's headlong rush and greeted little Cecily by taking her from her father as she begged he do, Tessa studied Christopher Steele.

His looks surprised her, for though he was attractive, he was not nearly as handsome as his brother. He'd Nick's dark hair, but his eyes were a pleasant brown, and though he was as tall as his brother, his slighter build was entirely less prepossessing.

It surprised Tessa when the two brothers embraced, laughing and pounding each other upon the back as they each informed the other he was looking fit enough. She had never seen men demonstrate such affection and was still marveling at the sight when a happy cry diverted her attention to the door again.

Her swirling taffeta skirts rustling, a pretty young woman came rushing lightly down the steps as she laughed and called Nick's name. Small, for she did not even reach Nick's shoulder, she was the epitome of English beauty with china-blue eyes and soft blond hair arranged in thick curls.

"We thought you would never get here!" she said, embracing Nick as she planted a kiss upon his cheek.

Tessa felt a catch in her throat. She had been loved fiercely by her grandfather, but an undemonstrative Scot, he had never accorded her even half such a delightfully exuberant welcome. The thought did not embitter her, for she was too taken with the scene. Rather, she resolved not to play a dour Scottish raven opposite the sunny Sassenach.

"You must be Tessa!" Keeping to her resolve, Tessa smiled. She could not know how her face lit when she smiled, but Tessa could not escape the effect she elicited, for the young woman clapped her hands together happily. "What a beauty you are, my dear! How delightful! Why, your eyes put me in mind of a Scottish mist! I found them so mysterious and enchanting when I went to visit my sister—"

"Susannah!" Her husband laughed. "The poor girl has

been traveling for days on end, and before you invite her inside, you begin to rattle on about her eyes. Miss Strahan''—Kit Steele's twinkling eyes begged Tessa's indulgence—''I hope you will forgive us all. We ought to have you sitting comfortably with your feet up, and instead we go into whoops over Nick and into raptures over you.''

Nick's younger brother possessed a smile that was, if not as bold as his brother's, in its own way entirely charming, and Tessa smiled in return. ''I have sat in a carriage so long, Mr. Steele, that I find standing positively delightful and being flattered to boot . . . well, it makes for a very nice welcome.''

''Prettily said!'' Susannah Steele grinned brightly. ''I can see we two shall get on famously by simply ignoring the men and doing precisely as we please.'' She giggled when her husband said mildly he thought that was what she did all the time, but subsided when he embarked on formal presentations.

''Your Aunt Honoria is not here as yet to greet you, I fear, Miss Strahan,'' Kit said next with an air of apology. ''Alderly has suffered a particularly vicious attack of his gout, but she stands ready to join us the instant she receives word you have come.''

Feeling as if she'd been granted a reprieve, Tessa managed to say, ''I see,'' affably enough, and then Susannah linked her arm through Tessa's and led her into the house.

''Shall I show you to your room, Miss Strahan?'' she asked. ''I should imagine you would like to bathe and change your clothes before you come down to dinner. We shall eat in an hour or so. I do hope you shall like your room. It is one of my favorites . . .''

Tessa was swept up a handsome curving stairway before she could reply. She'd an impression of elegant surroundings tastefully furnished. An Adam table stood in the hallway below, a painting she thought done by an Italian master hung on the wall, and overhead lay a delicately sculpted stucco ceiling.

Nothing, she thought, could have been further from the old, drafty barn of a castle that had been her home, and as her hostess continued to chatter vivaciously at her side, Tessa experienced a twinge of panic. She was succumbing to the Sassenach, allowing herself to be carried off to the heart of their well-ordered domain without even the pretense of battle.

Glancing a little wildly down to the entryway below, she found Nick, as she somehow had known he would be, watching her while his niece and nephew played around his legs and his brother gave some directions to a servant. The expression on his arresting face, clearly illuminated by the light from the doorway, completely routed Tessa's momentary panic.

Never before had she had the singular pleasure of seeing Nick thrown entirely off his stride. But he definitely was just then. His brow, as he watched her climb the stairs in apparently friendly accord with his very English sister-in-law, was lifted and his jaw was, if ever so slightly, still unmistakably, dropped.

Mischief prompting her, Tessa gave him a wide, sunny smile as if there were nothing the least remarkable occurring. She thought, but could not be certain because he was so far away, that his lips twitched.

Tessa quickly ducked her head in a display of listening to Susannah and attempted to dismiss both the interchange and her remarkably lightened spirits from her mind. That she would not put away all thought of Nick quite so handily, she realized when she took in what it was her hostess was chattering on about.

"It all seems like some story Sir Walter Scott might write!" Susannah Steele beamed happily at her. "A Scottish beauty must be brought south and a thrillingly handsome—Nick is that, don't you agree?—lord escorts her. They have adventure after adventure, but in the end . . ."

Tessa was not certain where Mrs. Steele's seemingly well-developed romantic imagination was leading her, but thought it time to introduce a dose of reality. "Actually," she interrupted her companion's flow of words with a wry smile, "Lord Kerne and I did not always see eye to eye. He can be most insufferably high-handed at times."

Susannah's blue eyes widened in unmistakable surprise. "Why! I do believe you have resisted Nick's allure." Seeing Tessa's brow lift, she shook her head with a laugh. "I see I must confess I worried that it was the height of folly to place a young woman in Nick's exclusive company for so long a time."

"Did you fear I should arrive upon the doorstep wearing my heart upon my sleeve?"

Eyes twinkling merrily, Susannah nodded. "And with a case of the worst mopes besides. Not that you lack the looks to attach any man's interest, of course," she hastened to add. "But Nick has never shown the least interest in young ladies—"

"Preferring instead, I should imagine, older, experienced females who would never be so absurd as to expect marriage," Tessa finished for her hostess.

Susannah gave a choked laugh. "I see you do not mince words, but yes, that is precisely what I might have said. He is a riveting man whom we all adore, you understand. It is merely that his heart seems immune to any truly long-lasting relationship. Perhaps it is that too many women, young and old, throw themselves at him. I've the greatest hope he'll come around eventually, however . . ."

Tessa hid a smile as Susannah frowned thoughtfully. No wonder Nick had called his sister-in-law scatterbrained. It seemed the affairs of his heart were a subject of serious consideration for her.

"Here we are." Susannah pulled herself from her preoccupation and led Tessa into a graceful, airy room whose walls were covered in pale blue silk. The Queen Anne furniture was as pleasing to the eye as the view of the flower gardens out the window.

"I hope you find it to your liking?" Susannah said with some concern.

Tessa smiled sincerely. "How could I not, Mrs. Steele? It is entirely charming."

"I am glad you think so! But if we are to be friends, surely I must be Susannah?"

Tessa hesitated. Friends? But not even when she summoned Angus's visage could Tessa find the heart to deny the appeal in Susannah Steele's very wide, guileless eyes. She inclined her head. "And I am Tessa to most."

Susannah left her when Nan arrived with her trunks, saying she would return in an hour to lead her to the salon below, where they would gather before dinner.

14

*W*hether it was fatigue that overtook her or shock at finding herself inclined to friendliness toward Nick's Sassenach relatives, Tessa laid her head down upon her pillow for a nap before dinner and did not awaken until late the next morning, just before Nan slipped in to see about her.

"Aye, 'tis a fine house this!" Nan informed Tessa before crossing to pull open the curtains. Noting her maid's brisk step, Tessa thought dryly that Nan seemed more pleased than otherwise to find herself in a grand Sassenach home. "There be windows at every turn"—Nan gestured to the five in Tessa's room—"but nae a draft to be felt! And mind ye, Miss Tessa, 'tis only one o' his lairdship's homes."

Discovering herself reluctant to marvel over the vastness of Nick's estate, Tessa diverted Nan by asking whether the others had already breakfasted.

Nan shook her head. "Nae, though 'tis past nine o'clock! Mrs. Steele be at the breakfast table still and awaits ye there. His lairdship and Mr. Steele did break fast earlier," she added with more approval. "And ye'll ne'er believe it, but his lairdship ha' gone out ridin' with his brother joost as if he did nae spend all these past days astride a horse. The maids say 'tis like him, though, for they say he 'twas fair born in the saddle."

It was easy enough to distract Nan from relating any further tidbits of wisdom she'd gleaned from Nick's staff on the subject of their master. Tessa had only to rummage in the wardrobe as if she looked for something to wear, and she was soon ready to descend to the breakfast room, where Susannah greeted her warmly.

"You are not to apologize for sleeping late," Susannah chided when Tessa began to do just that. "You are here to rest after your journey, and I am glad you did. Now, what shall you have? As you can see, I have only toast points and coffee, but I am struggling to keep my waist at the size it attained after James's birth. You, I cannot think, have such worries."

"I have always enjoyed a good breakfast," Tessa allowed, deliberately ignoring the one morning she had had to be persuaded with a tankard of ale to eat. In the twinkle of an eye, she found a plate laden with eggs, ham, rolls, and fruit placed before her.

Though Susannah gave the plentiful display an avid look, she spoke not of food as Tessa ate, but of Honoria. "Your aunt should arrive some time before tea, I imagine," she said, causing Tessa's fork to waver momentarily. "The roads between here and her home in Leicestershire are quite good, and I know she is only waiting for the summons. She is thrilled at the thought of meeting you, you know."

Tessa searched her hostess's face as she nodded politely, but Susannah's smile was entirely innocent. Merely making conversation with a guest, she seemed sunnily unaware of any tensions that might affect the imminent meeting. "And I am interested in meeting her." It was not a lie, Tessa thought wryly. How would she not be interested in meeting a woman those father had forbidden even her name to be spoken?

"I have always found her to be the kindest and most generous of women," Susannah mused. "She was, before Alderly became ill, one of the great hostesses of the *ton*, as you must know, but I hope you do not imagine she is as frivolous as many who dote upon the social scene are." Laughing unself-consciously, Susannah appended, "As I am! In comparison to Honoria, I am a mere butterfly. Nick and Kit, as you must know, hold her in the highest regard, for she was quite wonderful to their mother."

A footman entered then with more coffee, and Tessa was obliged to wait, more impatiently than she cared to admit, for him to depart so that Susannah might divulge the details of her aunt's devotion to Nick's mother.

Indeed, her interest was such that when Susannah did not return to the subject after the man had departed, Tessa condescended to prompt her. "Was the marchioness ill, then?"

"But did Nick not tell you?"

Susannah was clearly amazed, and Tessa realized that in the normal way of things, she and Nick would have discussed the connection between their families during their journey together. But then, from the first nothing between them had conformed to tidy convention. With just the ghost of a smile Tessa said simply no, and waited for Susannah to continue.

Susannah stared a moment, obviously torn by a desire to ask what it was Nick and Tessa had discussed if not the bond connecting them, but something in Tessa's expression subdued her curiosity. "Ah, well, when Nick had only been at Cambridge a year or so, his father and mother were injured in a carriage accident. The marquess did not survive, but Lady Emmaline was not so fortunate. Oh, I know it seems a cruel thing to say, but in truth it is a great deal worse to be left an invalid, unable to walk or get about without someone to come and lift you. She was a very brave woman, however. She'd her bad days, when she missed her husband terribly, but generally she was amazingly cheerful."

Susannah tipped her head consideringly. "She and her husband were very much in love, you know. Kit says it is his parents' felicitous marriage that has caused Nick to be so wary of the institution." As if they'd a will of their own, Tessa's gracefully arched eyebrows lifted, and Susannah, pleased by this show of interest in a subject she clearly adored, nodded eagerly. "Yes, you see, it is Kit's theory that, having seen at close hand a union based on the deepest affection, Nick finds it impossible to accept anything less for himself. He is searching for the perfect woman, you see."

"A most exalted mission." Tessa could not but smile wryly at Susannah's dreamy expression. "How fortunate for him it demands a thorough acquaintance with the spectrum of England's mature beauties.''

Susannah attempted to look offended, but her giggle spoiled the effect. ''I can see you think me as intolerably romantic as Kit does! But, nonetheless, you will not dissuade me. Though I admit Nick is not rushing himself, I insist that when he does find the right woman, he will settle down and make an exceptionally fine husband.''

The thought of Nick married did not amuse her as it ought to have done, and Tessa thought it time to return the conversation to her aunt. ''We have disgressed, you know. I am still ignorant how Honoria assisted Lord Kerne's mother.''

''Oh, do forgive me!'' Susannah threw up her hands in an extravagant gesture. ''I am a chatterbox, but I shan't waste another moment holding forth on the subject of my brother-in-law. Instead I shall tell you, simply, that Honoria took charge of Lady Emmaline's care at a time when no one else could. Nick and Kit were both in school, you see, and Lady Emmaline was made more anxious than she was soothed when Nick left Cambridge, for she dearly wished him to complete his studies.''

Feeling no small twinge of guilt for having believed Nick's life had lacked all adversity, Tessa said quietly, ''It must have been a very difficult time for everyone.''

''It was, yes. But it was not without some benefits. Nick and Honoria, particularly, grew closer together. Their relationship is quite famous, you know.'' Susannah gave a little laugh. ''Indeed, the esteem in which Nick holds Honoria is such that no one will question the wisdom of sending him after you.''

Tessa was on the point of saying Susannah herself had admitted to reservations, but Susannah was already waving her hand. ''Oh, I do not mean that there will not be those who are as surprised as I that you have escaped succumbing to Nick's legendary charm. You will be quite a curiosity in that regard, my dear.'' Susannah grinned when Tessa grimaced. ''I see the prospect does not please you, but at least you may be grateful that though you've beauty to spare, no one will suggest Nick may have overstepped the bounds while you were in his care. Everyone knows he would never betray Honoria's trust in him."

Perhaps he would not, Tessa conceded, but she knew perfectly well that Nick's famous esteem for his godmother had never been put to the test during the entirety of their trip. Had he not slept beside her on a tiny pallet with only the rain to chaperon them and done nothing at all but fall into a sound sleep?

No, whatever Susannah might think of her beauty, and there had been others as well to say she was a "fair lass," Nick found her only a troublesome chit who did not tempt him in the least.

Nor did he tempt her, Tessa addressed a mental image of Nick sharply. Granted, that particular night when she had slept in his arms, she had felt safe and warm and, perhaps, just for the briefest tick of time, something more unsettling, but all her reactions were entirely understandable. When she had been in a most harrowing situation, he had appeared very like a knight of old to rescue her.

Now, Tessa lectured herself as Susannah chattered on about her children, it was time to put Nick Steele from her mind and prepare herself for her introduction to Honoria.

"Honoria's nae daughter of mine!" Angus had railed when once Tessa had asked about her aunt. "Marryin' a Sassenach! Ne'er speak her name to me again, Tessa Ross Strahan. She's as one dead."

But in the end the old man had left her to her aunt's care. Why? Had he merely refused to admit how gravely ill he was? Or perhaps he had wished to reunite his daughter with her family, but had been unable to admit as much to anyone, himself least of all.

Angus gave her no answer, and Tessa, her mouth curving slightly thought she could hear him growling, "Think to worry me in paradise, do ye hinny? Well, ye won't! 'Tis yer own guid mind ye'll have to rely upon today."

Honoria arrived, as Susannah had predicted, just before tea. Taking it upon himself to act as messenger, Nick found

Tessa in the nursery, where she was reading a fairy tale about princesses and dragons with Cecily on her lap and James by her feet. Their eyes wide, they listened intently as Tessa revealed in a low, dramatic voice the magic words that would save the princess.

The story completed, Tessa saw Susannah wave and looked toward the door to find Nick propped there, observing the little scene with an enigmatic expression.

She stiffened, preparing herself should he dare to gloat over finding her so cozily ensconced with his young Sassenach kin, but looking over the heads of the two children who had run to greet him, Nick merely announced Honoria's arrival. Their gazes locked, then, after an indeterminate amount of time, Nick gave a brief nod that seemed to signal satisfaction. "Shall we go down, Miss Strahan?" he asked politely.

Tessa made him wait as she bade the children farewell, and all the while, under her breath, she damned Nick for holding her helpless with his blue, Sassenach eyes. Unimpeded, he had read her mind in that infuriating way he had and had decided, it seemed, that she could be trusted with Honoria. It would serve him right, Tessa smiled grimly to herself, were she to stomp into her aunt's presence and roundly condemn the woman for being a heartless traitor.

With Susannah accompanying them and mercifully chattering all the while, they reached the salon in due time, and when the footman threw open the door, Susannah hurried forward and greeted Honoria with a fond kiss upon the cheek.

Following behind, her step deliberately slower, Tessa took in her first glimpse of her notorious aunt and was surprised to find Honoria rather small, though she sat erectly upon the edge of a straight chair. She also gave the impression of being older than her years, for her auburn hair was streaked heavily with white, but she did not lack an air of fashion. Her hair was worn in a soft, becoming knot that Tessa had seen in fashion plates, and her tasteful but obviously expensive dress of gray, watered silk was cut in the latest style.

Closer now, Tessa watched Honoria lift her cheek to

Susannah, and following the movement, Tessa suddenly caught her breath. Her aunt's profile was, with the addition of a few wrinkles added by time, feature for feature, the exact image of Joanna Strahan's.

Tessa swallowed past a sudden, disconcerting lump. She'd not expected such a remarkable likeness to her mother.

In the next moment, when Honoria turned to her, she was somewhat better prepared for her aunt's eyes. Mrs. Dunadee had told her both Ross girls had gotten their blue eyes from their mother. Still, she found it impossible to remain unmoved by eyes that called up a host of painfully good memories.

"We meet at last, my dear. I own that I am very, very pleased."

"Ma'am," Tessa dipped her aunt a proper curtsy, glad of the excuse to look down. Honoria's eyes were misty with unshed tears.

"You must both excuse us now." Honoria turned to Nick and Susannah, each of whom regarded the scene in his own way: Susannah with sentimental tears to match Honoria's and Nick with a quite unsentimental directness. "We Scots, you know, prefer to make our greetings in private," she added with a touch of gentle humor when her godson did not leap to obey her.

Nick's mouth curved faintly, and he bowed. "Of course, my dear," he said. He strolled from the room behind Susannah, but only after he had taken the time to favor Tessa with a bland look that she read, correctly, as a warning.

She tossed her head ever so slightly at his retreating back and only heard her aunt say, "I hope your trip was not unduly difficult, Thérèse."

As Tessa turned to her, the words "Being dragged by a high-handed Sassenach lord does not make for an unduly easy trip" were on the tip of her tongue.

She subdued the retort, however. Honoria's blue eyes, mercifully dry of tears now, wavered with an eloquent mixture of wariness and pleading that could not but affect Tessa.

"No, the journey was not unduly difficult, ma'am."

"I am glad. I know Nick can be high-handed, and I worried how you'd take to him, but after the way you sent poor George packing, I thought I'd need of a stronger emissary."

"I should say you succeeded."

Poor George Pierpoint had been the merest milquetoast. When she had said, "I'll not be going anywhere with you, Sassenach," he had gaped and spluttered, but ridden off the very next day quite—but for his valet—alone. Nick, by contrast . . . Tessa's eyes, despite the tension of the moment, lit with wry amusement as she thought how very differently her first meeting with her aunt's second emissary had proceeded.

"Oh, Thérèse!" Her aunt's soft exclamation recalled her from the banks of Skelgara's burn. To Tessa's surprise, Honoria's hands were clasped tightly together. "My dear child, you quite undo me. Do you know how like you are to my mother—your grandmother?"

Tessa tipped her head slightly. Others, even Angus once, had said the same, but Tessa had recognized little resemblance between herself and the slender, blue-eyed woman with the vivacious smile who had existed for her only in a miniature Angus kept in his room.

"You've the same sparkle in your eye," Honoria said half to herself as she studied her niece. "And her refined features. Did you know Mama was a much acclaimed beauty in Edinburgh in her youth? The young men said she was all Scottish fire cloaked in French grace." Tessa had not known. Thérèse Ross, born of a French mother and Scottish father, had rarely been spoken of at Kilmorgan, for Angus had taken her loss very hard. "At least that was what our nanny told us." Honoria smiled. "Joanna and I got our looks not from Mama but from her mother. Strange that you would repeat our pattern. You even have the beauty mark Joanna and I would have given our eye teeth for." She chuckled, obviously at some memory. "Once we applied patches just at the corner of our mouths to see how we would look, but Nanny found us out and scolded us unmercifully for wanting what the good Lord did not see fit to give us.''

There was a moment's silence and then Tessa said, "I always thought Mama very beautiful, and you look, as you must know, quite like her.''

The intensity of Honoria's smile was out of all proportion to the compliment she'd received. "Thank you, my dear! We did have quite a time in our day.''

Tessa waited quietly while Honoria looked away to blink rapidly, but when her aunt's expression was again composed, Tessa thought it time to address the one whose name had not yet been spoken.

"However much I may resemble Thérèse Ross, it is Angus' eyes I have.''

Honoria stiffened. She'd not expected the remark. Slowly, not taking her eyes from Tessa's, she nodded. "Yes, you do. 'Eyes as mysterious as Scottish mist,' my mother used to say. Can yours be as flinty as his, Thérèse?''

It was Tessa's turn to feel surprise. It seemed her aunt was not all tears and sentimental memories. The query had been direct, even blunt. She answered truthfully, "I don't believe anyone's eyes could be as flinty as Angus' when he was in a temper. But . . .''

Tessa hesitated. Face to face with a woman who was quite different than she'd imagined her aunt would be, the words describing how strongly Angus had railed against his daughter and how deeply his attitudes had affected everyone within hearing did not roll off Tessa's tongue.

"But you've no notion how to deal with me, because Angus . . .'' Honoria's attempt to finish Tessa's thought faltered. Biting her lip, she turned her hands over almost in a gesture of surrender and finished tensely, ". . . remained so very angry with me.''

Tessa admitted to no small sense of dislocation as her aunt hastily withdrew a dainty handkerchief from the reticule beside her and applied it to her eyes. Always when she had thought of Honoria, she had imagined a willful daughter who had flounced off upon the arm of her wealthy Sassenach lord without the least care for how she affected her father.

The truth, it seemed, had been far different from that image. Though her hair was turned half white with the years, Honoria still mourned because her father had so fiercely rejected her along with her choice of husband.

Her eyes dry again, Honoria looked more the Countess of Alderly, and she leaned forward as if to bridge more than the physical distance between her niece and herself. "I know you have not wanted to come to England, Thérèse," she said in a steady, if low voice. "Why my father left me to be your guardian, considering how terribly I had angered him, I cannot know. I would like to think he made no specific provision for you, because though he could not bring himself to say it directly, he wished through you to make amends, but I admit I may well be allowing my own wishes to interfere with my judgment. Knowing as I do how painful it is to feel forced against one's will, I'll not force you to stay with me. I asked Nick to invite you here only that we might become acquainted."

"Invite me?"

"Why, yes. I hoped that if you could be persuaded to come, you would find me more tolerable than you had thought. You are my only relative, Thérèse," she finished simply. "I should like to know you."

They were at the crux of the matter, and Tessa, looking deeply into her aunt's eyes, eyes so like her mother's, found herself saying, "And I you, Aunt."

"Oh, my dear!" When Honoria, smiling tremulously, held out her hands, Tessa had no thought but to clasp them in her own. "I have longed to hear you say that and feared I should not! We shall have such a very good time. You'll see. Truly the English are quite fine people."

A spark flashed in Tessa's eye, but fresh tears blinded Honoria so she did not see it. Even had she noted that dangerous light, she'd not have known what to make of it, for she could not know she had reminded Tessa of a particular Englishman—the one who had been instructed to invite her south. Invite her!

15

*T*essa was obliged to wait much longer than she had anticipated to discuss with her aunt's godson the vast difference
between "invite" and "force." Nick was not in sight when
she returned to her room, and not forgetting Susannah's
propensity for matchmaking, she decided against asking for
him.

With a wry grimace she conceded there had been some
compensations to traveling with the man. Then at least, he
had always been at hand when she wished to vent her ire.

When the dressing gong rang, Tessa allowed Nan to choose
a soft muslin gown for her. The light material was entirely
appropriate for the southern climate she now inhabited, but
accustomed as she was to the necessity for heavier clothing
and shawls even in summer, Tessa hesitated over the effect
of her scant costume.

Nan was not so uncertain. " 'Tis the verra thing these
Sassenach wear," she avowed stoutly. "Ye did nae see her
last eve, but Mrs. Steele wore a dress as flimsy."

Admittedly more comfortable, Tessa allowed herself to be
persuaded and hurried down to the salon, where the little
party was to gather before dinner, in the hopes that she would
find Nick alone. That she had not been prompt enough she
could tell from a distance, for the evening being warm, the
doors to the salon had been left open and she heard
Christopher Steele exclaim, "Damn, Nick! You've the
devil's own luck. First the heiress, who might as easily have
been poker-faced and squint-eyed, turns out to be a raving
beauty, and now I learn that while you were engaged upon
the onerous duty of escorting her south, you had the out-

landish luck to win a stallion as fine as any in your already
renowned stables. Blast, but the stakes must have been
exorbitant! I thought you had given up playing so deep.''

"The man needed a lesson.''

Tessa, her grievance forgotten for the moment, stepped
quickly through the door. Her eyes flew to Nick, but she
was not to learn if the man he had trounced at cards was
the same man he'd knocked down for insulting her.

Lounging with his shoulders propped against the mantle-
piece, Nick's eyes met hers only for the briefest moment
before, his brow lifting faintly, he lowered them to her dress.

At once Tessa turned her gaze to Christopher Steele. Even
when she had stood before her pier glass she'd not felt as
uncertain over the delicate airiness of her muslin as she did
just then with Nick's eyes raking her, but she'd have fallen
in a faint upon the floor before she let him see how uncertain
he made her.

"Good evening, Miss Strahan,'' Christopher Steele gave
her a warm smile as he extended his arm. "I hope you feel
as fresh and rested as you look, my dear. You made a very
long journey, and I am aware that traveling with this dog
would be no easy task.'' He gestured to his brother with an
easy laugh and then shook his head. "Egad, but Nick never
gets paid back in his own coin! Imagine that such a loose
screw should earn the honor of escorting you.''

Seeing no need to disabuse so kind a man of his fantasies,
Tessa smiled a most appealing smile and forebore to mention
that Mr. Steele's brother had most likely found the task of
escorting her south more tribulation than honor. "You are
very kind, sir, and yes to your question. I feel entirely
restored.''

"Good evening, all!'' It was Susannah who breezed in with
a bright smile before she turned to her husband. "And no
more flattery, Kit. I heard you doing it up too brown from
the hallway, and I believe we must both take ourselves to
task. We wish to make Tessa feel at home, not the prize piece
in an exhibit.''

Chuckling, Christopher conceded that hanging framed upon a wall would be a most uncomfortable position, and asked the ladies if he could make amends by bringing them a glass of ratafia. They said yes, seated themselves, and after he had served them, Kit inquired if he could not be on the same familiar terms with Nick's guest as his wife was.

"I cannot have the two of you upon close terms while I languish at the edge of such intimacy as the cold Mr. Steele," he explained with such a lugubrious expression that Tessa laughed and said he had her permission to call her by her pet name, if she were allowed to address him as Kit.

From the corner of her eye Tessa slanted Nick a quick look to see what he made of the concession she had so easily granted his brother but had made every attempt to withhold from him. That she thought she detected a gleam of amusement glinting in his eye prompted her to add, addressing his brother, "And may I say, 'tis a delight to meet an Englishman with such polish, sir. I had feared you might one and all be a race accustomed to overlooking the desires of those around you as you order things to your precise liking."

Kit's response was to round upon his brother with an enormous smile. "Oh, ho, Nick! I do believe you've suffered a reprimand by a lady. And about time, too, at least one of the species saw your faults. As his younger brother, I echo your sentiments entirely, Tessa. The brute can be a high-handed taskmasker, indeed."

Nick inclined his head quite unperturbed. "When there is a need," he agreed equably, his eyes going from his brother to Tessa. "I can be, I quite agree, most firm of, ah, hand."

Tessa blushed fiercely. And she flashed Nick a dagger-sharp look, informing him with her eyes as she could not with her tongue that he was no gentleman for referring to that mortifying moment when his hand had firmly handled a most unmentionable portion of her anatomy. Nick, to Tessa's fury, only reacted by compounding his offense.

Seeing her stormy expression, he actually had the ill grace to grin wickedly.

Their interchange could not be overlooked, and both Susannah and Kit regarded Tessa with considerable surprise. Though she had maintained Nick had vexed her considerably upon their journey, neither of his relatives had truly believed her. Too long they had been treated to young ladies who either threw themselves upon one of the marriage mart's most elusive catches or retreated from him in blushing confusion. Looks that promised a lingering, painful death were not in their ken, and a startled silence reigned until Honoria entered a moment later.

Elegantly turned out in a dress the blue of her eyes, Honoria gave them all her gentle smile. "I apologize for my tardiness. I was detained in the nursery by a most unusual game of chess. You must speak to your son, Kit. By means of a magic spell he reduced all my pieces to pawns. It was most disconcerting."

Kit gave a great laugh, and Susannah admitted ruefully that her eldest child did change the rules of games to suit himself. "Sometimes I believe from his autocratic ways that he is related to the royal Stuarts by more than his name."

There was a general chuckle, and then the conversation turned to Lord Alderly and his condition, but while Honoria related that her husband was much improved, Tessa sat unattending.

The easy reference to the Stuarts, whose cause had brought the Highlands out so disastrously against the English, amazed her. That no one, not even her aunt, made the least stir about the reference to a royal line whose claims to the throne had cost so many of her countrymen's lives informed Tessa more clearly than any lecture could have done just how passé the issue that had so deeply affected her was here in the south.

Thoughtful, not certain how the discovery affected her, Tessa glanced up to find she'd erred. One person had remarked the moment, and he was watching her now. Perhaps Nick only wished to forestall any undue reaction from her, but if so, his eyes reflected no hint of warning. Instead, his gaze was steady, almost—if Tessa could allow herself to believe it—compassionate.

She looked away, uncertain whether she wanted Nick's understanding, to find her aunt regarding her quizzically. "My dear, you have not been attending," she said with a smile that robbed her words of any scolding. "I have been telling Kit and Susannah how very like my mother you are."

"Then I hope you have been saying how closely you resemble my mother, Aunt Honoria," Tessa replied quickly, hoping to distract her aunt from further discussion of the raving beauty of Edinburgh. Though not particularly vain, Tessa still had little desire to be held up to a standard before which she thought she must inevitably pale.

"I second your niece's opinion, you know." Tessa marked the smile with which Nick favored his godmother. It was devastatingly sweet—even then Honoria was straightening before its warmth—and it was not one he had ever bestowed upon his troublesome charge. "I identified your sister's portrait at once. She is almost as lovely as you."

Honoria beamed. "You've a gentle tongue, Nick, and I love you for it. But"—she turned eagerly to Tessa—"is the portrait a good one? I should dearly like to see a portrait of Joanna."

Tessa's hesitation was imperceptible. Who was she to deny her aunt the sight of her sister's portrait? But Honoria crossing Kilmorgan's threshold? Tessa might have forgiven her aunt, but she doubted that the old stones of the castle had.

"You would also see your niece at about the age of thirteen, I think?" Nick looked at Tessa and his calm gaze steadied her so she nodded. "They are together, you see, with an enormous hound that looked to have just emerged from Hades."

"Nestor was a babe!"

Nick's mouth quirked. "Who looked a scoundrel," he insisted before adding mildly: "But Honoria could judge for herself if you had the portrait brought down to London. I

have been meaning to say the *Sea Witch* in a month or so
will be ready to fetch down anything you may have left
behind.''

Tessa could not but appreciate the easy solution Nick had
provided to her difficulty, but she could not be so pleased
by yet another demonstration of his facility for reading her
mind. A stiff thanks, therefore, was all he received before
his butler, Booker, came to announce dinner.

As they ate in the most informal of the Hall's dining rooms,
much of the conversation centered upon the seemingly
limitless acquaintances the Steeles and Honoria had in
common. Though she'd nothing to add, Tessa found herself
content to listen. As Nick might have pointed out, a great
many Sassenach ways were revealed.

Rules and decorum were as important, she found, as Ivey
had always maintained. When a certain Assembly they referred
to as Almack's came up for discussion, both her aunt and
Susannah defended the policy its hostesses had of turning
away any gentleman who was not dressed in small pants.

''If a man can't come and go as he pleases, he's no more
than a babe,'' Kit argued with Tessa's sympathy.

Honoria disagreed, though with an unruffled mildness.
''No, dear boy. There must be standards. People might come
looking any which way and that would not do at all.''

When Kit looked at his brother, Nick laughed. ''Oh, I
support you, Kit, never fear.'' Turning a roguish grin upon
his most proper godmother, he said, ''Surely you will agree,
my dear, that it would do a great deal toward relieving the
deadly tedium that currently reigns in Almack's hallowed
assembly rooms if people were allowed some latitude. Just
think of the variety of costumes that might appear to amuse
us.''

Honoria smiled, amused despite herself, but it was
Susannah who responded, shaking her finger at her brother-
in-law even as she giggled. ''I don't doubt my cheeks would
burn if I could see the sort of costumes you've in mind, Nick
Steele! But you can be no authority on the atmosphere of

Almack's. I am persuaded you've not been to an Assembly in an age.''

"Are tepid lemonade and stale cakes the refreshments?" he queried, and when Susannah, laughing, admitted they were, he nodded wisely, point made.

"Well, I think, we are all giving Tessa a very bad impression of what she may expect in town." Susannah looked at Tessa with a smile. "Nick notwithstanding, Almack's is a glittering assembly, where only the finest people gather, my dear, but you needn't fear you will only rusticate away up here in Cheshire. There's a rather exalted assemblage very nearby.''

"Oh?" It was Honoria who spoke up with interest.

Susannah nodded, pleased to have an entertainment worthy of the Countess of Alderly. "The Clarstons are having a house party. They've a mix of people. Sally Jersey is there, Charles Bascom, the Carstairs and their two daughters in one or the other of whom Nicola is attempting to interest her son, Peter, and to keep the boy company, she has invited Sir Malcolm Fraser.''

"Malcolm! But that is famous." Immediately Honoria turned to Tessa with a pleasant smile. "My dear, Malcolm Fraser is one of the young men I hoped might interest you. He's quite handsome and exceptionally courteous, and, best of all, he's entirely Scottish.''

Tessa blinked, absorbing her aunt's announcement only slowly, but when she had, she smiled a smile of such brilliance she might have lit a dudgeon and laughed aloud.

"But I thought you would be pleased, Thérèse," her aunt said, concerned by the mirth she'd elicited. "Did I mistake the matter?''

Tessa, struggling to sober, shook her head. "Oh, no, not at all, Aunt. It is only that . . .'' Another laugh welled up in her, and she turned her sparkling eyes upon Nick. The joke was at her expense, true, but it was too rich not to share with him. He would scarcely be called upon to save her from the loathsome match she had pictured in her gloomy imagings. To her surprise, however, Nick's look was entirely impenetrable and conveyed not even a hint of the smugness he'd every right to feel. Puzzled, Tessa turned back to her aunt's more scrutable expression. "I shall be very happy to meet a gallant, handsome Scotsman, ma'am."

Pleased by the reassurance, Honoria asked who else was present at the estate that Tessa gathered was only a few miles distant. "Sir Giles Bayesford is among the party as well," Susannah said, looking less than pleased. "I cannot understand why it is people invite him about. He's the most unpleasant manner."

"Nor can I say I find Giles particularly endearing," Honoria agreed. "However, he has been all the fashion since Prinny took his advice on a waistcoat."

"But the man's dress is outrageous. I've never seen such a man-millner!"

"You would be quite amazed, Kit," Nick addressed his brother. "But there are a good many seemingly intelligent people for whom Giles is the very embodiment of how an English gentleman must look."

Kit made a strangled sound of disbelief, but Nick turned to look at Tessa, a mocking light glinting in his eyes. So he had meant her, she realized, when he had said, "seemingly intelligent." Because the appellation did not sit at all well with her, her brief feeling of goodwill dissipated entirely. She returned Nick a most cool look and reminded herself of her desire to rake him over the proverbial coals for his failure to merely invite her to England.

"The only person whose presence comes as any surprise is Madelaine Landon's," Susannah said, drawing Tessa's attention from Nick. "I had thought she would remain at home this month as her husband was expected home from the Peninsula at any time."

"I cannot think Richard's return would figure heavily with Madelaine," Kit remarked dryly. "She's scarcely wanted for companionship these two years."

Mindful of Tessa's innocent ears, Honoria immediately

turned the conversation from the murky waters of the Landons' marriage. Though Kit, realizing his error, followed suit, Tessa was only vaguely aware of their discussion upon the superb dinner Nick's French chef had served.

As Susannah had made mention of Lady Madelaine Landon, who had presumably so little reason to be in Cheshire, she had turned a most speculative look upon her brother-in-law.

Tessa had followed that look. It was impossible not to. Susannah's thinking was easy to follow.

But Nick was well up to his sister-in-law and replied to the question in her eyes with a faint, enigmatic smile that gave neither Susannah nor Tessa any answer at all.

16

"Welcome home, my dears." Kit, reclining on a settee across from Honoria, smiled up at his wife and Tessa as they entered the salon. "I trust Mrs. Archmore had an inspiring selection of ribbons."

"She did, indeed," Susannah replied to her husband and again to Nick when he strolled in and repeated his brother's inquiry. "We found just the color for my new dress as well as a comb for Tessa."

After Tessa had brought out her comb to be duly admired, Susannah remarked of the visit she and Tessa had made to the nearby village of Corymede, "I know we are a trifle late for tea, but I declare half the county seemed to be in the village today."

Kit laughed. "And it would not do but that you must acquaint poor Tessa with them all, I suspect."

Susannah chuckled when Tessa gave an emphatic nod. "Now, you cannot say you minded all the pleasantries I forced you to, my dear," she admonished. "I thought you liked Sir Malcolm Fraser very well."

"You have met Malcolm! And what did you think of him?"

Tessa gave Honoria a smile. "He was quite as handsome as you promised, Aunt, and most agreeable."

"Agreeable!" Susannah, her eyes dancing, shook her head. "Smitten at first sight, I should say. He could scarcely take his eyes from you, Tessa. Even before he and Peter caught up to us, he was so entranced, he upset those crates standing in plain sight before him."

"How adept."

Not caring to hear a Scotsman disparaged, Tessa shot Nick an unfriendly glance. "Only one of the things spilled, and it was a child, not Sir Malcolm, who ran into it." Before Susannah could speak up to point out that the young man had started the train of events by bumping the child and sending the lad into the stack of crates poised rather precariously on the walkway outside Boodle's Tavern, Tessa turned back to Honoria, beside whom she had taken a seat. "Sir Malcolm asked after you, Aunt, and I told him you would be delighted to see him, should he have an opportunity to ride over."

"We shall see the boy tomorrow, mark my words," Susannah remarked with considerable certainty.

"When, if he can remember to do so, he shall at least incline his head toward Honoria?"

Kit's eyes twinkled so merrily, Tessa could not but give him a reluctant grin, while Susannah laughed. "If he can remember," she agreed with her husband. "You had best be prepared as well, Nick." When her brother-in-law lifted his brow quizzically, Susannah nodded. "Malcolm will be accompanied by Peter, who is, I warn you, quite in awe of you."

"Peter?"

Susannah bestowed a tolerant look upon Nick. "Peter Derwent, Matthew's son and has lived no more than five miles from here all his life. Though you may have taken little notice of him, he has followed your career closely. When he learned Tessa had journeyed south on the *Sea Witch*, he would have all the details from her and then held forth for what seemed at least a quarter of an hour upon your exploits at Trafalgar."

"Did he?" Nick glanced in a seemingly idle fashion to Tessa. Her head was bent over the cup of tea she'd been passed, but as if feeling the pull of his gaze, she looked up. The flash of resentment in her eyes was unmistakable and seemed to amuse Nick, for his mouth curved as he turned back to Susannah. "I hardly know the boy, but now you mention it, I recall him prosing on one day about the navy.''

"He said you were badly wounded.'' Tessa bit her lip. She had not meant to say a single word on the subject of Nick's heroic and heretofore unmentioned navel career. She had wanted to pay him back in his own coin. He had made her feel a fool by saying nothing, allowing her to continue in the belief he had shirked his duty by not fighting for his country.

She had had to learn the whole from a stranger. "They say he's as capable on a ship as on a horse, though I should have to see it to believe it,'' young Mr. Derwent had exclaimed. "Still, he was one of our heroes at Trafalgar. He must know what he's about at sea.''

"A hero at Trafalgar?'' Tessa repeated rather sharply, or so she guessed, for Mr. Derwent had looked slightly taken aback. "I am sorry I did not mean to pounce upon you, Mr. Derwent. It is just that I did not know.''

"I find it no surprise Kerne kept a closed mouth!'' The young man nodded forcefully. "He never boasts of his feats, though he was much decorated. Served with Nelson from the Nile to that last engagement when they put Boney's navy under once and for all. Kerne was badly wounded in the affair—took a ball in the shoulder, you know—but remained at the helm of his ship.''

"Nick was dreadfully wounded, my dear.'' It was Honoria, not Nick, who answered Tessa's query as to the extent of Nick's injuries. "After the battle he collapsed from loss of blood, and his life hung in the balance for some time.''

"As you can see, however, the question was resolved in my favor.'' Nick's expression was amused and revealed none of the pain Tessa guessed he had suffered.

"Only because you were too pigheaded to give in to a French ball.'' Kit looked at his brother with more than a little affection. "The word from your fellows was that in your fever you raved most adamantly about not succumbing to the frogs.''

"Enough, dear boy.'' Nick lifted his hand to halt Kit. "I

am told I raved about a good many things, and I am certain few of them were fit for the ears of ladies.''

"Well, what I want to know is what in the world did the two of you discuss over the course of your journey?'' Susannah looked inquiringly from Tessa to Nick. "It seems no mention was made of the connection between you, or of family, or of past history. I should have thought you'd have learned all there was to know of each other on such a long journey.''

"Oh, I should say we learned quite a bit,'' Nick said most uninformatively from Susannh's point of view, but in such a way that Tessa was inexplicably reminded of the night they had spent in each other's arms in the hut in the Lammermuir Hills.

Feeling a blush rise in her cheeks, she made a great show of nibbling the seed cakes that Booker had brought along with the tea, while she avoided everyone's, but most particularly Nick's, gaze.

Susannah looked as if she might tax Nick for particulars, but before she could, Honoria spoke up to ask whom else Tessa and Susannah had encountered in the village. "You did say you met up with half the county,'' she reminded Susannah.

Diverted entirely, Susannah at once took up the thread of their visit to Corymede, but Tessa listened only absently while Susannah gave the names of the mostly women they had encountered. With a half smile Tessa summoned to her mind a more entertaining subject: her introduction to Sir Malcolm Fraser. As her aunt had said, he was quite a handsome young man, and if his coloring was more Sassenach than Tessa had envisioned it would be, she forgave him, for his blue eyes had reflected such unmitigated admiration, she could not but be flattered.

As Susannah had suggested, Sir Malcolm collided with a child playing before Boodle's Tavern because his eyes were not upon his path, but upon her. His golden hair in some disarray after his encounter with the child, Sir Malcolm had

not been able to suppress a look of surprise when he caught
up with his friend, Mr. Derwent, and Susannah made the
introductions. "Miss Strahan?" he repeated with such
wonder that Tessa taxed him as to the cause.

His fair skin, already flushed, turned even warmer, and
he allowed that Lady Alderly had spoken to him of her niece.
"She spoke highly of you, Miss Strahan, but you will understand, I hope, if I say I did not pay great heed. It is rare
that an aunt's praises fall short, as they have done in this
instance."

"I thank you, sir." Tessa had smiled warmly and was
rather amused to see her smile cause the young man to flush
again, but he managed to collect himself sufficiently to offer
her his arm as Mr. Derwent and Susannah made to stroll
ahead.

"You are from Scotland, I believe?" Tessa asked as she
took Sir Malcolm's arm and noted he was of slender but not
negligible build and a little above her in height.

"Aye." Sir Malcolm's smile was more sure now. "My
home is near Edinburgh. But you are from the Highlands,
I believe your aunt said."

"You are doing very well at recalling a conversation you
must have attended only marginally," Tessa teased and was
rewarded with an abashed grin. "But, yes, Skelgara is in
the far north, with only sea and sky and heather about it."

"And bonny lasses."

The fervent declaration made Tessa laugh. "For a dour
Scotsman, ye've a sweet tongue, Sir Malcolm."

They'd no other opportunity for private talk, as they had
reached the little shop that sold the ribbons Susannah desired.
Tessa had only the time to invite Sir Malcolm to pay his
respects to Honoria, and then she was whisked away to decide
whether sky blue or periwinkle blue would do best as an
accent for Susannah's new dress.

On the whole, if she had not fallen head over heels for
Sir Malcolm, Tessa had found him a most pleasant boy who
had all the prospects for being a most amiable ally in the
midst of the Sassenach surrounding her.

". . . the only untoward occurrence was that we chanced to run across Giles Bayesford as he escorted Nicola Clarston about."

Her attention caught, Tessa looked up sharply. She had hoped Susannah would not relate in detail this particular encounter, but saw at once that her hopes would be denied. Susannah was in high gear. "The man is quite as nasty as ever! I tell you, I cannot understand why Nicola tolerates him. No sooner had he made me that affected sort of bow that is more a mockery than tribute than he asked me where on earth I had got my bonnet. But I did not allow his sneer to rout me. I returned him my loftiest stare and informed him that I had it from Ardling's in Bond Street. As they are the most fashionable of milliners, he could not say a thing to that."

Kit grinned. "I am relieved to know you set Giles in his place, dear. But I do wish I had been along. What an eyeful he must have been for the locals!"

Susannah giggled. "Mr. Johnson's bespectacled eyes did widen quite amazingly when he took in the coat Giles wore. I suppose he thought puce colored satin a little much for a village stroll, but what can a poor cobbler know of the refinements of dress?"

"And that was all to your meeting with Giles?" Nick asked.

"It isn't the half of it, really. But the rest is Tessa's story."

Susannah looked cheerfully to Tessa, but that young lady found herself reluctant to repeat the remainder of the encounter and only shrugged. "It was nothing, really."

"Nothing! My dear, you served the gentleman a riposte he is not likely to forget soon."

"Do tell!" Kit's accents were as blithe as Susannah's but Honoria's query was more anxious.

"Oh my, I do hope nothing too unpleasant occurred?"

"What took place?"

Responding to the clipped query, Tessa's gaze swung around to Nick, but when she continued to hesitate, Susannah could not longer contain herself.

"The rodent gave Tessa quite the full Giles Bayesford treatment, raising his quizzing glass to his eye in that absurd way and looking her over as if she were some prize mare he had it in mind to purchase. Smiling ever so languidly, he then remarked that he had not known the Celtic race could produce such a pleasing form." Susannah paused, glancing curiously at Tessa. "I saw at once you were displeased, my dear, though I must admit I could not see precisely why. It was a complimentary remark for Giles, but then, I suppose you could not know that. At any rate," Susannah looked back at the others and was gratified to see that no one's attention had wandered, "Tessa was not well pleased. I imagine he expected her to blush or some such nonsense and thank him profusely. Instead, maintaining a speaking silence, she fixed the supercilious cad with a look so cool his brow lifted. Later, just before we departed, he addressed Tessa again, though everyone knows Giles detests ladies below the age of five and twenty and never says above two words to them."

Susannah lifted an imaginary quizzing glass to her eye and twirled a make believe walking stick in just the way Sir Giles Bayesford had done earlier. " 'You spent quite some time in Kerne's inimitable company, Miss Strahan. Quite an effect the marquess is reputed to have upon the ladies. I imagine, like all the ladies in London, you are past your prayers over him.' Such a rude remark, really, but the sort Giles might make. And in that insufferable drawl!" Susannah lifted her eyes to the ceiling. "I am proud to say Tessa never hesitated. Her voice as cold as an icicle, she said, 'I beg your pardon, Sir Giles, but I must tell you that a good Scotswoman never passes her prayers.' And then, dipping Giles and Nicola a curtsy worthy of a princess, Tessa made our excuses and swept me away as if she had been the eldest present, not the youngest."

Christopher Steele applauded loudly, and Tessa was emboldened to flash him a mischievous grin, though she was aware Honoria was frowning. "I have never liked Giles above half, you know. There was some dust-up between you at school, was there not, Nick?"

"We've never seen eye to eye, no," Nick said to his godmother.

Kit was more informative. "Don't you recall, Godmama?" he asked Honoria. "Nick forced him to forfeit a stallion he had abused. Won the animal from him at sword point. They still tell the story at Cambridge. I don't believe Giles has ever forgiven him. He's always after Nick in one way or another, though my brother frustrates him at every turn."

"While Nick may choose to frustrate Giles, I do hope you will choose the wiser course, Tessa, and avoid his company as much as you are able. I cannot like to think of him as an enemy to you."

"It was nothing at all, Aunt. Do not vex yourself. Truly, nothing untoward occurred." Tessa knew as she spoke that she lied. While Susannah had merely listened to the words exchanged, Tessa had watched Sir Giles. In response to her retort, an unsettlingly hot light had flared momentarily in his narrowed eyes.

The reaction had come and gone too quickly to label, but Tessa did not think it the displeasure she had expected. Made uneasy for some indefinable reason, she still could not regret her remarks. The dandy had been impertinent and had deserved to be put in his place, but she was enough of a realist to know that she had made an impression she might well come to regret.

It seemed, though he had not been present, Nick guessed as much, for with more force than tact, he directed Tessa, "You will heed your aunt, Miss Strahan, and avoid Giles. You do not know him, but Bayesford is not the merely idle dandy he looks to be. He can be quite dangerous, in fact."

Tessa glared at Nick, resenting his arrogant tone. She could not say aloud that she would never allow such a miserable Sassenach to get the better of her, but her expressive eyes communicated something of her thoughts. Nick was not moved and returned her a look so set, it was Tessa who conceded. Aware Honoria was looking on with real concern while Susannah and Kit watched with something more like curiosity, she inclined her head in Nick's direction. "I cannot promise to shrink from the man, my lord, for I believe such a course would only encourage him, but I promise to be wary of Sir Giles.''

Not blind to the fact that Tessa had promised nothing more than she had likely already determined to do, Nick responded with silence, but Honoria, who knew her niece a great deal less well, said she thought Tessa had hit on a very nice compromise.

17

*B*y noon of the third day Tessa had been at Tarlton Hall, she had come to the surprising conclusion she was vastly pleased with the results of her journey south. She had met a quite eligible young Scotsman, who had all the makings of a fine friend. Then, when she had encountered an Englishman who was—and she would inform Nick so when she at last had the opportunity for a private interview with him—even worse than her direst imaginings of a Sassenach lord, she had shown the sneering dandy a Scotswoman, of Celtic heritage, was no silly miss to be thrown into confusion by his every sneering remark.

Best of all, however, her Aunt Honoria had proven to be the dearest lamb. They had spent the whole of the morning reading the letters Tessa's mother had written to her sister over the years. There were dozens of them, for Joanna had disregarded her father's insistence that Honoria was to be shunned. Each reflected affection for the sister who had been swept away by her handsome Sassenach lord, and a complete absence of Angus's sense of betrayal. The two sisters had even met twice after Honoria departed for England, Tessa learned.

The certain knowledge that Joanna would have approved her instinctive reaction to Honoria made Tessa's spirits lighter than they had been since she had received her first letter from Honoria, and Susannah's suggestion that they take a stroll through the grounds after luncheon accorded perfectly with her mood. She did not even protest when Susannah insisted they take parasols along, and jauntily twirled the handle of hers as they drifted through the sweet-scented rose gardens Nick's mother had made her especial project.

"I know you shan't mind climbing the hill here a little way," Susannah remarked as they turned out of the flower garden and followed a gravel path up a gentle slope behind the Hall. "The view of the grounds from just a little farther on is superb, and Nick says you are quite accustomed to walking the steeper inclines near your home. He says there are crags all around it . . ."

Tessa nodded absently as Susannah rattled on. The mention of Nick reminded her that he had not appeared at breakfast, when Susannah had said he and Kit were out riding, or at luncheon, when Susannah gave it as her opinion he had gone off to the Clarstons'. It was odd to have gone so long without any sight of him, but Tessa had not the opportunity to dwell on the thought or upon her slightly lowered spirits, for Susannah was saying she would dearly enjoy a visit to Kilmorgan.

"The landscape there is not so tame as it is here," she warned with a smile. "It is stark and very bold. My grandfather never commissioned Capability Brown as Nick's grandfather did."

"Do you like his work, Tessa, or is it too mild to you?" Susannah asked curiously.

"I love Kilmorgan and its wildness, of course, but it is very lovely here, too," Tessa replied and found she meant what she said. The gently rolling lawns accented by ornamental lakes and perfectly placed stands of trees could not but please the eye. She even liked the two quaint arched bridges she could see. "But what is that, Susannah?" When Tessa pointed to a stand of trees in the middle of which sat a queer little hexagonal building that seemed to have only a roof and no sides, Susannah laughed. "It's the Folly. Come along a little farther, and you will see it better. It was built by a Steele ancestor who thought he saw his wife too seldom, for they had eight children . . ."

Susannah's voice trailed off, and Tessa saw that something in the area of the Folly had caused her to crane her head forward. Following Susannah's lead, Tessa found she had seen only a portion of the glade in which the building sat. Now that she was more directly above it, she could see there were two horses there tethered close to the trees. One was Saladin.

"Oh!"

Tessa registered Susannah's delighted exclamation in silence, for just then Nick emerged from the shelter of the Folly hand in hand with a lady. From her vantage point Tessa could see only that his companion was tall, slim, and fashionably dressed. When they reached the horses, Nick did not immediately lift her onto her mount. He turned to her, and though it was impossible from a distance to say who was the instigator, it was no difficulty to watch the couple kiss full on the lips.

Susannah gasped. Tessa knew it was not she who made the sound, for she had bitten her own lip so hard she tasted blood. Then Nick tossed the woman onto her mount, and after he had swung up onto Saladin, he rode out of the glade beside her.

"Well! Madelaine! And I had heard . . . ah . . ." Susannah recalled Tessa's presence and faltered. "I mean . . ."

"That was, then, Lady Madelaine Landon whose husband is shortly returning from the Peninsula?" Tessa asked, disregarding entirely Susannah's distraction. "Is she Lord Kerne's mistress?"

Susannah drew a shocked breath. "You ought not to ask such questions, Tessa," she moaned. "It is not accepted for a young lady to know of such things!"

"Come, Susannah. If you do not make mention of it, no one else will be the wiser, for I shall have no reason to put such a question to them—if you make me an answer, that is."

"You are threatening me, I think!" Susannah sounded aggrieved, but when Tessa only cocked her head, she gave a reluctant smile. "Oh, drat! I should be the greatest hypocrite on earth if I did not admit I asked the same questions when I was your age."

"A veritable eon ago, of course."

Tessa's dry remark caused Susannah to laugh. "Four years is a veritable eon when one has married and had two children in the interim. Oh, la! I may as well tell you, for you know almost the whole. Though Madelaine and Nick were discreet, there were rumors earlier this summer about an affair between them. Then, a little later, just after Nick left to fetch you, Madelaine was seen wearing a quite magnificent bracelet. It is the sort of gesture Nick makes at the end of a liaison, and I, along with everyone else, assumed that the affair was over."

"You were premature, it would seem," Tessa said. Looking out over the grounds, she could see two riders emerge from the woods. They rode close together, or so it seemed from Tessa's vantage point. "Lord Kerne and Lady Madelaine do not appear at all estranged."

"No, they do not. But really," Susannah continued with what for her was exasperation, "Nick ought to set up his nursery and cease wasting his time with . . . with . . ."

"Other men's wives?" Tessa asked coolly.

"Oh, my dear! I can see you will shock me senseless if we do not turn the subject, though I suppose that is precisely what I meant to say. Nick can be a devilish rake," she added with something of a sigh. Tessa thought the sound absurdly wistful, but said nothing as Susannah turned and retraced their steps down the hillside. "You'll not take it amiss if we return to the Hall now, will you, Tessa? I promised Cecily I would read to her this afternoon before her nap."

Schooling herself to politeness, Tessa made no objection, though she felt restless enough to walk for miles more. As the Hall loomed larger and larger before them, she experienced less and less inclination to shut herself up inside, a surprising sentiment, for the grounds seemed to have lost some of their magic for her.

The very studiedness of their arrangement grated on her now. With discontented eyes Tessa took in the scene she had admired not half an hour before and decided its artistry was little more than an example of Sassenach wiliness. Rather than a wild park, the grounds were in reality a tame garden arranged to give the effect of wilderness.

The grounds deceived much like the lord of the manor did. The thought made Tessa grimace to herself. She was, she knew, being dramatic, but still she did not recant her sentiments. She did acknowledge that not all Sassenach men wrapped their unworthy, roguish natures in gentlemanly manners. Kit, for example, would never, under cover of the woods, cavort with the idle wife of a man gone off to fight for his country. True, Nick had never held himself up as saintly, she admitted, but almost at once challenged herself. He had taken care to be discreet, and that proved he did not care to be known far and wide as the betrayer of a fellow officer.

"Mama! Mama!"

Looking up, Tessa realized she stood in the entryway of Tarlton Hall. She had not heard a word Susannah had spoken, or even noted where she walked. It had taken young James' piping voice to rouse her from her consideration of Nick's dishonest character.

The young boy was racing headlong down the stairs toward his mother. A short distance behind him trotted his governess, Mrs. Hudson, whom it seemed the boy had escaped.

"Mama, have you seen Uncle Nick? He promised to take me fishing, but he has not come!"

"I am sorry, my lady," Mrs. Hudson, puffing audibly, began an apology for having allowed her charge to make such a scene in the front hall.

Tessa did not allow the good woman to finish. She felt such anger toward Nick at the thought that he would deliberately disappoint his devoted nephew in favor of trysting with his mistress—his married mistress—that she had to force herself to smile, but she managed to acquit herself well enough that no one looked at her oddly. "I know how to fish, James. We fly fish a great deal in Scotland, and I should be pleased to show you how."

"You would, really, Miss Strahan?" James looked doubtful.

"You would not mind, Tessa?"

Tessa addressed both mother and son together. "I should be delighted. I was accustomed to fishing almost everyday, you know."

"Miss Strahan." The newest entrant upon the scene was Booker. The dignified butler bowed carefully when Tessa turned to him. "You have a caller, miss. A Sir Malcolm Fraser has come. I have put him in the yellow salon."

Tessa stared blankly a moment. With her mind clouded by the events of the previous half hour, it took her a moment to think who Malcolm Fraser was and why he had come.

"Oh, yes. Yes, of course," she said slowly even as she saw a fair-headed gentleman appear around the corner.

"Miss Strahan." Malcolm Fraser was attempting a confident smile, but his fair skin betrayed a flush. "It only just occurred to me that I might be presuming upon your time. Rather than wait for you now, I thought I would leave my card and return another day, closer to receiving hours."

"Nonsense, Sir Malcolm." Tessa held out her hand and gave him her most piquant smile. "We are in the country, and I cannot believe we are so formal here as to have only certain hours for visitors."

"Certainly not," Susannah brightly assured the young man she considered prime material for Tessa. "We are delighted to have you, Sir Malcolm. Won't you return with us to the salon that we may have a comfortable coze? I shall send up to tell Honoria you are here."

Just then Tessa caught sight of James. His hand captured by the stout Mrs. Hudson, he listened to his mama with a crestfallen expression.

"Perhaps my aunt could wait until another time to greet Sir Malcolm, Susannah. You see"—Tessa's laughing eyes invited the young Scotsman to understand—"I promised James I would teach him to fly fish, and as he has already been disappointed once today, I do not believe I can go back on my word. Perhaps you would care to join us, sir? Two teachers must be even better than one.''

The prospect of having Tessa all to himself but for a child and his governess prompted Sir Malcolm to agree to the plan at once, though he did think it wisest to disclaim any ability at fishing. ''I was never very proficient, I fear,'' he announced with taking honesty. ''Rather than two teachers, it is more likely that there will two pupils.''

''But this is famous! An impromptu outing.'' Susannah clapped her hands together out of sheer delight. ''If you can wait a moment, I shall send Mrs. Hudson up for Cecily, and we shall make a party of it.''

Tessa saw Sir Malcolm's expression fall slightly, but she welcomed Susannah's suggestion nonetheless. There would be time enough to be alone with the young Scotsman, she knew. Anyway, just then she was not feeling much like carrying on a private tête-à-tête with anyone.

''Your pole is bobbing, Jamie! You've got one. Pull sharply to set the hook.'' Tessa cast her own pole down upon the bank of the little stream where Susannah said generations of Steeles had pitted themselves against the local trout and rushed to Jamie's side. The boy was biting his lip as he strained to hold out against the fish which was twisting and heaving mightily in an effort to escape, but Tessa knew better than to take the pole from him. ''Hold steady,'' she advised. ''He'll tire himself soon.''

''He's awfully strong!'' James was panting from his exertions. ''I don't know if I can—''

''Of course, you can,'' Tessa encouraged. She had caught four fish and Malcolm one, but this would be Jamie's first, and like his mother, who watched with her hands clasped tightly together, she hoped he would win through. ''Give him line that he may heave and tire the more easily. That's it. Good! Now, he's coming to the bank. Quickly, before he entangles himself in the brush, heave hard!''

Tessa mimed the motion she recommended, and Jamie,

following her example, swung the fish high in the air before bringing it down on the bank with a hard thud. "I did it! I did it!" he shouted, hopping wildly around the flopping prize.

"You did do it, indeed."

"Uncle Nick!" If Jamie had been happy before, he was ecstatic now. His uncle had come in time to witness his moment of victory. "Look what I caught!"

Tessa could not control a start. Concentrating on Jamie's catch, she had not heard Nick approach. Jerking her head up, she saw he came accompanied. On his arm hung the elegant brunette Tessa had seen him embrace.

Lady Madelaine Landon, seen at close quarters, was striking. Almost as tall as Tessa, with her dark hair and eyes set off by an exquisitively cut riding habit of deep burgundy, she carried herself with a fashionably languid air that proclaimed she knew very well how desirable she was.

As Lady Madelaine flicked her liquid brown eyes over Tessa, they widened slightly, almost as if she were surprised. But Tessa could not imagine that anything about her could surprise such a sophisticate, and she assumed the lady was taken aback to encounter a woman who would appear in public looking as flushed from exertion as Tessa knew by the heat in her cheeks she was. Even when Lady Madelaine's eyes, narrowing the least bit, lingered upon her beauty mark, Tessa imagined that the woman was finding fault with her, and therefore she liked Lady Madelaine even less than she had when she had thought her merely an adultress.

Tessa's gaze, with a will of its own, slipped in Nick's direction. She would know if he shared his mistress' disgust. More than probably he did, for she realized they had both seen her jumping about to help James bring in his catch, but Nick was not looking at her, as it turned out. He had gone to examine James' fish.

"Madelaine, allow me to present Miss Strahan, Honoria's niece," Susannah said after greeting the lady without giving the least hint she had been seen breaking her marriage vows. "Tessa," she continued in the same superbly even tone, "this is Lady Madelaine. She is visiting with Lady Clarston, whom you met yesterday in the village.''

"How do you do, ma'am? Perhaps you would care to try your hand at fishing? We've an extra pole.''

Tessa was not as able as Susannah to hide her knowledge. She smiled sweetly enough, but she was not displeased to see Lady Madelaine's air of nonchalance shaken. "No, no, I don't think so,'' Lady Madelaine replied rather more quickly than was strictly polite, and Tessa had to look off to hide her grin.

"You know Sir Malcolm Fraser do you not, Madelaine?''

When Susannah drew Malcolm forward, he made a hurried bow. "We met at the Albermarles' rout last spring, my lady, though I doubt you recall. It was a shocking squeeze.''

"You are kind to remember, sir. Eugenia entertained half of London that night,'' Lady Madelaine replied with a tact that even Tessa could not fault, though she did think it an example of how the lady was able to handle men. "Have you done well this afternoon?''

"I fear not.'' Malcolm glanced a little ruefully at Tessa. "As I told Miss Strahan when we set out, I am no angler. I have caught only one.''

"But he is a fine, fat one, if not as large as Jamie's.'' Tessa's smile caused Sir Malcolm to brighten perceptibly. "And besides, we came not to engage in a fishing contest, but to rescue James from disappointment.''

"At which I should say you succeeded admirably.''

Again Tessa was not prepared for Nick's voice. His examination of Jamie's prize completed, he had strolled up behind her. "My thanks,'' he added, making it impossible for her to avoid his gaze unless she wished to appear sullen. Nick's eyes seemed very blue and misleadingly clear, and Tessa found it difficult to look into them with any degree of equanimity. She wanted to shout that she knew all about his tryst with his mistress, but instead was obliged to listen calmly while he said, "As I explained to Jamie, something arose that prevented my returning by the hour we had appointed. I am pleased he was fortunate enough to find so accomplished a replacement."

"Tessa is prodigious good, Uncle Nick! She caught four."

Tessa summoned a smile for James and gave him a little curtsy in return for his praise. As a result her eyes were lowered and no one saw the disgust sparkling in her eyes. Something came up, indeed! she fumed to herself. The rogue ought either to have said nothing at all or to have been honest enough to admit that Lady Madelaine's charms were more potent than a fishing expedition with a worshipful little boy.

"I am not surprised that Miss Strahan caught so many, Jamie," Nick replied to his nephew. "The first time I, ah, met her, she was fishing. Is that not so, Miss Strahan?"

The direct question forced her to look at him and to see the devilish gleam in his eye. Abruptly Tessa bent down to pick a leaf off the edge of her hem. "Yes." It was all she could say. His roguish gypsy's eyes had reminded her, as clearly as if he had spoken, how he had kissed her that day, and she found she was so furious she could not but wonder how everyone failed to note it. Yes, he had kissed her in that secluded place, just as he had kissed Lady Madelaine only a little earlier today. He had a positive penchant for secluded places, it seemed, though whose lips he tasted seemed of no particular import to him. They might be Lady Madelaine's lips, or as on that day Tessa remembered more vividly than she cared to, the lips might be hers—it was all the same to Nick Steele.

At the thought that Nick had treated her as he would any other woman—Lady Madelaine most recently—Tessa's head came up, and she met Nick's gaze head on. "As I recall, Lord Kerne," she said in a cool voice that did not match the hot sparkle lighting her eyes, "you interrupted my amusement that day. Thankfully, nothing so unfelicitous occurred here, as it did that day."

"I know I have never enjoyed angling more." Tessa could have kissed Malcolm for speaking up just then, and she sent him a particularly pleased smile that caused him to flush with pleasure.

"Nor has Jamie ever been more pleased with himself," Susannah said with a laugh. She pointed to her son, who had departed to watch the gamekeeper string his prize that it might be taken home to show to Jamie's father. "He's as proud as I have ever seen him."

"Will I get a fishy, Mama?" Cecily cried. "I want one. Will you get me one, Tessa?"

"I should like very much to come fishing with you, Cecily. Perhaps we can try again tomorrow." Tessa congratulated herself on the steadiness of her voice. She could feel Nick's searching glance upon her, for he had not missed her own, bitter, reference to the kiss he'd stolen, and she was torn between coolly ignoring him or flinging him a look full of all the loathing she felt. Lady Madelaine's watchful gaze decided her against joining battle just then.

"You had better make your plans for a little later than that, I'm afraid." It was Nick, but Tessa found a piece of lint on her sleeve that needed removing, and so only heard him give the reason she must delay her fishing expedition with Cecily. "We have been invited to dinner tomorrow at the Clarstons'."

"But how delightful!" Tessa was grateful Susannah could make an appropriate response, for she felt only distaste at the thought of dining in company not only with Nick's insufferably "tonnish" mistress, but also with the dandy, Sir Giles, to whom she'd taken such a dislike. "Nicola said she wished to get up a party, but I did not realize she meant to act so soon."

"She is always restless," Lady Madelaine remarked offhandedly. "She sent me over today as a sort of footman."

The remark was intended to amuse, and Susannah laughed as did Sir Malcolm. Tessa turned away with the pretext of speaking to Jamie as his fish was held up by the gamekeeper. She knew very well why Lady Madelaine had come to the Hall that day, and for reasons unclear to her, her knowledge rendered her furiously angry.

18

"*O*ch, Miss Tessa! Were Laird Angus to see ye noow, 'twould be proud, he'd be.''

Nan stood with her mistress before the pier glass and smiled with pleasure, while Tessa, searching for flaws, frowned. She found nothing amiss in the color of her dress. Of a creamy white, the silk dress heightened the translucent quality of her complexion and brought out the bronze tints in her chestnut hair. The underslip beneath it was of a particularly pretty shade of sky blue that Tessa decided Nan had been correct to say deepened the gray of her eyes. Nor could Tessa fault the gown's cut. Its tiny, high waisted bodice was all the fashion, and now that she had spent a few days with Susannah, whose evening dresses were all similarly cut, she was not made self-conscious. Even the effect of the transparent lace edging the low, square neckline did not appall her as it might once have done. Though in some mysterious way the flimsy bit of material seemed to draw the eye to the gentle swell of her breasts, Tessa had only to imagine the sort of dress Lady Madelaine would wear that night to decide she was entirely within acceptable limits. When her eye fell on the hem of her dress, she smiled. At last she had found something of which Angus would approve. Embroidered about the hem in gold thread was a broad border depicting the Scots national flower, the thistle.

Tessa met her maid's eye in the glass. "Ye really think I shall pass, Nan? I've a mind to give these lofty Sassenach we dine with tonight a start. I daresay they expect a Scottish lass to appear before them as dowdy as a wren.''

Nan wagged her head. " 'Tis ignorant they are, then, o'

the reams o' dresses Madame Reevoaks sends up from Edinburgh for ye, Miss Tessa, and I'll be bound ye'll be the fairest lass at table this evening, for the French seamstress' eye be keen indeed for what suits ye.''

Tessa's lips twitched at Nan's mangling of the French modiste's name, but encouraged by her maid's belief that Mme. Rivaux's efforts had been to some effect, she hastened down to the yellow salon to test her appearance again, this time before the members of the household.

When she found only an empty room awaiting her, Tessa chuckled at the deflation she experienced. Angus had told her vanity could do naught but sow disappointment, and now knew him to be absolutely right. While she awaited the others, she drifted out to the terrace to enjoy the summer's twilight, a scene of far more enduring beauty, as she told herself, than any looks she might possess.

Absorbed in the different shades of lavender and pink streaking the horizon, Tessa did not hear Nick come onto the terrace. He saw her at once, a slender figure in creamy satin silhouetted against the purple hues of the dusk. As he approached, the last of the sunlight was caught by the hundreds of tiny seed pearls Nan had wound through Tessa's hair. He noted the effect, then followed the elegant line of her neck and shoulders down to the delicate lace that gave such a tantalizing glimpse of the high breasts rising and falling beneath it.

Tessa did not hear Nick's steps for another moment. Therefore, when she did turn to make a greeting, Nick had had sufficient time to study the gown she wore, noting particularly its colors and the thistles ornamenting its hem.

"Oh . . ." Tessa exclaimed in an uncertain voice when she saw who approached. Since she had seen him kiss Lady Madelaine Landon the day before, she had avoided Nick's company as completely as she was able, and when she had had to acknowledge him, she had found it almost impossible to speak in a civil tone.

Tessa was also taken aback because Nick was regarding

her with an unmistakably stony expression. She had not long
to wonder why. He did not greet her but said brusquely, "I
trust those thistles and that blue and white you wear do not
bode ill for this evening, Tessa. This is your first outing in
society, and you would disappoint Honoria immeasurably
if you were on your Scottish mettle. You did promise, you
will recall, to avoid Giles."

"I cannot see that my dress has aught to do with Sir Giles,"
Tessa snapped with an indignation that arose in part, though
she did not acknowledge as much even to herself, from disappointment with Nick's response to her appearance. Far
from being stunned by her radiance, he was so unmoved that
he could carp at what she had chosen to wear. "I daresay
that fop will not recognize Scotland's colors or her flower."

"You underestimate Giles, Tessa. He is a treacherous
man."

There was a note of urgency in Nick's voice, but Tessa
was too displeased with him to attend. "I did not expect else.
He is so very Sassenach."

Nick's gaze sharpened. "Whence the biting tone, Tessa?"
he demanded. "I thought you were finding England not as
bad as you had feared. Am I mistaken in thinking that you
have taken to Honoria?"

"I like my aunt very well. And I have found the Kit Steeles
all that you said I would, but nothing has persuaded me to
trust the Sassenach in general any more than I did. Quite
the opposite in truth. Take you, for instance, Lord Kerne."
Tessa lifted her chin because Nick's eyes narrowed threateningly, and she would not be cowed by him. "I have it from
my aunt that she bade you to do no more than invite me south.
Can you explain how it is you saw fit to fairly drag me down
here instead?"

One of Nick's black eyebrows lifted slowly. Oddly Tessa
had to fight the feeling she was being petty, and so she tipped
her nose even farther into the air as he spoke in a carefully
controlled voice. "I kept in my mind that Honoria added
before I left that she hoped I could persuade you to come

to her. I interpreted her remark liberally. Do you regret coming, Tessa?''

Tessa found she could not hold Nick's challenging look. ''I am glad I have met Honoria,'' she said and stepped by Nick before he could object that she had not truly answered his question. Just then she did not quite have the courage to tell the truth, that her only regret was making his acquaintance. He might ask what he had done to so disaffect her, and the only answer that came to her mind was that he had betrayed her. But that was too nonsensical an answer to entertain even privately, for Nick had promised her nothing, and so Tessa marched away with her mind closed to any thought but a desire to reach the salon, where she hoped she would find at least one other person to act as a buffer between her and Nick.

''Oh, there you are, children.'' Honoria, looking quite elegant in a beaded gown of blue satin, appeared through the French windows of the salon as if in answer to Tessa's prayer. ''I thought I could not be the first to descend.'' She stopped and, taking in the full effect of Tessa's appearance, clasped her hands together. ''Oh, my dear! You are lovely as can be, as I am certain Nick must have told you.''

''Nothing so gentle,'' Tessa returned a shade more sharply than she had intended. ''Lord Kerne has been informing me that the colors I wear—the blue and white of Scotland—will incite Sir Giles' animosity.''

Looking from Tessa, who was, Honoria realized belatedly, biting her lip almost as if she were distraught, to Nick, Honoria said, ''But that does not sound at all like you, Nick. Surely Giles will make nothing of Tessa's thistles or her colors. I have seen Scottish ladies in London similarly attired, though never to such a delightful effect.''

''Your niece mistook me.'' Tessa could feel Nick's gaze touch the exposed skin at the nape of her neck. ''It was not Giles's mood concerned me, but hers. I feared she flew her national flag as a provocation. Now that I am reassured, however, I will waste no time echoing your sentiments, Godmama. No flower Scotland has ever produced could be lovelier.''

"There now!'' Honoria smiled happily. "That is prettily done, and I am certain Tessa forgives you your lapse, Nick, now that she understands.''

However gently couched, it was a request, and Tessa knew it would distress Honoria if she remained churlish. Turning, she avoided meeting Nick's eyes by dipping him a pretty curtsy. "I thank you for your concern, my lord.''

"Do you?'' The question was lightly put and rhetorical to boot, but Tessa had to struggle to overcome a desire to fling the arrogant beast a most negative answer. No, of course she was not grateful for his constant meddling in her affairs. With Lady Madelaine in the vicinity, she could not understand why he did still concern himself with her. Likely he would not do so as much in future.

Eyeing Tessa's meekly bowed head with an enigmatic expression, Nick said, "Well, you are welcome for my interest, Miss Strahan. I give it quite free of obligation on your part.'' Mindful of Honoria, Tessa bit her lip and kept her thoughts to herself. Nick, however, seemed intent on trying her patience to its limits, for he went on to say, "My compliments are a different matter, however. It is the custom in England to thank a gentleman when he makes a lady a compliment. Is it not the same in the Highlands?''

Nick's chiding affected the last vestige of Tessa's restraint as hot sun does ice. Honoria's presence temporarily forgotten, she lifted her flashing eyes to him. "As you would say the same to any woman, my lord, I took your flattery for it was worth: nothing.''

"My dear!''

"I apologize,'' Tessa murmured at once, though she kept her chin up as she looked at her aunt. "I forgot myself, Aunt, but your godson is well aware I know him to be a rake and therefore practiced in the art of pretty words and seductions.'' Tessa was unable to keep from looking back at Nick, a spark kindling in her eye. He had deliberately provoked her and deserved some retribution. "If it comes to it, my lord, I think I may observe that it is not the least customary, in Scottish circles at least, for a gentleman to point out a lady's lapses. But now that you have, allow me to respond as it seems you would wish." Flicking her fan open, Tessa drew it up before her face and peeping over it, batted her lashes at Nick "La, my lord! You do say such sweet nothings."

Her accurate portrayal of a most empty-headed young miss surprised a chuckle from Honoria. Nick did not seem so amused. He only inclined his head, giving Tessa the point. Later, much later when she was lying in her bed reviewing the events of the evening, it occurred to Tessa that not once again that night had Nick addressed any remark at all to her. She had won the skirmish, it seemed, but at a cost. One she was willing to pay, she added quickly, for if the rogue did not care to speak to her, neither did she ever again wish to enter into conversation with him.

Lord and Lady Clarston's dinner party was a great deal more enjoyable than Tessa had anticipated it would be. The greatest surprise was that she liked their daughter, Hetty. In contrast to most of the Sassenach Tessa had encountered thus far, the girl possesssed a grave manner that was reflected in her large brown eyes.

Curious about Scotland, Hetty asked Tessa a good many questions, but, unlike every other female Tessa had encountered, she did not make a great to-do over Tessa's journey in Nick's company. The girl was sensible, Tessa decided, and immediately added appealing to Hetty's attributes when she blushingly revealed she was engaged to be married to Peter Derwent.

He was the young man who so hero worshipped Nick, but Tessa forgave him, for he was also Malcolm Fraser's host. No sooner had the thought occurred that the two young men might well have been invited to the evening's affair than Hetty said they were to come.

Deep in conversation with Hetty, Tessa gave little thought

to Sir Giles. Only later, when she went into dinner, did she think to be relieved she had not encountered him, for though she was not afraid of him, she was wary of him.

She did encounter Lady Madelaine. When the party from Tarlton Hall first arrived, Lady Madelaine joined them, ostensibly to bid Kit, whom she had missed the day before, good evening. The older woman was quite as magnificently turned out as Tessa had anticipated she would be. Her classically inspired dress was daringly cut to bare entirely one milky-white shoulder and to hang so close to her figure that it revealed what the diaphanous silk of her gown did not, and that, Tessa thought as the woman drifted away on Nick's arm, was not much, for in certain lights one could almost see through the material.

Tessa did not regret her own much less revealing dress, however, though Susannah did whisper that the transparent style was all the crack in Paris. It was, simply, not for her, and if any thought her sadly lacking in fashion, that—she found herself glancing toward Nick, where he stood with a group of friends—was that gentleman's jaded opinion, not hers.

Certainly Malcolm Fraser did not find her lacking. When he came, he called her a "Scottish princess come to life" in a breathless way she found quite taking. "I do not believe Scotland's colors have ever been worn to better advantage," he added most sincerely.

Tessa smiled brilliantly in return. Here was someone who not only recognized Scotland's colors but admired them! "Thank you very much, sir. I am pleased to see you here. I had not expected you."

"Because Peter is engaged to Hetty we are often included in Lady Clarston's entertainments. I said nothing yesterday only because I've an appalling memory and could not recall if Peter had said we were to come this evening."

Tessa laughed, liking the young Scotsman's frank manner quite as much as his open admiration. He was a good fellow with a most endearing smile and agreeably handsome features. She disregarded his light coloring. To some it might seem Sassenach, but Tessa had decided it was the legacy of some marauding Viking, not a conquering Englishman.

They talked easily, or rather Tessa did. Sir Malcolm asked her about her home, and she felt free to wax lyrical on the subject of Kilmorgan. She ended by telling how, though a large part of the castle had been burned after '45, her grandfather had rebuilt all but one tower, which stood as a reminder of the hostilities.

"Was your own home much harmed?" she asked.

Sir Malcolm shook his head. "We were fortunate. But for a freak illness it might have been the same as with Kilmorgan. The day before my grandfather intended to go out for Prince Charles, he was struck by a fever and could not leave his bed for months on end."

Their private conversation ended then, for Peter Derwent and Hetty joined them, but Tessa, though she sternly told herself she ought not to judge a situation she did not know well, could not help remembering how Angus had told her that the prince's cause might have been won but for the several Scottish lords who developed "rebellion yellow throat" in order to sit on the sidelines until they could determine how strong young Charles's cause was.

At table Tessa was seated between Peter Derwent and Malcolm. At first she spoke the more with Malcolm, and he displayed a happy ability to entertain her with amusing observations on Sassenach ways. She laughed particularly when he observed that though the English declared themselves enormously proud of their country, they'd a positive mania for all things foreign. "Just think," Sir Malcolm said, grinning, "they have imported a German king to rule them as they wear their Belgian lace, enjoy their paintings by the Italian masters, and savor their turbot a l'orange, after which they sip their burgundies. And none of that is to mention their homes and gardens. Lady Clarston has an exact replica of an Italian ruin on the estate, while Mrs. Derwent's sitting room is done in the Egyptian style."

Tessa laughed delighted, but was obliged out of politeness
to turn to her other partner. She found Peter Derwent less
amusing, for he could not but go into raptures over Nick.
It was not a subject Tessa much appreciated. Every time Peter
extolled some accomplishment of his hero, she had to bite
her tongue not to point out that his paragon, possessing the
morals of a cat, was willing to seduce any female who was
married, preferring, of course, those whose husbands were
safely away at war.

She did not make Peter Derwent any cutting remark, however, for his enthusiasm for Nick was so genuine, Tessa
found she'd not the heart to disillusion him. Indeed, in the
end she found herself on such easy terms with him that when
Mr. Derwent asked for the details of her land journey, Tessa
found herself relating how Nick had won a fine stallion over
a chance game of cards.

"By jove!" The young man slapped the table in his
excitement. "A blooded stallion, you say? The wagering
must have been deep indeed. I heard tell Lord Kerne had
given up such reckless sport, but he must have found some
reason to revert to his old ways. Though," Peter conceded,
"perhaps it is not so wild to wager deeply when you invariably win. I can tell you there were some relieved sighs
in town when Nick took to showing up at his clubs less
frequently. He scarcely ever lost, you see."

Mr. Derwent's remarks once again piqued Tessa's
curiosity about Nick's motive for winning his fellow
Sassenach's mount out from under him, but she could not
look to Nick to read his expression. He sat on her side of
the table.

Glancing down to confirm the seating arrangement, Tessa
realized with a jolt she was being observed. Sir Giles was
studying her from his seat down the table. When their eyes
met, he smiled. It was not a warm expression at all, but rather
reminded Tessa of the look a cat might give its prey before
pouncing. She inclined her head only so far as to be just polite
before allowing her gaze to move away.

Later, after dinner, the gentlemen gave up their port to join the ladies earlier than usual because, Tessa learned from Hetty, Lady Madelaine had agreed to play the piano for the company. "You may well be surprised," Hetty smiled when Tessa's brow lifted. "Lady Madelaine does not seem the sort to exert herself to play, but she really does play well, or Mama would not inflict her upon us."

Hetty was quite correct, Tessa realized after only a few bars. Lady Madelaine was very good. With a sigh of pleasure Tessa settled back to enjoy the woman's unexpected talent.

At Kilmorgan there had always been music, for Angus had long provided a living to an elderly kinsman, Duncan Ross, a fine harpist who played all the old ballads of Scotland as well as the more rarified music of the courts of Europe. Every night after dinner he played for them, and Tessa had missed his entertainment.

When the justly earned applause for Lady Madelaine had died away, Tessa felt the hairs on her neck lift. Glancing about for the reason, she again found Sir Giles Bayesford, now with his quizzing glass lifted to his eye, examining her.

Displaying a theatrical sense of timing, he addressed her when the general praise of Lady Madelaine quieted. "Will you not play for us, Miss Strahan?" he inquired in a thin, drawling voice that grated upon Tessa. "I have been told all you Celts are musically inclined."

For the slight but unmistakable mocking emphasis the dandy placed on the word "Celts," Tessa longed to slap him. She thought he'd not have looked so superior with a red handprint on his cheek.

"You honor those of us with Celtic blood, Sir Giles," she said, a dangerous light in her eyes, though she did manage to smile charmingly. "You must know we Celts echo the sentiments of your own bard, Will Shakespeare: a man without music can only be base and untrustworthy." Tessa paused almost imperceptibly, but managed to suggest she imagined Sir Giles languished in the category of those "unmoved by concord of sweet sounds."

Well satisfied with the faint flush that rose in her
adversary's cheeks, she added in a more accommodating
tone, "And I should be honored to play for you tonight, Sir
Giles, though I warn you I shall not be up to Lady
Madelaine's standards." Tessa turned to incline her head
with real respect toward the woman who had gone to arrange
herself upon a settee beside Nick. "It was a great pleasure
to hear you play, my lady," she said, her eyes not straying
from Madelaine.

"Play us a Scottish ballad, my dear." Honoria smiled
confidently as Tessa rose, for she had known Dunstan Ross
and harbored no doubt her niece would at least play
adequately.

Tessa, a small smile curving her lips, went to the piano
and did just that. Dunstan had taught her well, and though
Tessa had truly mastered only the harpsichord and the harp,
the two instruments Angus thought the most pleasing to the
ear, she had had sufficient opportunity to experiment upon
a piano at her mother's home in Edinburgh to find the notes
to accompany herself.

The first song Tessa chose, Sir Giles in mind, was a
rollicking ballad all in Gaelic that recounted Robert Bruce's
rout of the English at Bannockburn.

The company, captivated by her clear, lilting voice,
clapped in delight, but it was Honoria's look that meant the
most to Tessa. Her aunt's blue eyes sparkled with suppressed
mirth, for unlike the others, she'd understood what Tessa
had sung. Tessa marked the conspiratorial look they
exchanged as the first true sign they shared Scottish blood.

Having had her admittedly obscure revenge, Tessa accommodated the company's request for another song by choosing
a Robert Burns ballad about unrequited love.

She'd sung the haunting piece often for Angus, and that
night, though in the company of Englishmen, she sang as
if she were in the hall at Kilmorgan with its flickering torches
and heather-scented drafts. Tessa did not possess an opera
singer's power by any means, but her rendition was so pure

that at the end her audience accorded her high praise indeed. After the last, rich strain had died away, there was a moment of total silence.

When the applause burst forth, Tessa bowed her head briefly in acknowledgment, then took particular care to look at Sir Giles. Why she must taunt him, she could not have said. She only knew she could not return quietly to her seat without forcing some public recognition from him.

She succeeded. In acknowledgment of her skill Sir Giles nodded. It was a brief, clipped gesture Tessa thought grudging, but she did not concern herself overlong with that. The man's eyes, as they beheld her, concerned her a great deal more, for they glittered in such an odd way, she was reminded, too late, how treacherous Nick believed him to be.

Tessa resisted an urge to look at Nick and send him an unspoken plea that he come and shield her from Sir Giles's disconcerting regard. Through her dark lashes, when she accepted the company's applause, she had looked at Nick, where he lounged beside his mistress. She thought his hands had moved only perfunctorily when he clapped, and he had broken off his applause before anyone else. With Lady Madelaine beside him, it seemed he could not be bothered to think of anyone else.

19

*W*hen she awoke, Tessa found her sleep had not much refreshed her. She had tossed and turned all night, and now her spirits were as dull as the overcast sky out her window. Even the prospect of riding out with Sir Malcolm later that day failed to cheer her, and that though she felt restless as well as gloomy. She longed just then—more strongly than she had done since coming into England—for the sharp, tangy air of Kilmorgan, where everything, despite the persistent mists, had seemed very clear indeed.

Tessa kept to her room that morning, but the book she sent Nan to the library to fetch did little to hold her attention. Halfway down a page she would glance up and realize she had no notion of what she had read.

"Fie on it!" she cried at last, casting William Shakespeare aside and jumping from her chaise to pace the room.

A knock on the door preceded Nan. Her freckled face seeming to beam with goodwill, the girl smiled. "And do ye feel well enow to go down for luncheon, Miss Tessa?"

"I have never felt badly, thank you, and so, of course, I shall go down." Seeing Nan's eyes widen, Tessa shook her head. "Och! Forgive me, Nan. I did nae intend to snap at ye."

"I don't doubt ye are merely tired. Your aunt has na come down from her room either and will take luncheon there. But Mr. and Mrs. Steele be waitin', if ye intend to join them."

Tessa did not ask where Nick was. She thought she could guess. Susannah confirmed her suspicion as they sat down at the table. Nick was at the Clarstons', but the circumstances of his visit did come as a surprise.

"It is all too famous!" Susannah enthused. "There is to be a race."

"This afternoon?"

Kit laughed. "Not quite so soon as that, my dear. Five days hence, Nick will race Saladin against Sir Giles's bay, Apollo."

"You see," Susannah explained, taking pity on Tessa's bemused expression, "Giles learned somehow or other about Nick's winning the stallion and would not rest until he came to judge Saladin for himself."

"That bit was my doing," Kit admitted with a grin. "Giles questioned me about him last evening, and when I saw it needled him that Nick should come by a fine piece of horse flesh without the least expense, I prosed on and on about Nick's good luck. Giles rushed over first thing this morning with Clarston and after one look challenged Nick to a race. It will be at the Clarstons', for both Nick and Giles are familiar with the course there. They are meeting now to arrange the details."

"Does Sir Giles imagine he shall win over Lord Kerne?" Tessa asked, her tone indicating she thought Sir Giles mad.

"His bay is swift, I will say that," Kit told her. "He's never lost a race, and you must not imagine Giles will be riding him on the fateful day. He employs a man for the very purpose of racing his mounts."

"The coward!"

Kit laughed. "Giles could never out ride Nick and knows it. There was no question of it, really. He did not challenge Nick's horsemanship, only Saladin's speed. And you must concede, my dear, if that is to be fairly tested, the ability of the riders must be equal." Kit shrugged. "It is a common enough arrangement, really, particularly where Nick is concerned. He's the ablest rider I know."

"But we have not told you the most delicious part!" cried Susannah with such relish that Tessa could not but smile.

"And what is that?"

"Do you recall the waistcoat Giles wore last evening?" Tessa nodded. "I could scarcely have missed anything so colorful. Crimson and black striped satin with gold thread through it is not precisely to my taste.''

As she spoke, an image of Nick as he had appeared at the Clarstons' dinner rose in Tessa's mind. Compared to Sir Giles, he had been plainly dressed in a black satin coat, black small pants and a white satin waistcoat. Understated, but of the finest materials and most superb cut, Nick's clothes were the essence of elegance, and when he had stood beside Sir Giles, he had rendered the fop absurd.

Susannah's giggle recalled her to the present. ''Gaudy wasn't it? Well, if Nick wins, Giles must forfeit the thing. Not that Nick will wear it. He told Giles directly that he intends to burn the thing! Oh, my, I'd have given anything to see the look on Giles' face. Kit said he became so suffused with color, he thought the man might choke.''

''Indeed I did,'' Kit agreed, but with a frown not a smile. ''I have never seen Giles so angry, and for the life of me I cannot understand why Nick went to such lengths to provoke him. In the past he has gone out of his way to avoid Giles, or so it has seemed to me, yet in this instance he made a remark—in the presence of witnesses, yet—that not so long ago would have been cause for a duel to the death.''

Tessa recalled how often she had looked up to find Sir Giles' gleaming eyes on her and only just kept from shivering. ''I find him a most disagreeable man,'' she said with considerable feeling. What did he wager, by the by?''

''Nick put up a painting he recently acquired by a new artist, Turner,'' Susannah said. ''I cannot say I like the man very much. I can never make out what it is he has painted, he is so indistinct, and the colors he uses! Very bright, my dear. But Nick admires his work and for that reason, I suppose, Giles was well content.''

''A garish waistcoat for an artist's work seems a singularly lopsided wager,'' Tessa said, and had her suspicion that the full wager had not been revealed confirmed when Kit shifted uncomfortably in his seat.

Susannah, however, had learned that the effort to be discreet with Tessa was a wasted one. "Giles must also forfeit a costly emerald pendant Madelaine lost to him earlier this summer if his bay comes in second," she divulged smiling knowingly to Tessa.

"Ah," was all Tessa said, but she thought it unnecessary to look further, as Susannah had done, for the motive behind Nick's actions. He had baited Sir Giles for his own pleasure, but had wagered the Turner he admired for the honor of returning his mistress the pendant he had likely bestowed as a companion to the costly bracelet that had not been a farewell gift but an indication of approval. Perhaps he had meant the pendant to signify his desire to continue his liaison with the lady even after her husband returned home from war. Yes, that was it, Tessa declared, believing the notion true, the moment she conceived it.

After luncheon, when Susannah announced she had need of a nap, Tessa gave thanks. She did not think she would have been a pleasant companion for anyone just then. Even the thought of gossip set her teeth on edge. She wanted only to ride as hard and as fast as she could. To feel the wind in her face, that was what she needed.

Racing upstairs after luncheon, she called for Nan to bring her habit.

"But ye're to ride oout wi' the Fraser, Miss Tessa," Nan objected.

Tessa had forgotten Malcolm, but only shrugged when she was reminded. "It may be raining by the time he comes," she said impatiently. "And I must get out of the house for a time."

Nan simply nodded, seeing it was not the time to question what it was had caused her mistress to be as taut as a bowstring. Dressed in a soft green habit and a rakish little hat to match, Tessa soon departed for the stables. The grooms were uncertain about sending her off alone, but Tessa gave them a credible imitation of Augus's flinty glare to tip the

scales in her favor, for she did not want anyone, even a
groom, tagging along at her heels, and soon she was riding
out on a fine, responsive filly.

As soon as her horse was warmed, Tessa urged her into
a gallop. Across the fields they went so fast the air could
be heard rushing by. "Come on, my sweet," Tessa whispered in the filly's ear, and they took a stone wall easily.
When a time of decision came, Tessa chose to climb a hill,
reaching the top and continuing along the ridge for some five
miles or more. From her height Tessa could see the Hall,
its old ivy-covered walls, the rolling, spacious grounds, the
prosperous Home farm beyond, and further out, the tidy
tenant farms.

Despair, unexpected and frightening in its intensity, swept
through Tessa. She had never felt so empty, except when
first her mother and then Angus had died. The reason for
her distress had been easy to understand then, but now she
had no understanding of why she felt so desolate. She only
knew the scene before her gave her the feeling she had tasted
ashes.

Grasping for straws, Tessa decided it was the contrast with
the Highlands that affected her so adversely. So secure and
fat these Sassenach were with all their wealth. True, she had
wealth too, but not as much as Nick, and in the Highlands
most people, even the clan chieftains, were not so lucky
as she. People there had to work hard for what they
had.

Not at all like the Marquess of Kerne who had been raised
to the enormous wealth she saw before her. But had not been
taught the responsibilities that must come with wealth? Tessa
demanded. Her ire against Nick flaring, she answered un-
equivocally no. He knew naught of responsibilities. Oh, he
managed his estates well enough—with the aid of an over-
seer—but what did he know of his tenants? Likely nothing.
Unlike a Scotsman, who knew his crofters and even their
bairns by name, Nick only knew of the pleasures of wealth:
the fine horses it brought, the impeccable clothes, the rich
wines, and, of course, the women.

Abruptly Tessa tugged her filly's reins and headed down the side of the hill away from the sight of anything belonging to Nicholas Steele. She would not think of him, would not think how silly Susannah was to wish to see him marry. He would only make a wife miserable. He'd too great a taste for a variety of women. True, he had not touched her that night when she had had to sleep wrapped in his arms. Tessa bit her lip, willing the sudden, sharp memory of how Nick's arms had felt about her away.

It was the man's roguish qualities she would think of. He had not dallied with her because he found her uninteresting. He had called her a babe, and babes interested him not at all. Too marriageable, they were. His tastes ran to experienced women, women who would make no demands upon him. Look whom he'd chosen for his mistress: a woman of the first stare of fashion who was married to a man conveniently away at war.

Tessa spurred the filly to a faster pace, for they were on level ground again. It was that last which disgusted her most. Nick had been away at war himself, and though he had not been a married man, he must have known men who were. He'd have seen how they worried over what awaited them at home, and yet he had no compunction over taking advantage of such a one himself.

She ought not to have been surprised to discover a Sassenach lord would have so little honor, but, Tessa admitted with some bitterness, she was. She had thought better of Nick. An image of Nick's lips descending to Lady Madelaine's arose in her mind. At once Tessa set the filly to a reckless pace that demanded complete concentration.

"Miss Strahan! I say, Miss Strahan!"

Above the sound of the filly's hooves, Tessa heard a voice, and when she realized it was Sir Malcolm calling to her, she pulled up. "Greetings, good sir." She smiled at the young man who rode up looking at once pleased but puzzled to see her. Dressed in a coat of blue, with his hair slightly ruffled by the breeze, Sir Malcolm looked boyishly handsome. "This is a pleasant surprise."

"I am pleased to see you as well, Miss Strahan, but, ah, I mean, well, had you forgotten our appointment?" Sir Malcolm's cheeks heated in a way Tessa thought endearing. "I had understood, that is, we did agree, I believe, to ride out together at four o'clock."

"But of course I had not forgotten!" Tessa assured him hoping her smile would help to put him at ease. "I only feared it might rain, and I should never get out of the house if I did not ride early. I thought you would not mind a game of chess rather than an outing."

It was a question as much as a statement and Sir Malcolm was prompt to say that he would enjoy any activity Tessa suggested. "You are very kind, sir, if not wise." She laughed. "I fear I shall take shameless advantage of you."

"You could never take advantage of me, Miss Strahan," Sir Malcolm averred quite earnestly. "Your wishes are my desires, you know."

Sir Malcolm, though he gazed with youthful fervor at Tessa, never noted the second's hesitation before she smiled. It had been on the tip of her tongue to say he gave her a great deal of license, but she bit the remark back. Sir Malcolm was, Tessa realized, being quite sincere. Why the discovery made her uneasy she would have to consider later. Just then she inclined her head and smiled again. "You are very kind. But why have you come early? Or are you on your way to the Hall?"

"But I am not early. It is only a little before the hour of four."

"It cannot be!" Tessa cried with no little consternation. She had left at close to two o'clock and had never meant to be away so long. "Dear me, I believe I have allowed the time to escape me. Well," she brightened, "there is no harm done. I am not late for our appointment at any rate, and we shall have the opportunity to ride together a time."

"But should we not await your groom, Miss Strahan?"

Sir Malcolm asked, looking back over his shoulder as Tessa kneed her mount.

"We should be waiting a long while, if we did." Tessa grinned. "Will I sink beneath your estimation entirely, Sir Malcolm, if I admit I have ridden out quite alone?"

It did not surprise Tessa overmuch that, though his eyebrows lifted briefly, in the end Sir Malcolm grinned. "I think you are a brave Scottish lass, Miss Strahan, who has no use for meddling grooms."

"You do understand!" Tessa's gray eyes sparkled with such approval, Sir Malcolm wished she might always look at him just so. "In truth, I had no desire at all to slow my pace in deference to a sluggish groom."

They were trotting in tandem now, and Sir Malcolm glanced with approval at Tessa. "You ride wonderfully well, Miss Strahan. Surprisingly well, really. I thought Highlanders were accustomed to riding nothing but ponies."

"My grandfather got in the habit of riding true horses, when he fled to France for a time after '45. When he returned, he had a pair of horses brought over from that country."

"No Sassenach horses would do?"

Sir Malcolm was rewarded with a delighted laugh. "No Sassenach anything would do for Angus!" Tessa agreed, liking very well that with her compatriot she could be quite as straightforward as she pleased about her grandfather's feelings toward the English. "In plain words, he detested everyone and everything below the border."

The truth was Sir Malcolm's branch of the Frasers had long been an ally of the English, but the young man cast off his family's ancient allegiance with no qualms at all. Instead, calling upon dim memories of his mother's father's brother, he was able to respond to each grievance Tessa's grandfather had harbored with one his own relative had stated. As a result, when they came out of the trees lining the drive to Tarlton Hall, they were walking their mounts at the slowest of paces and were laughing together in the delighted way people do when they have a bond that sets them apart.

20

*I*t was Malcolm who first saw the knot of people standing in the drive before the Hall. Glancing forward, he inquired, "Are you expecting company, Miss Strahan?"

Before Tessa could make an answer, they heard Tessa's name called out and saw the little group surge forward toward them. There were no strangers, only Susannah and Honoria and behind them Kit and Nick, both holding the reins of their horses as if they intended to mount up.

"Therèse!"

It was Honoria who had called out, Tessa realized. She waved and urged her filly forward, but as she neared her aunt, her smile faded. Honoria's brow was knit with concern, and no one in the group was smiling.

"Yes, Aunt? Has something occurred?"

"We have been so worried about you, child! You have been gone for hours. Nick and Kit have only just returned from looking for you."

Recalling very well what had occurred the last time Nick had been obliged to ride out after her, Tessa darted an uneasy glance to him and was not reassured. He stood behind the others, regarding her with cold blue eyes that did reflect a forgiving mood.

A groom came then, providing a distraction, and when Tessa had dismounted, she hurried to take her aunt's hand. "I am sorry!" She looked unhappily at everyone but Nick. "I did lose track of the time, and then, when I met up with Sir Malcolm, we enjoyed ourselves too well to hurry back. I never thought I should cause you worry."

"But you ought not to ride out without a groom, Tessa!"

Susannah looked as if she had imagined a good many quite unpleasant reasons for Tessa's delayed return. "You are certain you are unharmed?"

Susannah's concern was so palpable, Tessa instantly forgave the public chiding and went to give her a quick embrace. "Yes, my dear, I am entirely well. You forget that I grew up at Kilmorgan. I never had an escort there and did not think I should need one here. But I am sorry you gentlemen"—Tessa glanced in Nick's general direction, saw one black eyebrow arch uncompromisingly and quickly turned from him to address Kit exclusively—"were put to such trouble on my account."

"You needn't make any apologies to me, my dear." Kit shook his head as he tossed the reins he held to a groom. "I went to no trouble at all. The truth of it is, I had a roaring time following this fellow's hell-for-leather pace across the fields."

He gestured to Nick, but Tessa kept her gaze from following Kit's hand. "You are very kind to let me off so easily, sir," she told him, giving Kit a quite beautiful smile for his gallantry. "But, nonetheless, I promise that in future you will race your brother for nothing more than the sheer joy of it."

No proof at all against Tessa's most appealing look, Kit gave a chuckle and clapped her around the shoulders. "You have a way with you, Tessa Strahan, I must say that! I imagine that grandfather of yours had cause to pull out his hair more than once. But come, let us not stand out here any longer. I have worked up quite a thirst with all my riding about. I imagine you could use a drink of something or other, could you not, Malcolm?"

With a quick smile the young man said he would find a refreshment most welcome, and Kit led him into the house. Tessa at once linked her arm with Honoria's, leaving Nick to lead Susannah in ahead of them.

"Truly I am sorry to have worried you, Aunt." That Tessa was sincere could be seen from the expression in her eyes.

"I had no notion I would cause such upset. Having left word with Booker as to my plans, I assumed all would be well."

"Well, well, you must not take on too dreadfully, my dear." Shaking her head, Honoria heaved a sigh. "In truth I hold myself at fault. I had forgotten how different life is at Kilmorgan, and never thought to say to you that young ladies here are escorted at all times."

"You must not blame yourself, Aunt! It is my fault entirely. Lord Kerne did give me some instruction to that effect." Tessa sent up a prayer that he not be moved to instruct her as thoroughly again. "But I did not realize I could not ride out alone in the area around the Hall."

That she had, in fact, ridden well away from Nick's estate; that she had had no intention of burdening herself with an escort no matter Nick's admonition that she must have one; and that she truly thought all the fuss absurd, for what could happen in broad daylight on a sleepy summer day, Tessa forbore to say. Her aunt was too genuinely distraught to be burdened with either the full truth or an argument.

"Now that I know, however, I shall not cause such worry again."

"It would be best if you take a groom, my dear, though I fear you will find such conventions constricting after the freedom you have been accustomed to." Honoria's expression cleared after a moment. "Perhaps you could make it a habit to ride out with Nick each morning. It is his habit, and I daresay he would not hold you back as a groom might. And there is young Malcolm as well. You looked as if you were enjoying yourselves very well when we first caught sight of you."

"We were," Tessa said, smiling to herself as she thought how amusing cataloguing Sassenach sins could be. "He is a very nice young man."

Honoria looked pleased, but said nothing more, for they had reached the salon, where the others were. A quick scan of the room showed Nick to be absent, and when Susannah spoke up to say some estate business would keep him from joining them, Tessa breathed a sigh of relief. If no one else had noted his speaking silence outside, she certainly had. He was furious with her, though he had no right at all to be. Honoria was her guardian, not Nick. All the same, rights aside, Tessa was glad to be spared the ordeal of making amiable conversation while attempting to ignore his threatening glare.

Only a little later, Tessa learned she would not have to worry over Nick for the remainder of the evening. Susannah announced in her breezy fashion that Charles Bascom and Lady Madelaine were coming for dinner, and Tessa smiled cynically to herself at the news. With any luck at all she realized she could avoid Nick until his mood had been sweetened by a prolonged visit with his mistress.

Though his eyes lingered with mingled pleasure and regret upon Tessa, Malcolm disciplined himself to observe the proprieties and rose to leave a half hour later. Tessa accompanied him outside and waved him farewell from the steps.

A piquant smile lit her features as she turned to retrace her steps inside, for after he had mounted, Sir Malcolm had leaned down to whisper low in her ear, "Your grandfather would be proud of you, Miss Strahan. What he may have lost at Culloden Moor, you have regained in Cheshire. You've all the Sassenach here eating out of your hand."

"Such a sweetly handsome boy young Fraser is. And by the looks of your smile, it would seem his tongue matches his features."

Startled, Tessa jerked her head up to find Nick looming above her and missed the step she had been about to take. Nick's hand shot out to save her from sprawling flat upon the hard steps, but Tessa did not thank him, only attempted and failed to wrest herself from his grip.

"Malcolm is no boy. He has reached his majority. And he is rivetingly handsome with a most courteous and kind Scottish tongue."

"Ah, yes. His coloring is so fair, I had almost forgotten that Malcolm was birthed north of the Border." Nick's smile mocked Tessa as did his eyes. "The boy's mother was English, did he say? As were three of his grandparents. I should say only his name is Scottish, really. Certainly his sympathies are not." Nick lifted Tessa by the arm and half dragged her up the stairs while he continued to address her in a light, pleasant tone that set her teeth on edge. "He did tell you he has never attended a school but that it was here in the south, did he not? His choice is no reflection upon the quality of the schools in Scotland, you understand, only the result of considerable tradition. If you ask, I do believe he can do no less than admit he came down for his schooling because his branch of the Frasers has sent its sons to Cambridge for well nigh two hundred years."

"You are insufferable, Sassenach!" Tessa did not dispute Nick's revelations. He would not lie, particularly when the matter was so easily verified. Unreasonably, the knowledge that Malcolm had been less than entirely truthful with her made Tessa angry not at the young Scotsman but at Nick, for it was obvious he was vastly enjoying the task of disillusioning her. "Vile cad! Release me!"

Her gray eyes flashing, Tessa gave another jerk but to no avail. "I've no intention of releasing you. I wish to speak with you in private. I think the library will do. Thank you, Booker."

Nick nodded casually to his butler, who held the door for them while he carried Tessa along, forcing her to skip on her tiptoes to match his stride.

"I do not care to talk to you!" Tessa hissed, mindful enough of Booker's presence not to shout.

"That is neither here nor there. I will speak to you." Throwing open the door of the library, Nick thrust Tessa inside.

Stumbling off balance, she caught herself and whirled about in time to see Nick slam the door behind him with a crack as sharp as a rifle's discharge.

"You . . . !" Her hands balled into fists, Tessa faltered for lack of a sufficiently scathing word.

"Yes, Tessa?" Nick's smile did not reach his eyes but did bare his teeth. "Is Sassenach too tame for you?"

Tessa saw a light leap to life at the back of his blue eyes. Slowly, purposefully, Nick pushed himself away from the door and began to advance upon her with the beautiful, pitiless stride of a cat. She retreated a step, then another. "You arrogant, pigheaded beast!" Tessa found her tongue, though she continued to give ground as Nick came steadily on. "I am not a child to be hauled about. And I am not your concern. It is my aunt who is my guardian!"

"Honoria does not have it in her to rein you in, Tessa, but by the devil, I do! You are in sore need of a firm hand."

The open threat sent Tessa flying to the far side of the settee. "I shall think you like whipping me more than is seemly," she warned, "if you take a hand to me for what I did today."

"What a lurid imagination you have, my dear." Nick's mouth curled sardonically as he approached her refuge. "I've no intention of spanking you again. The effects of that punishment lasted far too short a time. I intend to shake the necessary sensibilities into you this time."

The seemingly substantial settee proved to be no defense at all. With dreadful, graceful ease Nick vaulted it. From the corner of her eye Tessa saw that a window only five feet away was open. Rounding upon Nick, she took a step backward toward the promise of freedom.

"Sensibilities!" she echoed, hoping with her bluster to distract him from her purpose. "You've the effrontery to think to school me in sensibilities? I did nothing worse than ride out alone. You, on the other hand, my lord, are the seducer of a married woman, the wife of a fellow officer, a man who is away at war and cannot defend himself!"

The light in Nick's eyes flared. "You have been listening to the gossips, Tessa. I have seduced no one."

Incensed by his lie, Tessa forgot the need for retreat. "I saw you kiss her!" she shouted.

"Spying, Tessa? I'd not have thought you had prurient interests. Someday I shall clarify for you the difference between seduce and mutually please, but for the time, suffice it to say my liaison with Madelaine Landon is of no consequence. Madelaine and her husband have an understanding the entire world accepts."

"Understanding?" The blood in her veins pounded so loudly, Tessa could scarcely think straight. Certainly she had not the patience to come to terms with a type of marital arrangement of which no one had ever told her. "No husband wishes to be cuckolded. You are only trying to escape being called the worst sort of dishonorable rake!"

Before she even saw them coming, Nick's hands had caught her shoulders in a punishing grip. Hauled up close to him, Tessa thought for a wild moment Nick's eyes would set her on fire, they blazed so brightly. "You self-righteous little witch, condemning without the least understanding," he snarled down at her. "But then you are a narrow-minded Scot, are you not? And a self-centered one. While you are weighing our sins, Tessa Strahan, put this thought on your balance scales. My behavior has hurt no one, while yours has caused your aunt, one of the kindest women who ever lived, hours of anxiety. You did not think of that, did you?" Nick was shaking Tessa violently enough to rattle her teeth, and though she struggled, he did not seem aware of her efforts to escape him. "For hours today I looked for you," he went on, his jaw clenched, "thinking at every turn I should find you lying battered upon the road, but you must defy convention. You could not be bothered to care in the least whether those you leave behind are senseless with worry. I vow I do have a notion to turn you over my knee," he warned grimly.

"You-you are being absurd!" Though she was dizzy from the throttling he'd given her, Tessa was not bowed. "I have apologized to Honoria and have promised not to worry her so again. You only want to play the high-handed lord with me!'' She pounded his chest with her fist. ''There was no likelihood I would be attacked on your estate in broad daylight.''

Her answer had the effect of making the light in Nick's eyes blaze so that Tessa's heart raced in earnest. ''Little liar! I rode over the entire estate. You were nowhere to be found, and none should know better than you what dangers lie in wait on the open road. But you do not think of danger or of the dangerous passions you excite! No, you plunge on heedlessly.'' Nick shook her so her head bobbed. A handful of her pins loosened and thick strands of her hair fell to her shoulders, but neither Nick nor Tessa noticed. Each was aware of nothing at all but the other's furious eyes. ''If I say that for safety's sake you must have an escort, you ride out alone; if I suggest that you would do best to avoid Giles, you purposely taunt him with unexpected talents before an audience! But perhaps I have misunderstood all this time. Perhaps you relish the avid gleam you excite in Giles Bayesford's eyes!''

''No!'' The shocked denial was punctuated by a loud, sharp slap.

Time seemed to stand still as the handprint Tessa left on Nick's cheek turned from palest white to red. Though his head jerked back, Nick's eyes never left Tessa, and she stared back at him, frozen in place.

Vaguely Tessa became aware that she was breathing hard, then, more distantly, she heard voices in the hallway. At first, as she awaited Nick's retribution, she registered no recognition.

''. . . no need, Booker. I shall show myself in.''

''Tessa, I . . .''

Whatever Nick had intended to say, it was lost. Simultaneously Tessa broke the hold he had unknowingly loosened and the door to the library opened.

''What the devil!'' Nick swung around. ''Madelaine!''

Even distracted as she was, Tessa noted Nick had exclaimed his mistress' name with no pleasure at all, and it must be said she derived a grim satisfaction from her observation.

"Oh!" There was nothing languid in Lady Madelaine's tone as she looked from Nick to Tessa. "I seem to have interrupted."

Perhaps it was Nick's place to make the woman an assurance, but Tessa spoke up first. She had seen in an instant the contrast in their appearances. Once again Lady Madelaine put her to shame. Dressed in gold silk that fit like a sheath, with her hair carefully coiffed, she was impeccably turned out. Seeing her, Tessa became aware that her own hair tumbled around her shoulders, that her cheeks were unnaturally hot, and that her eyes stung with something she feared might look suspiciously like tears.

However, the thought of playing an embarrassed mouse before a woman who would betray her own husband stiffened her spine. "You have not interrupted at all, my lady," Tessa said in a voice as haughty as any Angus had ever used. "My business with Lord Kerne is quite ended, I assure you. Until dinner, my lord, my lady."

Concentrating carefully, Tessa found she could curtsy with proud grace to Nick's mistress first and then to Nick before, with her head held high, she walked over the hairpins lying in full view on the floor and made for the door.

"Tessa."

She stiffened. Nick spoke her name as if she were a recalcitrant child and he her father. Another step brought her nearer the door, but a sound from behind her decided her against attempting to bound through to freedom. "My lord?" she inquired, turning.

"You will not forget: an escort at all times. You may take a groom with you, or if you choose, you may ride with Kit and me in the morning."

"You are too kind, my lord," Tessa murmured in a gracious tone that did not match at all the frigid look in her gray eyes. She could not believe Nick was as oblivious to the position he had put her in before Lady Madelaine as he seemed. "But I could not presume so upon your time. Nor will I need a groom from your stables. Sir Malcolm has graciously offered to provide me escort in the afternoons. As to the other matter to which you refer, bear with me, please, as I repeat that Honoria, my guardian, and I have discussed it and have come to an agreement. You needn't fear I shall break my word to her. I would never care to disappoint anyone whom I respect."

A sudden, sharp intake of breath reminded Tessa Lady Madelaine stood witness to the scene. A giddy laugh threatened to overwhelm her. It seemed she had shocked an adultress. Tessa's eyes met Nick's. Flint could not have been harder than the look in his eyes. Again the laughter threatened, only now Tessa was not certain it was not tears that would disgrace her. Quickly she inclined her head and rounding on her heel, made good her escape.

21

"Clarissa Derwent must be enormously pleased that her party has chanced to fall the week of the race." Susannah looked at Honoria and Tessa, her companions in the morning room. "Everyone is so excited, her affair cannot help but be a success!"

Honoria glanced up from her needlework with a smile. "I think you are right in saying this race of Nick's will add a measure of excitement, but to be fair, you must admit that each year Clarissa has been up to holding her lawn party, it has been a success. Perhaps it is the beauty of the setting. I have always liked the stream that runs by Hartsford Manor."

"It is delightful," Susannah agreed readily. "All those willows are so picturesque. I think you will enjoy it particularly, Tessa."

"I think Tessa may be a bit fatigued by all our social gatherings." Honoria looked with some concern at her niece. "Life at Kilmorgan may be a trifle more difficult than here in comfortable Cheshire, but I know very well it is does not require half the stamina. There are not so many neighbors."

Tessa smiled as she was meant to, but Honoria's observant eye remarked that if her niece's expression was sweet enough, it yet lacked its customary vitality. "You are right, aunt. There have been a great many entertainments, but I have enjoyed them. Everyone has been most cordial."

"They adore you, my dear!" Susannah laughed. "Perhaps it is that slight hint of brogue in your speech that intrigues the young men so, but I have seldom seen a girl so sought after. You will be the rage in town, I wager. That is if you are not snatched up by that handsome Malcolm before you even see London. Your young Scot cannot take his eyes from you, as you must know.''

Tessa only knew with certainty that Susannah enjoyed no activity more than matchmaking, but even so she was taken aback by the suggestion, however playfully spoken, that Malcolm might ask for her hand before she repaired first to her aunt's estate and then to London. They were to depart only a fortnight hence. ''You jest, Susannah,'' she said, though there might have been just a touch of uncertainty in her eyes. ''Malcolm has been attentive, I admit, but only in a friendly manner.''

''Friendly! He has devoted himself to you this entire week. And do not say there are not other young ladies about. There is Amelia Harkness, Julia Cardowe, and even Mary Marching. All of them are very nice, rather pretty, and well enough dowered. But it is only you Malcolm stood up with twice at the assembly in Barncastle, and only you he has ridden out with daily.''

''Oh, well, as to that, you will remember he came that day I upset everyone so by riding out alone. He only wished to provide me a companion more compatible than a groom.''

''May I remind you, Nick is one of the finest whips in the country?'' Susannah laughed. ''No, it won't wash, Tessa. Unless Malcolm wished to keep you from Nick's company— which amounts to the same thing—he escorts you because he enjoys the opportunity to have you to himself. Ah, here you are, Mrs. Hudson. Come in, Jamie! And Cecily, my sweet! How do you, my darlings?''

Tessa greeted the children, who had come for their regular morning visit with their mama, with pleasure not unmixed with relief. She wanted time to consider the merits of Susannah's remarks about Malcolm. True, she knew he admired her. His eyes told her as much, but she had not thought much beyond that. For herself, she enjoyed Malcolm's company. He was handsome, attentive, danced well, laughed with her . . . in short, he was the perfect companion. But husband? She had not thought of him in that light.

Perhaps she had been remiss. Likely so, for now she thought of it, she realized that on the several occasions that week when she had been in company with other young Sassenach ladies of her age, they had done little but speculate about who intended to ask for whom. Tessa had only listened absently to their chatter.

A faint line of pink tinted her cheeks. The truth was she had only the haziest recollection of her conversations with anyone, even Malcolm. Several irreverent remarks he had made about the Sassenach had caused her to laugh, but the knowledge that he was playing to her prejudices more than expressing his own had dampened her enthusiasm for the sport. Nick had taken the bloom off that rose.

Nick. He was all she had been able to think of. There, she had said it. Tessa watched as Cecily climbed into Honoria's lap to show off a picture she had drawn, and Jamie displayed his own composition for his mother, but she did not really take in the pleasant scene. She instead saw Nick as he had looked when he was shaking her for having ridden about the countryside all alone.

Now, with the clarity of hindsight, she could see he had been afraid for her. Just as Angus had been angriest with her when she had climbed the highest crag behind Kilmorgan, though she had been told the rocks were uncertain there, so Nick had been angry because he had been worried for her safety. There was the incident in the Lammermuir Hills to spur his imagination, but Tessa believed, after a great deal of thought, it was not ruffians that had concerned Nick the most. Her impression, her intuition told her Nick's anxieties centered around Sir Giles.

She herself found it difficult to imagine the mincing dandy would be so brazen as to attack her anywhere or time, but she did not know what had led Nick to distrust the man so. She'd have liked to have asked.

Tessa bit her lip. She'd have liked to apologize to him,

too. Even when she closed her eyes, she could not shut out the sight of her handprint on his cheek. Nor the shuttered look on his face when she had declined his well-intentioned invitation to ride out in favor of accepting Malcolm's.

But Nick had given her no opportunity to approach him. In the five days since then she had seen Nick only when they were in company with at least two and usually a good many more others. Once she had asked Booker where she might find his master, but the butler had told her Lord Kerne was not in. Later she chanced to see Nick crossing the yard to the stables and knew Booker had lied, but knew as well he'd have done so only on Nick's orders.

There was only one conclusion to be drawn: Nick had no interest in speaking with her. Even in public he had not addressed more than a perfunctory "Good evening, Miss Strahan" or "Good day, Miss Strahan" to her. Certainly he had not requested a dance of her when they had attended the Assembly at which Malcolm had asked her to stand up with him twice. Nick had honored Lady Madelaine, of course, then Honoria, Susannah, and an assortment of other ladies, but Tessa's card he had ignored.

But he had not disregarded her entirely. On more than one occasion Tessa had glanced up to find Nick's eyes upon her. She knew why, however. On each of those occasions Sir Giles Bayesford had somehow gained her side.

The party from Clarstons appeared at all the gatherings the company from Tarlton Hall attended, which, simply put, meant that as the Sassenach seemed unable to spend even one evening in solitude at home, Tessa had seen Sir Giles in one setting or another every evening that week. Some evenings she had been successful at avoiding him, but other times she had not. He reminded her of a wolf laying in wait for the lamb. Hidden by a group of guests, he would step out suddenly to block her path.

Though she strove to maintain an aloof air, Tessa knew she failed. Her chin invariably lifted, and she'd the notion that her eyes flashed. The dandy no longer openly needled her, forbearing to refer to Celts as if her ancestors had been a tribe of savages, but still he put her back up. It was the way he looked at her, his expression tense and avid all at once, that made her dislike of him more intense than ever. At the assembly it had been all she could do not to shudder when he'd asked her to dance.

She had told him her card was filled, though it was not, and turned away abruptly to find that Nick, lounging negligently against the wall, was watching her interaction with the man. Undeniably heartened, Tessa had thought to smile to convey her gratitude, but before she could, when he saw she had caught the direction of his gaze, Nick had turned away and entered into conversation with some woman beside him.

"See, Tessa! Ish a fishy!"

Tessa blinked, and Cecily's cherubic face swam into view. In her fist the child held a paper upon which she had drawn a large, vaguely round shape colored in bright red. "Yes." Tessa deemed a nod appropriate. "I see, sweeting. So shiny it is, too."

As Susannah had predicted, a very great deal of the talk at Mrs. Clarissa Derwent's annual lawn party, prettily situated beside a stream that wound through the Derwent estate, was of the upcoming race between the Marquess of Kerne's black stallion and Sir Giles Bayesford's bay. The fine points of the horses were discussed; the relative abilities of the riders weighed; the course was taken into account; and, of course, the forfeits wagered were remarked upon.

To Tessa it seemed that no sooner did she begin a conversation than it turned to the race and inevitably either sooner or later to the pendant Nick hoped to win back for his mistress. Not that anyone, even in the murmurs of conversation she caught as she passed by, openly declared that Madelaine had some especial relationship with Nick. No one was so boorish, but Tessa read that very suggestion in the speculative glances that cut first to Madelaine and then to

Nick. As the two never seemed to be far apart that afternoon, the knowing gazes had not far to travel.

The relentless discussion quickly became tedious to Tessa,
though she kept her smile in place. She'd more pride than
to wish others to remark a mood she did not care to account
for, but when Hetty Clarstons invited her on a walk by the
stream in company with Peter Derwent and Sir Malcolm,
Tessa did not hesitate.

"Come along," Peter directed with mock gravity as
Malcolm, looking quite fine in a green coat that contrasted
with his fairness, fell into step beside Tessa. "I do not like
to dawdle when I've ladies who wish to see my fleet."

"I must admit this talk of a flotilla intrigues me, Peter,"
said Hetty with a quiet twinkle in her eye. "I'd no notion
you harbored naval interests."

"But I have, my dear, and as you will see, my interests
are of long standing." Peter smiled mysteriously upon his
beloved before turning his attention to Tessa. "I fear my fleet
will likely be the merest nothing to you, Miss Strahan, as
you have sailed upon the *Sea Witch*, but I do what I
can."

"I appreciate that, sir," Tessa replied with a grin. "And
though I have sailed on the North Sea, I have never been
upon the River . . . ?"

She looked significantly to the willow-lined stream whose
bank they had reached, and Peter, his lips twitching slightly,
finished, "Derwent! The River Derwent, wide and swift,
upon whose bosom a fleet may drift."

Hetty playfully hit him while Malcolm put his hands to
his ears. "Stop! We pray! Torture by dreadful poesy is too
much!"

Laughing outright, Peter stooped and whisked the cover
off an old, musty box. "Behold my fleet. See it and weep
for joy!"

Peeping inside, Tessa giggled unrestrainedly. There were
some five toy boats whose chipped paint, frayed lines, and
limp sails testified to their age. Peter fixed her with a

narrowed look. "Not going to look down your tipped nose
are you, Miss Strahan?"

She laughed and shook her head. "No, indeed, sir! I would
not be so vainglorious. I may have ventured aboard the *Sea
Witch*, but I did not captain her as you do your fleet."

Only a hint of smile betraying him, Peter nodded crisply.
"Actually, I believe I should be addressed as Admiral, for
I've five ships under my command. Two of them I shall
captain today, while each of you, my underlings, may captain
the ship I choose for you."

"Why, thank you, sir! Very generous, I must say,"
Malcolm teased.

Peter bowed gravely and forthwith gave his good friend
the oldest, most dilapidated boat. "Only a good sailor can
master her, my man," he said by way of reason. To Tessa
he gave a jaunty yawl whose trim matched her muslin of
daffodil yellow, and to Hetty, the girl he held very dear, he
presented his third-best schooner. The best two he kept for
himself, for, as he pointed out, he was the admiral.

They had a gay time rigging the boats out and setting them
adrift upon the current. Whose traveled the farthest depended
upon any number of inconsequential things: twigs in the
stream, eddies to tip them, the far bank. As there was a little
footbridge nearby, Tessa and Malcolm crossed over to rescue
the three ships that lay, as Peter put it, "beached unhappily
on yon far and treacherous shoal."

A particularly thick stand of willows at one section of the
stream obliged them to detour inland before they came again
to a clearing.

As the sound of Hetty's squeals and Peter's shouts dimmed,
Malcolm, taking Tessa's arm, slowed her pace. "Peter will
not miss us soon, I think. He's his boats and Hetty to occupy
him, and I should be grateful, Miss Strahan, to have you
to myself a time. It has been the very devil, if you will pardon
me for speaking so, to have you before me all this afternoon
but surrounded by a crowd of impenetrable thickness."

Tessa smiled and slowed her pace to match his. "I believe

that at least half the people here are on intimate terms with Honoria, and they desired above all things to meet her long-absent niece.''

Malcolm took the liberty of interlacing his fingers with hers, but Tessa scarcely noted, for as he did so, Malcolm crowed with pleasure, ''I vow you may be a gudgeon, after all!'' When she looked at him in surprise, the young man smiled charmingly. ''Allow me to enlighten you, Miss Strahan. No one desired an introduction to you on account of your aunt. They thronged about you because you are by far the most entrancing lady present this afternoon.''

The speech was very gallant, but Tessa was reminded of Susannah's remarks on the extent of the young man's interest in her. A polite smile on her face, she attempted to extricate her hand from Malcolm's. She went about the task gently, for she did not wish to wound him, and therefore she failed.

Indeed, Malcolm was so moved by how beautifully the little glade seemed to set off Tessa's appearance—she looked so slim and golden, almost a fairy queen among her boughs, he thought—that he threw all caution to the winds. Carrying her slender hand to his lips, he told her in a rush of feeling, ''I have watched you all the afternoon, and you've the brightest, most bewitching smile I ever saw, Tessa. May I call you that? I long so to be on the same terms of intimacy as your friends.''

''Malcolm, the sentiment does me honor, but—''

''You are more than very beautiful. You've a gift for life, Tessa,'' Malcolm continued, as if his ears were fashioned of lead and he had not heard the prologue to a dismissal. ''Though it may be unmanly to admit it, I cannot but reveal that you have swept me off my feet!''

While Tessa was still registering shock that so brief an acquaintance could produce such an effect, Sir Malcolm, in an excess of enthusiasm, swung her into his arms and lowered his lips to hers.

It is true that Tessa ought to have pushed the young man away at once. Lamentably, she did not. Tessa's first kiss had been a mere peck and of little interest. But her second kiss had been a different matter. When Nick had kissed her, though he had been a stranger to her, he had made her heart race and her blood pound. Tessa wished to know if Malcolm could produce the same effect. If so, she would know her response to Nick that day by the burn had had nought to do with the man.

Only a moment later a rustling in the willows by the stream advised Tessa to end her experiment. She did not wish another to come upon them and more to be made of the kiss than it warranted. There might be a push to pair her off with the young man who held her so intimately, and Tessa knew with certainty now that she would never marry Sir Malcolm Fraser.

He was as handsome as any girl could wish, good humored and Scottish, but she could not marry a man whose embrace had left her entirely unmoved. As to Nick . . . Tessa's mind veered away from finishing the thought.

Freeing her lips, she pushed against Malcolm.

"Tessa!" Malcolm's eyes were glazed and his breath came in rapid gasps, all in sad comparison to Tessa's calm, unruffled state. "Never say I have offended you!"

Tessa stepped away, though she did smile. "No. I am not missish enough for that, Malcolm, but . . ."

A voice, Peter's, rang out from a distance, interrupting Tessa. "Malcolm! Miss Strahan! Can you find the path? It is by the witch hazel, there!"

"Oh, lud! Peter! I had forgotten him."

Malcolm's cheeks reddened, but Tessa said they'd not been gone an unconscionable amount of time. "Though I do think we should go down at once now," she added and suited her actions to her words. Peering through the thick canopy of leaves, she did not see anyone lurking in the willows watching them. Likely it had only been an animal they had startled, she reasoned, and then she caught sight of Sir Peter and Hetty and waved to them.

As Tessa stepped onto the path, Malcolm hurried to her.

"Tessa, I must speak to you. Surely you can see that."

She could see he was somewhat put out at her offhand manner, but Tessa thought that not so bad. Perhaps he would be better prepared for the outcome of the interview he desired.

"I shall be free tomorrow at two o'clock to go riding, if you like."

An uncertain look in his nice blue eyes, Sir Malcolm nodded to confirm their appointment before they rejoined the game of boats they'd temporarily abandoned.

22

"Do ye mean to turn away the Fraser lad, then?"

With considerable surprise Tessa looked up at Nan. "How did ye guess? Have ye the second sight?"

" 'Twas naught to guess." Nan shrugged her plump shoulders as she settled a small, feathered riding hat upon Tessa's burnished curls. "Ye've chosen to appear before him in yer dourest habit—'tis more soldier's wear than lady's dress."

Nan gave the habit, cut in the exceedingly stylish military style, so disapproving a look Tessa smiled, though only faintly. " 'Tis an appropriately dour color, too," she murmured, fingering the slate-colored cloth.

A frown etched a line down the middle of her brow when she looked up again at her maid. "What shall I say to him, Nan? I feel quite at a loss."

"Ye be certain aboot him?" Nan asked.

"Aye." Tessa nodded. "He kissed me, Nan, and I felt naught. I like him well enough, but . . ."

Shrugging, she left the thought to finish itself, and Nan nodded briskly, convinced. "Ye'll be firm but gentle. Say he's fine, o'course, but nae the lad ye'll wed. Ye'll find ye must repeat yersel'. The gentlemen do nae take nay for an answer easily."

Nan's prediction would prove true, entirely too true to Tessa's mind. But she was not to know that as she greeted Malcolm and, after consulting Booker, decided with her companion that the heavy clouds covering the sky did not portend immediate rain.

Tessa pushed for a ride, as she wanted more privacy for

their interview than they would have in a salon at the Hall, where the door must be left open for propriety's sake.

Malcolm was not as cheerful as usual. Nervous, he watched her closely, and his smile of greeting was strained, but Tessa knew she appeared no more lighthearted. The business of dampening a conquest's ardor did not fill her with the least sense of victory, only a sadness that their friendship would likely soon end.

Malcolm was the first to raise the subject that lay between them. When they came to the crest of the hill Tessa had explored the week before, he spurred his mount alongside hers. "I-I believe you are put out with me, Tessa," he stammered, flushing painfully.

Heaving an inward sigh, Tessa drew up and Malcolm followed suit. Below them lay Tarlton Hall, but neither of them noted the charming picture it made. "I am not put out with you at all, Malcolm." Tessa gave him a gentle, almost wistful smile, for he really was handsome and just then seemed very young.

"You are not the same, however. You think I presumed."

"No, it is not that. I, that is, you see, I am honored by your feelings for me. But," she added quickly when Malcolm's eyes widened, "I do not return them in the same measure. I wish us to be friends—"

"Friends." He said the word quietly, but his gaze revealed the true measure of his disappointment. "I thought . . . we have been on such good terms, I had hoped . . ."

Malcolm took a deep breath to collect himself, and a line of pink rose high on Tessa's cheeks, for she thought herself at least in part responsible for his discomfort. She ought to have been more aware of the young man and how attached he was becoming. "Oh, Malcolm, I do like you very well. You're a fellow Scot, after all, and I do enjoy your company."

"But then . . . !"

"No, Malcolm." Tessa shook her head firmly. "It is not the same."

"There is someone else, then! Lord Kerne!"

"No!" She said it too swiftly, but in his preoccupation Malcolm did not notice. "There is no one else."

"Then, surely, you are being overly hasty, Tessa," Malcolm said, reaching for her hand. "I forgot myself yesterday. I did not take into account how sheltered you have been in that Highland castle of yours, and I frightened you. But we will forget that and go on as we were. Eventually, you'll see, you will come to feel for me as I do for you."

The happy prediction was tempting. Even if she never came to feel more for him, going on as they had done would be pleasant. But she would be leading him to believe the impossible might be possible.

"No, Malcolm." Tessa took Malcolm's hand in hers to impress upon him the depth of her belief. "It is no good. I know I shall only feel as I do now: that you are very like a close cousin."

When Malcolm stiffened, Tessa realized she had not been as gentle as Nan would have wished. "Cousin?" he demanded, his young man's pride obviously wounded. "You felt no more than cousinly in my embrace?"

To her intense relief Tessa was spared having to answer. Even as she searched for something to say that was at once honest and tactful, a smattering of raindrops startled her.

The clouds had darkened considerably while they had been absorbed with their discussion. More raindrops came, and her horse moved restively as Malcolm, following her lead, glanced at the sky.

"It is going to rain, after all!" Tessa said, feeling somewhat guilty over the excitement a storm always stirred in her. "We must find shelter. The nearest place I know is the Folly."

Malcolm nodded once, and Tessa turned her mount down the hill.

Dispirited by the thought that if she'd been wiser, she might have avoided things coming to such a pass, Tessa almost welcomed the deluge that came when they were only halfway to shelter. It seemed her due.

Wet to the skin by the time they reached the Folly, she shivered as the air, cool from the rain, raised goose bumps on her arms. His boyish face unnaturally shuttered, Malcolm did the gallant thing and removed his coat to give to her.

Tessa attempted a smile and thanked him as she struggled into it. The coat was wet, but it did help protect her from the breeze.

They were stranded there some twenty minutes in all, while the sudden squall vented its fury before passing on to inundate the next county. It was for Tessa the longest span of time she had ever endured.

They neither one spoke. She searched for some way to break the tension, but each gambit she considered seemed ludicrously inane in the circumstances. For his part, Malcolm remained half sitting on the edge of a table, his hands in his pockets, staring morosely at the floor.

Feeling the worst sort of villainess, Tessa was more than prepared to brave the elements when the rain faded abruptly to a misty drizzle. Malcolm seemed to desire more fraught silence no more than she and went without objection to help her mount her filly, being careful to hold her at an exaggerated distance. She thanked him, and he inclined his head stiffly.

When they reached the Hall, Malcolm announced he would not come inside. "You may send my coat over to the Derwents later."

"But, Malcolm," Tessa protested. "Surely you wish a dry one for your ride?"

"No. Thank you."

And he was gone even before Tessa, with a young lackey's assistance, had dismounted.

Distraught by the thought she was responsible for his bleak expression, Tessa wished only to escape to the privacy of her room and never imagined that a reception committee might be awaiting her. When Booker opened the door to her, therefore, she was obliged to stifle a groan. Not only was Susannah there, looking anxious, but, worst of all, Nick. He was dressed to go out in a coat with an impressive number of capes and a top hat.

As Susannah cried with considerable relief, "Oh, here you are!" Tessa felt Nick's gaze rake her.

Until then she had not given any consideration at all to her appearance. There had been other matters to think of, but now, as she gave Susannah a reassuring smile and said as lightly as she could that she was indeed there, Tessa felt keenly how she must look garbed in a jacket reams too large for her, with the feather of her little hat drooping limply over her ear, and her wet skirt plastered to her legs.

"I was just coming to look for you."

It was the first full sentence Nick had addressed to her in a week, and it was the final straw for Tessa. "I am sorry you were put to the trouble of donning your coat, my lord, but as you can see, I did not need assistance. I only got caught by the rain."

"Yes, I see that."

When Nick allowed his gaze to travel deliberately over her, Tessa had an urge to stamp her foot. She felt a fool with a puddle of water forming at her feet. Her eyes flashed a warning, but before she could put words to her look, Susannah asked, "Where is Malcolm, dear? Never say he rode home without a coat!"

"Yes. He, ah, did not care to appear disheveled before everyone here.

"Well!" Susannah looked rather impressed by such thoughtfulness. "He's nice manners to spare us so, but I think he will take a cold for his pains. Where were you all this time, my dear? We were becoming worried."

"I think I shall be the death of you," Tessa apologized ruefully. "You needn't have worried, though. Malcolm and I were on the hill when the rain started, but managed to make the Folly before the worst of it."

"How convenient."

Tessa closed her eyes and took a breath before she turned to Nick. He had given his coat and hat into Booker's care and stood before her looking quite immaculate, not to mention dry and warm in his coat and buckskins.

"Yes. It was deuced convenient not to be obliged to sit almost bareheaded in a deluge, and if you are thinking anything . . . untoward occurred at the Folly, may I suggest, my lord, that is only because you are thinking of your own visits there!"

Hearing Susannah gasp, Tessa bit her lip. She had meant to hold her temper. "Truly," she addressed Nick's sister-in-law exclusively, "Malcolm was every inch the gentleman."

"Of course he was, my dear." Susannah darted a brief glance at Nick's stony expression, then added, rushing her words, "I would not think otherwise. And I am certain your disrepair was of no moment to him at all. He himself must have been sadly in need of repair."

If she had needed confirmation that she looked a complete sight, Tessa had it then. Susannah's attempt to reassure her only made her aware how past repair she was in all her dirt.

"I believe you worry unduly, my dear Susannah." Nick's remark surprised Tessa into glancing at him. She was in time to see him flick his gaze to her legs before he impaled her with a look so mocking, she flushed despite herself. "I very much doubt the pup objected to the sight of Miss Strahan soaked to the skin."

Tessa felt a bracing wave of anger quite submerge her earlier embarrassment. Why Nick was being so entirely hateful she could not imagine; she only knew she had had enough. "You are right, my lord," she informed him as her gray eyes clashed with his very blue ones. "Malcolm never made one objection to my ragged appearance." Let the beast make of that what he would, Tessa thought, tossing her head. "And now, if you will excuse me"—she pulled her gaze from Nick's and essayed a smile for Susannah—"I should like to go up to change. I am wet and a little cold."

"Of course, you are!" Contrite at how they'd kept Tessa standing, Susannah hurried at once to put her arm about Tessa's waist as if a mere wetting had rendered the younger girl an invalid. After her first step Tessa was grateful for the assistance. The difficulty of mounting a flight of stairs while hindered by disgracefully clinging skirts had not occurred to her.

Tessa was keenly aware of Nick's gaze upon her as she lifted her skirts and hobbled her way to her room, and she'd have liked to glare at him. He'd been odious when she had obviously been in difficulties.

He seemed to hold her responsible for the rain, though even Booker had declared he thought the clouds would not let loose for some hours. That the old man's bones had misjudged the matter was not her fault.

She did not challenge Nick with a look, however. She was careful, in fact, to keep her head turned from him. To her dismay she found that tears were stinging her eyes. Unnerved by so unaccountable a reaction, Tessa bit her lip and blinked them back before Susannah could notice.

When they reached Tessa's room, Susannah insisted upon tucking Tessa into bed, not a surprising course for her to recommend, perhaps, but an astonishing suggestion for Tessa to follow. Nan was most alarmed, fearing her mistress was truly ill, but Tessa waved her away and pulled her bed covers tightly around her, needing their warmth more for her spirits than for her body.

She regretted very much having hurt Malcolm. He was a very nice young man who deserved better, she told herself miserably. Fresh tears pricked her eyelids, but when Tessa clenched her eyes tightly shut, she did not see Malcolm's injured expression.

It was Nick's scathing glance made her eyes fly open again. Her cheeks heated. She might as well have stood before him in nothing at all, the way he'd seemed to look through her wet clothes.

He had made her furiously angry again. Tessa bit her lip.

The truth was, a single raking look from Nick had affected her more deeply than all Malcolm's miserable expressions together.

Tessa's soft pillow received a blow as she rolled over. Double damn! She was crying. And she knew why. She could evade the truth no longer. She had wanted Nick not to harp at her, but to come and take her in his arms as Malcolm would have done, had he seen her wet, disheveled, and obviously miserable.

Malcolm had been closer to the truth than she had wanted to admit. She had found him lacking in comparison to another.

It was Nick she wanted. Tessa's pillow sagged from a rain of blows. Little wonder his affair with Lady Madelaine Landon upset her so! She was jealous.

What a fool she was! A Sassenach and arrogant to boot, Nick had called her a babe and did naught but find fault with her.

Tessa collapsed in a still heap upon her bed, seeing Nick as he been when standing upon the deck of the *Sea Witch*. Aye, he was a brae mon, as they would say in the Highlands. Brave and bonny, and he made her come alive as no other could.

23

Tessa seized on three sneezes as an excuse to keep to her room for the remainder of that day and all the next. She needed the time to come to terms with her emotions before she faced Nick again. His blue eyes could cut uncomfortably close to the bone, and she'd a mortal fear he would recognize the feelings he had stirred in her. Whether he would find her hopeless passion amusing or wearying, she could not guess, but either response would be more than her pride could suffer.

Tessa also needed time to consider what she should do. The prospect of remaining in Nick's company seemed too bleak for words. She had not the ability to playact indifference for any length of time. And the mere thought of bidding Lady Madelaine Landon a civil good day made her clench her teeth.

On the night before Nick was to race against Sir Giles, Tessa paced her room restlessly. Kit had had the inspiration to host a convocation for-gentlemen-only at the Hall, and she could make out the distant sounds of the men's revelry as they made their wagers in an atmosphere freed of the constraints female company would demand. Though she knew it was only her imagination, she thought once or twice she heard Nick's laugh. The sound lowered her spirits dreadfully, for she'd the notion that Nick would never again laugh with her. He seemed so utterly estranged from her since their quarrel in the library that Tessa could not believe they could be even friends again, and she was obliged to battle an impulse to rush to her aunt's rooms to announce she would depart for Kilmorgan at the first opportunity, taking anyone but Nick for an escort.

She might have given in to the desire, but she would not hurt Honoria so. Her aunt spoke with too great a pleasure of having her niece by her for a long time. Frustrated, Tessa flung herself down upon her bed and wrenched her pillow over her head. Wanting to cry out, she banged her fist against the bed linen instead and was startled to encounter a foreign object.

At the realization the thing was only a piece of paper, she nearly tossed it aside. She did not and even rose to light the lamp by her bed, because the mystery of a piece of paper appearing under her pillow on a day when she had written nothing took her mind off Nick.

The heavy, cream-colored vellum had been folded into a small square. Inside was a note penned in a wavering hand.

> My dearest love,
> I need you most urgently! If you love me as deeply as I love you, please come to me as soon as you may safely get away. I shall await you at the Folly until three o'clock. Do not fail me!
> Yours eternally,
> Malcolm

Tessa stared in amazement, for though she had never seen Malcolm's writing, it little mattered. He would not have written such a note. He knew very well she did not bear him a love to equal his.

Who had written the note and brought it to her pillow? She could not imagine Nick doing such a thing, or Susannah, or Kit. They'd none of them reason, nor such odd notions of humor, to tease her so.

After a time Tessa's eyes narrowed. There was one gentleman among those gathered at the Hall that night who, so she had been warned, wished to do her harm. But what could have given Sir Giles the notion she so loved Malcolm she would go alone into the night to meet him?

The only incident between them that even hinted at such

feelings was the kiss they'd shared at Lady Clarston's fete. Cocking her head thoughtfully, Tessa recalled the stir in the willows that afternoon. Would Sir Giles have followed them that day? From a distance it might have looked to him as if she returned Malcolm's embrace.

But how could he have gotten this note to her room, when she had gone no farther than the screen in the far corner for the steaming bath to which Nan had persuaded her?

Frowning, she considered all the questions the odd note raised and what she ought to do. It did not take her long to come to a decision. She would sneak down to the Folly, and do something—she was not yet certain what—to turn the tables on Sir Giles.

Soon, dressed in a dark muslin, her sturdiest pair of boots, and a thick cloak, Tessa stepped out the door of her room. No one was in sight. Honoria and Susannah had gone to bed hours ago, while Kit and Nick, she supposed, were below with their guests.

Secure in her assumption, Tessa took the shortest route to the servants' stairs, turning down the corridor that led past Nick's rooms. Her tread light but quick, she was approaching Nick's door when it was suddenly thrown open.

"Miss!"

Jakes executed a deft side step to keep from bowling into Tessa. Intent on some errand, he had not expected anyone to be in the hallway. As he caught her arm to steady her, Tessa sought some plausible excuse for being abroad at two in the morning dressed in a cloak, and sent up a word of thanks that at least Nick was not on hand. He would not tolerate some vague excuse.

"Jakes, what the devil's happened?"

"Damn!"

Taken by surprise to hear Miss Strahan swear, Jakes was a second too long answering his master. Nick appeared in the doorway to see for himself what occurred.

His brow lifted when he found Tessa standing cloaked and booted outside his door, but Tessa, in her turn, stared.

Nick had come to the door clad only in his breeches and

boots. His chest was entirely bare but for a towel rolled about his neck. Tessa had recognized he was well formed but she was not prepared for how he would appear in the flesh. He resembled a sculpture of a greek hero she had seen once in an old book, his musculature was so defined. Free of even an ounce of fat, Nick looked very supple standing there, almost as tall as the doorway. The candlelight reflected off his sleek skin, and as if she were afraid she might reach out to touch him, Tessa curled her fingers into her palms.

The mat of dark, curling hair that plunged downward drew her eye, and then Tessa's pulse leapt alarmingly. Nick's breeches did not fasten about his waist as she had presumed they would. To Tessa's consternation they hugged his lean hips in an unfathomably suggestive manner and directed her gaze to his exceedingly taut belly.

"Not expecting to see a man at his toilette as you snuck out of the house, Tessa?" Nick's mocking question had the effect of wrenching her gaze from his breeches. It was not bright in the hallway, but even so, Tessa was certain Nick could see her cheeks turn fiery red. "I must say you seem to have undergone a miraculous recovery, my dear," he went on in the same sardonic drawl. "Honoria gave such a dire report on the state of your health this evening, I recommended you be attended by a leech."

"I detest leeches! They make my skin crawl." Tessa shivered at the thought of having the blood suckers placed on her arms and back.

Nick grunted. "And would, therefore, have quit worrying your aunt half to death with your malingering. If you wished to avoid me, as I don't doubt, Tessa, you needed only to send me your day's schedule. I'd have contrived to be wherever you were not."

Tessa caught her breath, for Nick's bald statement hurt her more than she wished to admit to herself. Tears in her eyes, she turned on her heel, but Nick was too quick for her. Before she'd taken a step, he had her by the arm and then propelled her ahead of him into his room.

"Thought to get away under cover of umbrage, did you?"

he growled, half flinging her through the door as he sent
Jakes on his way with a brief bark. "You've some explain-
ing to do before you depart, my dear. Now . . ." He leaned
back against the door and crossed his arms over his bare
chest. Because her eyes followed the movement, she was
reminded she was alone with a man only half dressed.
"Where were you to meet him?"

For a moment Tessa wondered how Nick could have
known about Sir Giles, but then realized he must be referring
to Malcolm. "You are allowing your imagination to run away
with you, my lord," she said with as much dignity as she
could muster. "But even if you had the right to question me,
it would not be here in your bedroom when you are not even
fully clothed."

"Do I frighten you, Tessa?"

In truth, he did. It was the greatest effort merely to keep
her gaze above his neck, and Tessa was terrified she might
lose all control and fling herself into Nick's embrace. All
she wanted just then was to feel his arms around her. She
could see the strong muscles in them. They would hold her
securely. Jerking her gaze back to meet Nick's, Tessa
shivered. A strange light lit his blue eyes.

Her breath caught in her throat as he levered himself away
from the door. "Speak up, Tessa. Or would you find it
simpler to tell me why it is that pup intrigues you?"

Tessa shook her head, but could not seem to speak. Nick
had come so close, she had to arch her neck to look at him.
His smooth skin was only inches from her. She could feel
the heat of him, could recognize his male scent. She knew
it from that night in the hut, only now it was stronger, for
there was not even a shirt between them.

"Does he kiss you, Tessa?"

The husky question had only just registered with her when
Tessa saw Nick's hand come up and catch her chin, and then
his lips descended to capture hers. It was not a gentle kiss.
Nick's touch seared her, he was so forceful. Tessa's knees
trembled, and she felt herself sagging as Nick wrenched his
head back.

"Does he kiss you, Tessa?" he demanded again, harshly. His eyes seemed to blaze. No longer merely blue, they burned as an opal does. "No." Her voice came out a choked whisper. She shook her head swiftly and tried again. "No, you don't understand. I do not go to meet Malcolm."

Nick's head seemed to jerk back as if she had slapped him again, and his grip on her arm tightened. "I do detest liars, Tessa. There is no other you would go to!"

"No, please, you don't understand." Tessa addressed Nick's back, for he had abruptly let go of her and was now striding to a chair where his discarded shirt lay. He shrugged into it as he turned back to her. "Look," Tessa held out the note she'd received. It was very important to her that he believe her. "Read this before you judge me."

His expression set, Nick made no move toward her for a long minute, then with a muffled oath he took the piece of vellum and scanned it quickly.

If anything, his expression hardened. "A billet-doux. How nice for you, but if you wish my congratulations, you'll be disappointed. The thing's absurdly melodramatic and only confirms my suspicions. You are a fool to risk your reputation for a boy who gushes in this fashion. He may be a Scot, but I imagine you could find another, more worthy countryman in London. You've only to be patient." Nick took Tessa's arm and hauled her toward the door. "I'll listen to no more lies tonight. It is time I went to sleep. I doubt you remember it, but I've a race to run tomorrow."

"Arrogant Sassenach!" Infuriated, Tessa shook off Nick's hold and stamped her foot. "I am not so hen-witted I forgot your race, nor am I so wanting for sense I would think to prove my innocence of an assignation with Malcolm by showing off a love note from him. This thing is not from Malcolm Fraser."

Nick did not thaw. "He put his name to it."

"But we are not on those terms!"

"If you are not on those terms, why should some mysterious unknown person think you were?"

It was, of course, a good question, and it had a good

answer, but Tessa hesitated. She did not think the answer would much please Nick. "Ah," she said, faltering, trying to think what to say, but with an impatient oath Nick forced her hand. He reached for her again, and she only eluded his grasp by a quick step back. "I believe the writer of the note may have had reason to misinterpret something he might have seen," she said in a rush.

"Might he now?"

Goaded by Nick's disbelieving tone, Tessa flung her head up. "Yes! At Mrs. Derwent's lawn party I believe that someone drew the wrong conclusions when he saw Malcolm Fraser kiss me."

Tessa could not but feel gratified that she seemed to have earned Nick's full attention, but she acknowledged that his sudden stillness was, all the same, unnerving. "This embrace was so passionate that the unknown person who saw it believed you would slip out in the middle of the night to keep a tryst with your pretty lover?"

"You are absurd!" Tessa's hands were on her hips as, her temper flaring, she forgot discretion and leaned forward to set the Marquess of Kerne straight once and for all on the subject of Malcolm Fraser. "Malcolm Fraser is not pretty but handsome, exceedingly so, and he is not my lover! Nor was our embrace passionate, though it may have seemed so from a distance."

Nick's answer was a mocking laugh, and Tessa abruptly turned on her heel. "This is pointless. You are set against me, though I cannot understand why!"

She was halfway to the door when Nick caught her by her arm and whirled her around to face him. "I have not given you leave to depart, Miss Strahan. We had gotten as far as a passionate embrace with Malcolm Fraser."

"We had gotten as far as you not believing a word I say!" she corrected him furiously. "What do you want of me?"

"The truth."

"The truth is our embrace was not passionate, and that is precisely why I know this note is not from Malcolm."

"You mean that Malcolm did not kiss you passionately, only someone thought he did?"

"Yes. No! Oh, let go! You are hurting me."

Nick relaxed his grip slightly, but he neither apologized nor released Tessa entirely. "Out with it, girl."

He shook her impatiently, and aware his jaw had tightened ominously, Tessa allowed grudgingly, "I suppose one might say Malcolm kissed me passionately, but I returned it . . ." When, simultaneously, a light seemed to explode in Nick's eyes and his grip on her arm bruised her, Tessa cried out, "How else was I to know how I felt about him if I did not kiss him? He is handsome, personable, and admires me prodigiously. He will make a good enough husband. He is a Scot!"

Tessa glared defiantly at Nick, but his expression was unreadable. "Then we shall hear the banns read soon, I imagine."

"You are laughing at me!" Tessa accused.

"At this moment, my dear, the very last thing I have in mind to do is laugh at you."

When her heart skipped a beat, Tessa upbraided herself for a fool. The rough sound of Nick's voice meant nothing but that he was growing impatient. Applying her mind to his question, she shrugged half regretfully. "No, I shan't marry Malcolm Fraser. I found I felt no more when he kissed me than I might have if a cousin had kissed me."

"A cousin?" Nick asked, and when Tessa nodded, he released her and, glancing down at the sleeve of his shirt, carefully arranged it to his liking. After several moments he glanced up and said, "Now, let me see if I understand your story. Malcolm Fraser embraced you. You returned his embrace in a spirit of curiosity, found that you felt cousinly, and told him as much—or I suppose you did, for how else could you know this note referring to the love you bear him is absurd?"

"That's it exactly," Tessa sighed, relieved beyond measure to have the matter clarified at last. "I explained my

response to Malcolm yesterday, or the day before I suppose
it is now, when we went riding. It was our discussion of my
feelings or lack of them that distracted us so we did not take
notice of the rain clouds.''

"Ah . . .''

"What does that mean?''

Nick half smiled. "Several things, actually, but for the
moment only that I've a clearer understanding why Malcolm
arrived tonight at the Hall already half foxed. He was so far
gone he could scarcely walk when he left with Giles a half
hour ago.''

"Sir Giles! But I believe him to be responsible for my note.
There is no one else who has any reason to lure me away
from the house. Was he absent from your affair for any length
of time tonight, Nick?''

"You mean, had he time to slip up to your room to leave
this note?'' When Tessa nodded, Nick shook his head. "I
cannot say, but Giles is not the sort to act so openly anyway.
He'd have paid a minion to convince a maid to take you a
lover's note from Malcolm.''

"You do think it possible, then, that Sir Giles is responsible?''

Nick countered with a question of his own. "Why do you
believe Giles spied upon you at Clarissa Derwent's affair?''

"I wish I could say I saw him in the willows,'' Tessa
confessed ruefully. "But in fact I only heard a rustling that
might have been caused by an animal as easily as a person.''

"What did Malcolm think?''

Tessa flushed faintly but unmistakably. "Malcolm did not
hear it.''

Unable to parry Nick's searching look, she only heard him
say, "I see.'' Her eyes upon his boots, she was aware he
turned away. When she looked up, his head was bent as if
he were deep in thought. "I cannot conceive of Giles lurking
in the bushes, but he might have sent someone to spy on you.
He brought a dozen servants with him from town, and at
least one of them has been seen at odd hours in the vicinity
of the Hall.''

"To watch for me?"

Hearing the tension in Tessa's voice, Nick swung around. "That is my suspicion, yes. And that is why I have had you watched as well—though not at the lawn party. If there was a man in the willows, he was Giles's man, not mine."

"He is mad!" Tessa exclaimed, shivering. "Why should he go to such lengths?"

"You've several marks against you, I fear. Your association with me was the first. Our mutual ill-feeling is both considerable and of long standing. But I cannot take all the blame, for it was you who provoked Giles as publicly as possible, and he has ever detested losing credit to anyone."

Tessa searched Nick's grave expression closely. "There is something else. Something you are not saying."

"Perhaps," Nick admitted with a frown. "I cannot say anything certain but that Giles watches you when he believes he is unobserved, and the light in his eyes has a measure of . . . ah, interest."

"I have noticed," Tessa admitted in a small voice. Somehow she had held out her hands to Nick before she realized what she did. He did not reject her as she feared he would. His grip was strong and sure. "He must be mad, Nick. I've the feeling I may never be free of him."

Nick gave her hands a reassuring squeeze. "You were going out to surprise him, weren't you?" When Tessa nodded, Nick frowned but not in anger. "You would not have succeeded, I think. He'd have paid others to lurk in the shadows of the Folly and bring you to him. But perhaps, prepared as we are, we can succeed at turning the tables on him."

Tessa's eyes widened. Nick had said "we." "You've a plan?" she asked, her excitement making her eyes shine.

Evidently Nick did not approve of her high spirits, for he frowned. "I cannot see how to keep you out of it," he murmured half to himself.

"I shan't mind if you will be there, Nick. You will be, won't you?"

"Never doubt it."

"Then I shall do whatever you say."

A glimmer of what might have been laughter lit Nick's eyes, but it was gone so quickly Tessa could not be sure, and then he said sternly, "You had better, Tessa, or I shall make you very sorry you did not."

Making her expression as solemn as she could when all she felt was joy at the thought that Nick had made himself her ally, Tessa swore to do as she was bidden.

24

A half hour later, as Tessa made her way to the Folly, she was less sanguine. She clutched her cloak tightly about her, and though she called herself a silly gudgeon, she started at every strange night noise she heard. When at last she came to the edge of the clearing, she felt no easier. The darkness in the shadows under the trees seemed impenetrable. Prickles of unease raised goose bumps on her skin, and it took all her courage to call out Malcolm's name in a soft voice.

Silence greeted her. "Malcolm," she called again and waited tensely for she knew not precisely what.

When it came, it came with startling suddenness. One moment she was alone, anxiously scanning the mysterious darkness, and then she was jerked from behind by strong hands. She'd not the time to scream. A callused hand pressed a rag into her mouth, tied it, and swept a hood over her head. Fear engulfing her, for she had not expected to be rendered blind, Tessa struggled furiously, but soon her wrists were bound, and she was hanging facedown over a man's thick shoulder. Half trotting, the man made his way to a nag hidden in the woods, threw Tessa up, and swiftly mounted behind her.

In all, Tessa thought, they traveled a half hour or so, but she could not have said how far they went. The man might have ridden in circles for all she knew.

When they halted, she was lifted from the saddle and carried in burly arms through a doorway and up a short, narrow flight of stairs. Her beast of burden knocked twice upon a door, eliciting an immediate response.

"Enter!" Sir Giles's voice sounded more eager than usual, but it was nonetheless unmistakable.

Tessa swayed dizzily when she was set none too gently
upon the floor. Her attacker's hands steadied her, but lingered
overlong upon her slender waist, and Tessa followed an
impulse to lash out at him. She caught him by surprise.
Though the blow to his shin did not incapacitate him, it did
elicit a satisfying grunt.

"Delightful!" Tessa had nearly forgotten Sir Giles. He
clapped. "Spirited even now, my dear. You are a prize.
Unhood her, man!"

Though the room was lit by only a brace of candles, Tessa
blinked, for the hood she'd worn, fashioned of a thick woolen
cloth, had allowed no light to reach her eyes.

"Welcome, my dear! I apologize for the crudeness of our
surroundings, but you will not be here overlong, I fancy."

Tessa jerked her attention to Sir Giles, who lounged upon
a chair, his back to the wall. Arrayed in evening clothes,
with a dozen fobs hanging from his embroidered waistcoat,
he seemed an exotic bird in the rough room.

Recalling in time how ignorant he supposed her to be, she
bent a furious look upon him. "What can you mean dragging
me here like this?"

"Why, I mean to compromise you, my dear!" Sir Giles
laughed evilly when Tessa gasped. "You need teaching a
lesson, you know. You are far too forward for your own
good. Take off that cloak, Jennings! I wish to see precisely
what I've acquired."

Tessa made an attempt to struggle, but with her hands
bound, it was only a second before her cloak had been ripped
from her and she stood before Sir Giles in her plainest muslin.
He seemed to approve, however ordinary it was, for he
nodded as he allowed his eyes to roam over her.

"Where is . . . ?"

A snore drowned out her question, and Sir Giles laughed
again. "Your beloved, Malcolm?" he finished for her, but
Tessa scarcely heard him, for having traced the sound to its
source, she had found Malcolm Fraser. Curled on his side,
his boyishly handsome face to her, he was sound sleep.

"Is he ill?" she demanded of Sir Giles, though it made her skin crawl to look at the fop. He had his quizzing glass to his eye, the better to survey her as he smirked triumphantly.

"Only incapacitated for the moment," Sir Giles drawled after deliberately keeping her waiting. "He'll live to play his part."

"But why have you brought me here? What do you mean when you say 'part'?"

Sir Giles sighed loudly. "Such a deal of questioning! 'Tis unbecoming for a young maiden to demand so forwardly. I tire of it, my dear. Shall I have Jennings gag you again, or will you keep your place?"

"I do not care to be gagged!" Tessa spat, not caring that her tone would only anger Sir Giles. Nick would come soon, and the dandy's displeasure would not matter.

"By gad! You've need of a strong hand!" Sir Giles started forward in his chair as if he would whip her then and there, but the sound of a scuffle on the stairs arrested him.

"Hark!" He made a play of listening. "I do believe it is our third guest."

When the door behind her crashed open, Tessa's glad cry broke pitifully. Nick had come but not to her rescue. He was held by three brawny ruffians, and though he struggled against them, there could be no hope he would win through.

Nick cast Tessa one look. Direct, penetrating, it seemed intended to hearten her, but too soon Sir Giles forced Nick's attention to himself.

Smiling a silky smile that made Tessa grind her teeth, he inclined his head. "Welcome, Lord Kerne. I must say the little maid Jennings has courted so assiduously has proven remarkably capable. I shall have to think of some reward for her, as you both stand here through her happy efforts."

"This is an outrage, Giles. You shall pay!"

Nick's low growl did not give Sir Giles pause. Far from it, he laughed. "I think not, my lord! Any retribution you may wish to exact will rebound upon this young lady, and

I am confident you would not want that, Nick.'' Sir Giles laughed with evil triumph. The sound frightened Tessa almost as much as the realization that the dandy had fully expected Nick to come to her rescue. She did not know precisely what he had arranged, but it was not difficult to imagine he had paid a maid to raise an alarm at the Hall. He'd not needed to go to such lengths, Tessa thought bitterly. In her heedless way she'd been the one to deliver Nick's head to the dandy's platter.

His sneering eyes on Nick, he crowed again. "You'd never have made an actor, Nick! You thought you concealed your interest in Miss Strahan, but I saw through your act." Tessa jerked her gaze toward Nick, but his stony countenance revealed naught, nor did he take his narrowed gaze from Sir Giles. "From the first I saw how your eyes followed her. As, I admit, did mine. I don't dispute your taste, Nick. She's a rare beauty." Feeling dirtied by the hot, gloating look the man turned on her, Tessa flung up her chin. Sir Giles made a pleased smacking sound. "I do believe, my dear, it is the flash in those wide eyes of yours that has the three of us"—he gestured with his hand to include Sir Malcolm as well as Nick and himself—"at your feet."

"You are disgusting!"

Sir Giles's smugly satisfied expression vanished as he smashed his fist down upon the table beside him. "You want taming!" he screamed shrilly. Suddenly he grabbed up a pistol Tessa had not noticed from the table and waved it at Nick. "She's mine! Concede it. You'd not enjoy bridling her as I will. You would spoil her, let her run wild as she pleases. You would! You've a weakness for spirit. You remember that stallion as well as I. You took him from me, when I'd have tamed him!"

"You'd have beaten him to death. Is that what you intend to do with Miss Strahan? You are mad, Giles, if you imagine I shall allow it."

Though Nick did not move, the menace in his words was such that the men who'd wrestled him into the room tightened their hold.

"Look who threatens!" Sir Giles cackled. "Who wins now, Nick? You ought not to have thwarted me over that stallion! Oh, yes, it was years ago, when we were yet school-boys, but I never forget. Your time has come as I knew it would! Now you will forfeit the Scottish beauty, as you made me forfeit that rogue stallion."

"Never."

That Tessa was no one's to give or take seemed to occur to neither man. Sir Giles straightened in his chair and again waved his long, lethal pistol at Nick. "You will!" he screamed. "I've all the cards this time! I've the girl and this pup she's heated over." He waved the pistol toward the recumbent figure of Sir Malcolm, but he did not take his glittering eyes from Nick. "And I've a special license in my pocket, not to mention a curate of questionable conscience in easy reach." Tessa, her eyes flaring wildly, looked at Nick, but he did not allow himself to be distracted from Sir Giles. "You shall attend my wedding this night, Nick!" Sir Giles shouted triumphantly. "And tomorrow, when you race against me, you will lose.

"If you should prove reluctant to do the one or swear an oath to the other, I shall dispatch you and this worthless boy. Everyone will believe the two of you fought over the girl. I was not the only one who remarked your interest in your godmother's niece, and the boy's infatuation was clear to all. She will mysteriously disappear. Ha! Ha! No one will ever find her, and only I will know her whereabouts. I shall use her to my heart's content without the benefit of marriage while you will go to your death knowing my hands caress her the night through, and when she balks, as she is bound to do, that it is I who will instruct her in good manners!"

Nick surged forward, dragging his guards, but before he could reach Giles, they pummeled him into submission. Sir Giles howled with delight. "What is it to be, Nick? Your life, the boy's, and a respectable wedding, or the other? I confess I hope you choose death, for I should enjoy ridding myself of you. The only reason I do not shoot you outright is the greater enjoyment I shall derive in the future watching your face each time I enter a room with your little love on my arm. She'll have just come from my bed, and you'll know it!

"Now what is it to be? Come, come, man! Shall I wing you to prove I mean what I say?"

Tessa stared in horror as Sir Giles leveled his pistol at Nick's leg. When he cocked the hammer, she did the only thing she could think to do. Forgotten while everyone, including the brawny Jennings, focused in deadly fascination upon the lethal weapon, she screamed before launching herself at Sir Giles.

She did not reach him, for Jennings recovered himself in time to catch her in midair. As she went down, Tessa saw Sir Giles's pistol emit a flame. A man yelled from very nearby and then, with a bone-jarring thud, she hit the ground.

A shrill scream roused Tessa after she knew not how long. Dazed, the breath knocked from her, she felt the rough floor beneath her cheek. An experimental move proved no one held her. She had the confused impression of a crowd of people. There were shouts and grunts on all sides, and slowly she lifted her head. To her astonishment she saw Kit Steele cuffing a ruffian on the head, and then, nearer to her, she found Nick. A beefy man clipped him hard upon the jaw, but even as Tessa gasped, Nick returned his opponent a powerful blow that sent him reeling to the floor.

Tessa watched the man crumple, her eye only distractedly taking in what occurred until by chance she looked beyond the man Nick had bested and saw Sir Giles. He lay in an awkward pose upon the floor, a bloody hole in his chest.

As from a distance, Tessa heard herself scream. Scrambling to her feet, her hand on her mouth, she jerked her gaze away, only to see the villain Jennings. Horribly still, he lay dead at her feet.

For the first time in her life, Tessa reeled, saw the room sway, and felt her knees give.

"Tessa!" She was caught up in a pair of strong arms and thought dreamily that perhaps she, too, had died, for Nick's voice sounded as tender as a lover's.

That she was very much alive, she realized only after a time, when, as from a distance, she heard someone—it seemed to be Kit—say with satisfaction, "Well, that's the lot of them."

"Good. And the boy?"

That was Nick's voice. Her head was on his shoulder as they sat, she thought, upon a bed. Opening her eyes, she moved imperceptibly.

Instantly Nick pulled back and looked down at her. "You are safe, Tessa." His blue eyes studied her intently. "It is all done. Giles will not harm you or anyone else again."

Recalling the horrid man's fate, Tessa burrowed her head into the hollow of Nick's shoulder. Tears welled in her eyes as his arms closed tightly about her. "Truly, Tessa, it is better this way." His calm voice comforted her. "But you, you brave, daft lass. I thought you had gotten yourself killed."

Tessa sniffed as she looked up at Nick. The look in his eyes was so gentle it intoxicated her. "I thought he would—"

"I know. And he might have. Thank you."

Tessa nodded solemnly despite the surge of tears Nick's quiet thanks precipitated.

"You are not harmed, are you, Tessa?" Kit knelt on one knee beside her.

"No." Tessa shook her head slowly. "I am not harmed, merely bruised in spirit." Her eyes seemed to darken as she looked from one brother to the other. "He was very mad, was he not?"

"He was." Nick nodded gravely. "Far madder than I realized, else I'd not have put you in his power for even a moment."

"But how is it you are here, Kit?"

"And Charles and Jakes," Nick answered for his brother. Glancing about, Tessa saw Jakes tighten the bonds on a man's wrists before dragging him to join four of his fellows, all of whom lay trussed and propped against the wall. Much nearer, at the head of the bed, Charles Bascom was bent over Malcolm.

Sitting up, Tessa swept her tumbled hair from her brow

and took in with widened eyes the shambles that had been made of the room. The window was shattered, the table broken, both chairs lay toppled, and the door hung by a single hinge. A skittering glance to the floor assured her no one lay there, though two reddish stains told her she'd not mistaken what she had seen earlier.

"Luckily I mistrusted Giles enough to bring reinforcements," Nick explained, following her shocked gaze. "I suspected that he hoped to involve me in whatever he had schemed, because he had gone to such a deal of trouble to get you in his clutches the night before our race. I am sorry I could not tell you, Tessa. I feared you would not be sufficiently frightened to fool Giles if you knew the whole. We made quite a procession coming here. You and the villain who attacked you in the lead; I following you; another pair of villains behind me; and last, out of sight of Giles's men, these faithful three."

"Come on, boy!"

Tessa looked around and saw Charles Bascom lightly slap Sir Malcolm. The young man's head lolled at an odd angle on his pillow, and though his eyes fluttered open, they closed again.

"What is wrong with Malcolm? He seems more than merely in his cups."

Kit spoke, frowning. "Giles must have laced his drink with some sleeping concoction, the better to render the lad agreeable to his foul plans. Gad! but I have never heard of a more dastardly scheme." Tessa shivered and was unashamedly glad when Nick pulled her tightly against him. She lay her head on his shoulder while Kit told his story. "I climbed the tree outside the window there, and listened to Giles rave from the ledge. In the meantime Jakes and Charles dispatched the man left on guard below and crept up the stairs."

"Is there no one else in this place, then?" Tessa asked.

"It would seem Giles paid the host and his wife to find another bed for the night and took the inn for himself. I doubt they questioned him overmuch. From the looks of the place, they needed Giles's largesse."

"I cannot rouse him, Nick."

Charles Bascom turned from Malcolm to address his friend and then looked to Tessa. "My apologies for one of my countrymen, Miss Strahan, and my undying respect to you. You nearly took Nick's bullet."

Mr. Bascom's normally good-humored countenance looked so grave that Tessa battled another surge of tears. "I owe you a great debt for coming to my rescue as you did, Mr. Bascom. And you, too, Kit." She turned a tremulous smile upon Nick's brother.

Kit surprised her by gently grazing her cheek with his hand. "I can think of no one I would rather save, my dear. I heard Giles make his threat, but could not see that he'd cocked his pistol. Had you not acted, Nick might have lost his leg. But look how we repay you. It is past time we got you away. You are pale as snow."

One of the most difficult parts of the night came then for Tessa. She had to separate herself from Nick, for he and Mr. Bascom, it was decided, would stay while Jakes went for the magistrate, and Kit took her home.

"Keep your stout heart, Tessa. I shall see you as soon as I can," Nick told her softly before he tossed her up to his brother, mounted on his horse.

Another bout of tears assailing her, Tessa could only nod as she sniffed. Amazingly, Nick's smile flashed in the dark. "I did not ever think to see you such a watering pot," he teased.

"Nor did I ever think to be one," she admitted with such mournful sincerity as she accepted the handkerchief Nick held out to her that both brothers chuckled. At once Tessa felt better, as if the moment of humor had cleansed away at least a little of the horror of the night. Straightening, she managed her farewell in a much firmer voice. "Until later, then, my lord."

25

*S*wift and safe, the ride to Tarlton Hall differed entirely from Tessa's earlier journey. Her eyes, when Kit lifted her from his horse, were only half open, and to her surprise she fell into a deep, untroubled sleep almost as soon as her head found her pillow.

When Nan bustled into her room at nine o'clock the next morning to see why her mistress slept so late, Tessa came instantly awake, though she'd had only four hours' sleep.

"Ye'll nae believe it, Miss Tessa, but Sir Malcolm Fraser an' another mon were set upon by highwaymen last eve!" Nan's eyes were very wide as she relayed the amazing news. "The Sassenach wa' killed, but Sir Malcolm took naught but a blow to's head. Laird Kerne ha' missed his night o' sleep settin' the matter straight."

Tessa summoned a look of astonishment as she considererd the story Nick and Mr. Bascom had hatched up between them. A great deal of unpleasantness for the Bayesford family would be avoided if it were accepted. "Is Lord Kerne returned now?" she asked Nan.

"Aye. The laird ha' returned this hour or more, an' rests in his bed now."

Tessa welcomed the news. As long as she did not see Nick, she could cling to the hope that Sir Giles, if mad, had not lacked perception where his enemy was concerned. Abruptly Tessa put the cup of chocolate Nan had brought down upon its saucer. She was mad as Sir Giles to give a moment's credence to his wild ravings.

Tessa swung her legs out from beneath the covers and crossed to wash her face in the warm water the maid had brought for that purpose. Nick only felt an obligation to her due to Honoria. If he did feel any affection, it was only because they had been through a great deal together.

"I shall wear my rose muslin, Nan." Despite her very levelheaded thoughts, Tessa judged that no harm could come of wearing her favorite dress. It was not stretching the truth to say she needed all the assistance she could summon to feel even halfway presentable.

Though a simple thing with little ornamentation but a wide sash that marked its high waist, Tessa thought the dress's color deepened the gray of her eyes, and the scooped neckline, after Nan had pinned up her hair, showed the slender column of her neck to advantage.

And she was the biggest fool in Christendom, Tessa chided herself, to think the color of her dress or cut of her neckline could be to any point whatsoever. Nick's eyes had too long been upon Madelaine Landon's sophisticated elegance.

A knock at the door broke in upon that lowering thought, and in response to Tessa's call, Susannah rushed in to deliver, again, the news that Sir Giles had been sent to his reward. "Oh!" she shivered unhappily. "I can scarce believe so dreadful a thing could occur here near the Hall. I-I had thought highwaymen almost a thing of the past. What if the children had been in the carriage . . ."

"Then Kit would have been with you and half a dozen outriders as well," Tessa said at once and wondered if the sensibilities of Sir Giles's family could be worth causing Susannah worry.

Luckily, Susannah seemed reassured. "You are right, of course, and I am a silly goose to worry so. I don't doubt Giles said something nasty that provoked the men into firing at him anyway."

"Yes," Tessa said with conviction. "He was a most unpleasant man, and though it is a harsh thing to say, I do not believe I shall mourn his loss."

"No," Susannah agreed slowly. "I cannot say that I shall, either, though I would not be so bold as to admit it publicly.

Well," she said, smiling gratefully at Tessa, "now that I am much reassured, would you care to join me below for breakfast?"

"I should be honored," Tessa replied with mock formality, and departed from her room glad to have Susannah's chatter to occupy her.

Honoria, in the breakfast room when they arrived, had been told the shocking news by her dresser. "I can scarcely countenance such a thing happening!" She paled and shook her head. Tessa went to take her hand.

"Susannah and I are persuaded, ma'am, they were a gang of men who only passed through this area, for there have been no other attacks reported."

"Yes, there is that," Honoria agreed. "But to have two men shot quite dead!"

"I forgot to say that Giles's coachman was shot as well," Susannah said, mistaking Tessa's sudden intake of breath for surprise.

In truth, Tessa had forgotten Jennings, but now she could not but think how she had last seen him, lying grotesquely still upon the floor. Nodding briefly, she asked for naught but tea for her meal.

Neither Susannah nor Honoria noted how the color had left her cheeks. Honoria had asked if Susannah knew why the gentlemen had been taken to an obscure inn and not a nearby home, and Susannah was relating what Kit had told her before he tumbled into his bed. "Malcolm was lucky indeed, for the other servants had all fled, and he lay knocked insensible in the coach when Charles Bascom came upon them. Charles was the last to leave Kit's affair and had, at Nick's insistence, Jakes with him. Apparently they knew the inn was close by, and while one drove the carriage there, the other returned here for Nick and Kit."

"I am grateful Malcolm escaped with only a light injury," Honoria remarked.

"True!" Susannah nodded. "He recalls nothing, which I think is fortuitous. Kit says he had been drinking rather heavily here at the Hall, and that, coupled with the blow to his head, left him without any recollection whatsoever of all that occurred.''

''That is a blessing,'' Honoria agreed. ''One could not want the boy to live all his life with the memory of so brutal an incident. Does he recuperate at the inn, Susannah?''

''No. Charles took him back to the Clarstons' with him.''

The morning wore on slowly as the ladies, remaining together by unspoken agreement, continued their discussion of the previous night's incident and its ramifications.

At one point Susannah inquired of no one in particular, ''Am I childish to admit I had quite looked forward to the race?''

''No, my dear, not at all.'' Honoria gave her a gentle smile before returning to her needlework. ''I was quite curious how it would come out as well.''

''I wonder what Madelaine will do now.''

''You mean about the pendant?'' Honoria abandoned the sampler whose stitches she had reworked twice that morning. ''Is it so valuable?''

''Yes,'' Susannah said, and seeing she had Tessa's interest as well as Honoria's, she expanded upon the topic. ''It was set with quite fine emeralds, you see.'' Tessa's stomach dropped horribly. She had not known how fine the pendant was, and, made distraught by the thought that Nick must have loved Madelaine more than a little to buy such a thing, Tessa knew she did not hear Susannah's subsequent statement aright.

''I beg your pardon?'' She bent an intense look upon Susannah.

''Yes, I know it is absurd, considering how open they are with their affairs, but it seems Madelaine and Richard do retain some sentiment for each other. Charles Bascom, bless him, finally related the story to me last evening, when he came to Kit's affair. It was Richard, you see, who gave Madelaine the pendant before he left for Portugal, saying it was to be a reminder of him while he was away.'' Honoria

let out something very like a snort, and, Tessa, both amused
by such an unladylike display of feeling from her proper aunt
and made giddy by Susannah's revelation, laughed aloud.
"It is amusing, is it not?" Susannah smiled at them both.
"Madelaine ought never to have wagered the thing, of
course, if she felt so strongly, but Charles said she seemed
particularly reckless that night some month or more ago—
in June, I think—when she fell into deep play with Giles.
She regretted the loss instantly and tried to buy the pendant
back from him, but, of course, he relished being able to spite
her. She only came to Nicola's in the hope she could win
it back, or failing that, call upon Nick for help."

"And is it not very like my quixotic godson to essay to
return to Madelaine her husband's parting gift? There has
been talk about Nick and Madelaine, as I don't doubt you
know." Tessa dropped the ball of yarn she'd been rolling
for Susannah to the floor, so startled was she that even
Honoria knew of Nick's affair with Madelaine, and Honoria,
reminded of her presence, quickly changed the topic by
remarking how fortunate that the other gentlemen attending
Kit's party were not attacked.

Eventually Tessa recovered something of her composure,
and though at luncheon she could do little more than push
her food about her plate, she was able afterward to accede
to her aunt's request that she play the piano.

"I think music may help soothe my fretted nerves more
than anything," Honoria said, and Tessa agreed.

In consequence, she was the last to see Nick, though she
had been waiting all morning for him. In her concentration
upon her play, she did not hear Honoria call his name, or
Susannah Kit's, and it was not until she had finished one of
the most difficult pieces Dunstan had ever set her that she
realized from the volume of the applause she earned how
her audience had grown.

She swung about, startled, her eyes going unerringly to
Nick's. He was smiling, she saw, and she at once looked
away. She could not bear to see nothing more than affection
in his so very light blue eyes.

To her relief, she did not long have to bear Nick's scrutiny, for Honoria asked him to tell again all the particulars of the "frightful occurrence."

With Kit supplementing a word here and there, Nick did as he was requested. The story was just as Susannah had related, but Nick did add reassurances about the possibility of further lawlessness. "I am convinced these ruffians are not local men, for there have been no other such incidents and no one hereabouts seems to have the least knowledge of them."

Honoria asked after Malcolm and was told he was recovering nicely. "The boy can count himself very lucky, for the cut on his head is really quite small," Kit spoke up to say. "He did feel the worse for wear the last we saw of him, but that was a result of the drink he had consumed."

"I find it odd he should drink so deep." Honoria frowned as she looked to her godson. "I had not thought him a drunkard."

"I don't think one night of excess quite makes him that," Nick assured her with a faint smile. "I imagine there will be several gentlemen from last evening who feel similarly today."

Though Honoria seemed reassured upon that point, there were a dozen or more she had yet to raise, and by the time Susannah added hers, Tessa was torn between admiration for Nick's ability to treat a fabrication as if it were real and impatience for the amount of time the absurd recital consumed.

In the end, when Nick looked to her and said, "You have been very quiet, Tessa," she started.

"Yes." Her glance grazed his too briefly for her to read his expression. "It is an unnerving tale."

"I know how you like to be out of doors. Perhaps a walk would suit you?"

The suggestion caused her heart to pound fiercely, and, afraid she would reveal the tumult she felt, Tessa looked to the windows. To her surprise, the sun was shining brightly.

"Yes, thank you. I should like that," she said, feeling absurdly shy.

Utterly preoccupied by the coming interview, Tessa had already got halfway to the French windows before she heard Honoria remind her she needed her hat and gloves. "We've no mists like those at Kilmorgan to protect your lovely skin, my dear, and it would be quite a shame to turn it an ugly brown."

"I shall await you by the sundial," Nick said before Tessa could object. A skittering glance in his general direction and a nod confirmed the appointment.

Her feelings at such a pitch that she felt she might burst into tears if someone so much as looked at her oddly, Tessa thought the journey to her room and back down again took an age, but then found herself approaching the sundial, Nick very much in sight, before she was ready.

The roll of a stray pebble alerted Nick to her presence. When he turned, she was standing still, looking at him with eyes the color of smoke. He could not know how unsure she felt. To Tessa just then Nick seemed achingly handsome with the sun striking blue-black glints off his raven's hair and his mouth curved just faintly in the suggestion of a smile.

"I see you have complied with the letter of Honoria's wishes, if not the spirit," Nick glanced, amused, at the bonnet and gloves clutched in her hands.

Feeling suddenly foolish, like the child he must think her to be, Tessa could only shrug. "They—I was anxious to know how you are."

His gaze, steady and reassuring, met hers. "A little weary perhaps, no more. But what of you, Tessa? You feel no ill effects? You were very quiet inside."

"I suppose I, too, am tired, though I do not feel overly so." She felt on steady ground as long as they kept to the details of the night before. "Those men, Nick, what has happened to them?"

"They'll not worry you again, I can promise you that. I offered them the mercies of a British court or transportation on a ship of mine to the colonies. Not surprisingly, they chose the latter.''

Tessa's shoulders sagged with relief, for she had been thinking it would not be easy for her ever again to walk in the woods about Tarlton Hall. "I am glad."

As if he'd read her thoughts, Nick's expression tightened, and then he held out his hand to her. "Come, we'll walk into the woods and show you how safe they are."

Though it was only a handclasp, her slender hand fitting into his larger one, without her gloves between them, bare flesh met bare flesh, and Tessa experienced a startling sense of joining.

She breathed deeply and essayed to lighten her mood with a quip. "I shall welcome the protection of the trees, for then I shall observe even the spirit of Honoria's wishes without going to the bother of wearing these absurdly warm gloves."

From the corner of her eye she saw Nick grin down at her. "Minx," he said and her breath caught in her throat. Afraid he'd guess his effect, Tessa looked away nervously. "And, ah, Malcolm? He truly feels no undue effects of the potion Sir Giles fed him?"

"Nothing untoward, I think. He did sustain a cut where Giles's ruffians handled him roughly, but it is small."

Unaware she did so, Tessa tightened her hold on Nick's hand. "And you, my lord? I saw one of the ruffians get a blow in."

"You'll think I've feet of clay, I fear."

"You dispatched him with ease!" Her eyes, flashing in outrage, lifted to Nick's and saw only then the smile curving his sensuous mouth. "You've a bruise," she said, tearing her eyes from his to address his jaw.

Nick waggled his chin and touched the tender spot carefully. "He had a powerful left, I admit."

An image of the man lashing out at Nick recalled the man's companion, Jennings. Anguish mixed with revulsion made her shudder.

Muttering an oath, Nick whirled her into his arms. Almost

before she could take in what had happened, Tessa stood with
Nick's strong arms tightly about her and her head upon his
chest. "Ah, Tessa!" Nick's exclamation was harsh with
remorse. "I shall never forgive myself for what you endured
at my urging! 'Twas sinful folly to send you to Giles when
I knew him to be wicked.''

"I am no Sassenach miss, as you well know," Tessa said,
her voice throaty and decidedly unsteady. Hearing how she
sounded, she swallowed, then lifted her head from the
comfort of Nick's chest. "I have never been protected from
the fact of death, Nick. Angus did not believe in sparing a
child the gruesome details of Culloden Moor." When Nick's
expression remained grim, Tessa lifted her hands to his face
as if she would wipe away his remorse. "I'd have been
shadowed by that man's twisted desire and malice all my
life had I not agreed, with all my wits about me, to your
plan."

Nick turned his head so that his lips touched her palm,
but he was not convinced. "You are a hoyden incapable of
saying nay to an adventure, Tessa. Do not try to take the
blame on yourself. I was responsible."

Despite his kiss Tessa stiffened in his arms. "I am no child,
if that is what you are concerned about! I am a woman who,
desired by a madman, chose a course of action that would
expose his madness. Now, if you are quite done with treating
me as a babe, I think it time to return to the Hall!"

Nick's hold, if anything, tightened, and at the back of his
eyes a flame blazed into life. "Never in all our association,
Tessa Strahan, have I been in any danger of treating you as
a babe. Far from it."

The last was said in a low growl that lit a wild warmth
in Tessa's veins. Pressing her against him, Nick bent his head
and kissed her—softly at first and then, when she opened
her mouth to him, more forcefully. At last Nick lifted his
lips from hers and kissed her brow, her tilted nose, her
cheeks, her eyes and finally, to Tessa's surprise, the little
mole above her lip. "Scottish witch. You have bewitched

me, just as Giles said." Abruptly Nick drew back and looked directly into her eyes, eyes that were now the color of silver. "I am Sassenach, Tessa." His voice was rough and flat. "Can you forget Angus?"

"No." Tessa's voice matched Nick's for intensity. "I shan't forget Angus, nor do I wish to. But I shall not fight his battles any longer, either. You are a man he'd have been proud to know, and if you're Sassenach"—her eyes lit with a teasing sparkle—"then I shall have to take you to Kilmorgan as often as I can and make you a Scot."

With a laugh that made him look boyish, Nick whirled her off her feet before he took her lips again. After some time it was Tessa who broke their embrace. "What of Madelaine, Nick? Will you . . . ?"

Her voice trailed off, for Tessa realized of a sudden Nick had not spoken a word about marriage. Perhaps he only lusted after her.

"You wish to know if I will see Madelaine or any other after we are married?" Nick's eyes danced, albeit with a tender light, and Tessa waited tensely for his answer. He chuckled. "The truth in regards to Madelaine is that our affair was ended before I ever set eyes on you. That day you saw us at the Folly, Madelaine had come to implore me to find some way to win back that pendant of hers from Giles. Did Susannah tell you the story of the thing? Yes, I suspected she would when Charles told me she had wormed it out of him. Madelaine also warned me that day that Giles had expressed a strange interest in you. You are not his sort, you see, and she thought some concern would not be amiss. As to other women, I have had no thought for any other since I first saw your bare legs by the stream beneath Kilmorgan."

"For so long!" Tessa's great gray eyes opened very wide. "But why did you not give any indication? I thought you believed me a tiresome child."

Nick laughed. "Tiresome, Tessa? I think you could never be that. Nor"—the flame in Nick's eyes burned brighter as he flicked his glance to her soft lips—"have I ever mistaken you for a child, my love. The most excruciating night of my life was the three hours you slept so trustingly with your most unchildish body pressed against mine.''

"You are a superb actor! I thought you scarcely noticed me in that crofter's hut. But why did you not say as much?"

"You," Nick said, brushing her nose with his finger, "had made it very clear my Sassenach self was beneath your Scottish contempt. I thought to bide my time until you realized the error of that notion. And then!" Nick shook his head. "I came close to murder when Malcolm Fraser appeared upon the scene. He had the one advantage I could never overcome.''

Tessa's laugh was a gurgle of amusement. "Conceited Sassenach! You are not as beautiful as Malcolm, you know.''

"I wanted to throttle you, and did that day when, having worried more than I care to recall over you, I looked up and saw you dawdling along, laughing gaily in that pup's company. I am sorry if I hurt you, my sweet.''

"And I regretted hitting you as soon as I did it, Nick! But you would not let me come near enough to apologize.''

"Every time I looked up, that boy was about, and I was afraid I might either throttle you again or sweep you into my arms if I got you alone.''

Tessa smiled mischievously. "Then you do not want a marriage like the Landons', Nick?" she asked innocently.

"I do not." The answer was satisfyingly unequivocal. "I am too selfish. I want you all to myself.''

Nick grinned then, the bold gypsy's grin that made her heart race, and Tessa met him halfway when he swooped down to capture her lips again.

It was a long kiss, and Nick's eyes were a particularly vivid blue when he pulled away just far enough that his lips hovered over hers. Softly he said, "Will you be my wife, Thérèse?''

"I will, my lord," Tessa whispered before she stood on her toes to kiss him in her turn.